Simply Learning, Simply Best!

Simply Learning, Simply Best!

倍斯特出版事業有限公司
Best Publishing Ltd.

新制多益
閱讀題庫

文法 ✚ 單字 (附詳盡解析)

TOEIC

Amanda
Chou ◎ 著

四大特色

1 關鍵文法和單字考點強化：**提升閱讀各題型解題技巧**
迅速掌握常見文法和單字出題模式，提高答題正確性+閱讀測驗閱讀速度。

2 詳盡文法和單字解析收錄：**養成獨立自學的實力**
包含兩種解題模式，協助考生兼具快速答題和確實理解的能力。

3 寫作能力大幅躍進：**聽力輔助寫作和閱讀單項的規劃**
全書英文段落、單字和文法考題均附錄音，記誦數百佳句，出口成章輕而易舉。

4 核心文法和單字實力鞏固：**與官方公布主題完全一致**
紮實介紹常見考點，能觸類旁通、舉一反三，其他英語測驗高分
亦手到擒來。

MP3

作者序

　　新制多益閱讀將原先的文法單字題從 52 題調降成僅剩 30 題，這意謂著甜頭性、技巧性和快速能完成的答題被削弱了，也在表面上給考生一個錯覺，覺得文法、單字的重要性沒有這麼高了，但是文法和單字的重要性仍是不言而喻的。除了說文法和單字是一切的閱讀基礎之外，新制題型中的插入句等新題型和更大量的商用書信閱讀，都是需要更佳的字彙量和對文法句型的掌握。書中的規劃則包含了提升答新多益 part 6 的答題能力、聽力和閱讀的整合能力規劃、單字和文法精選解析以及五回單字和文法試題，能更有效的提升考生自學的成效。

　　除此之外，書中的規劃也能運用在其他各類型的考試，包含英檢、轉學考、公職、學士後中西醫等。單字和文法題仍會佔一定的比例，而有時候多對一題文法和單字題，就影響到正取或備取。有些考生在高中準備大學考試時不愛英文科，靠著數理或其他科等考上理想學校，但是在後續的人生規劃中卻又還是要面對英文科，因為英文還是這些大大小小考試中的共同科目。不管你是為了求職苦讀新多益、上了大學後想考取更好的學校而報名了轉學考、想洗學歷報考國立碩士班、在選擇文組

後為了未來出路想考學士後中醫、在選擇生物系後想要報考學士後西醫、又或是上大學後專心想考公職，相信除了寫歷屆試題之外，這本書都能在範圍之外的英文考試中，讓讀者考生有效掌握關鍵的文法和單字考點，獲取一定的英文成績。

Amanda Chou

使用說明

INSTRUCTIONS

piece is hand carved, each exhibits a unique facial expression or posture. For instance, the long neck of the fox extends into the band, and wraps around the wearer's finger gently as if it's part of the finger. The glittery refraction of the sapphire zircon adds an aura of sophistication to the owl, since owls are the symbol of wisdom. Our ring sand pendants complement both daily and formal attire. Each piece can be custom made, including the colors and types of gemstones. Or we can adjust the rings into earrings, pendants into brooches for you.

每個動物造型搭配的鋯石顏色都不同。以狐狸和貓頭鷹戒指來說，它們的眼睛分別由祖母綠和藍寶鋯石鑲嵌。因為每件珠寶都是手工雕刻，每件都展現獨特的表情及姿態。例如，狐狸的脖子延伸至指環，溫柔地圍繞手指好像它是手指的一部分。因為貓頭鷹是智慧的象徵，藍寶鋯石耀眼的折射增加了貓頭鷹優雅的氣息。我們的戒指及垂飾能搭配平日和正式服裝。每件可訂做，包括寶石的顏色和種類。或者我們能為您將戒指調整成耳環，垂飾調整成胸針。

031

UNIT ❸

東京國際珠寶展
International Jewelry Tokyo

▶▶ 影子跟讀「短段落」練習　🎧 MP3 003

此篇為**「影子跟讀短段落練習」**，規劃了由聽「短段落」的 shadowing 練習，強化考生定位和聆聽數個句子的專注力，除了強化聽力外亦大幅提升答閱讀 Part 5 和 Part 6 的答題能力，現在就一起動身，開始聽「短段落」！

A jewelry designer from Taiwan is introducing her latest series in IJT (International Jewelry Tokyo). All of the pendants and rings in the minimalist animal series are hand carved and made of the fine sterling silver. The minimalist and geometric style does not reduce the glitz and glamour, but rather accentuates the zircons embedded as these animals' eyes.

一位來自台灣的珠寶設計師正在東京國際珠寶展介紹她的最新系列。所有這一極簡風動物系列的垂飾及戒指都是由手工雕刻，以最高品質的 925 銀製作。極簡風和幾何風格並不會減少耀眼的光采及魅力，反而強調了鑲嵌為動物眼睛的鋯石。

The colors of zircons vary from one animal to another. Let me take the fox and the owl rings for example. Their eyes are emerald and sapphire blue zircon inlays respectively. Since every

030

聽、讀雙軌規劃 ❶：

· 閱讀內文中英對照且均附錄音，除了閱讀文章之外，搭配影子跟讀法的學習修正聽力核心能力，聽、讀雙修，聽力核心能力，例如專注力提升的同時，聽力成績就開始有顯著的分數增幅。

聽、讀雙軌規劃 ❷：

· 考生先初步閱讀文章和使用影子跟讀學習法提升聽力能力後，搭配「填空題」規劃的學習，修正字彙拼字能力、內建語感和強化商業字彙能力。此外，更能輕鬆應付聽力或口譯測驗中的 spot dictation 等的測驗，在學校英文測驗中均大放異彩。

▶▶ 聽、讀雙效「填空」練習 🎧 MP3 003

此部分為聽、讀雙效「填空」練習，現在就一起動身，開始聽「短段落」，提升常考字彙、語感等答題能力！

All of the 1.＿＿＿＿＿＿＿ and rings in the 2.＿＿＿＿ animal series are hand carved and made of the fine 3.＿＿＿＿ silver. The minimalist and 4.＿＿＿＿＿＿＿ style does not reduce the glitz and 5.＿＿＿＿＿＿＿, but rather 6.＿＿＿＿＿ the zircons embedded as these animals' eyes. The colors of zircons vary from one 7.＿＿＿＿＿ to another. Let me take the fox and the owl rings for example. Their eyes are 8.＿＿＿＿ and 9.＿＿＿＿＿＿ blue zircon inlays respectively. Since every piece is hand carved, each 10.＿＿＿＿＿＿ a unique facial 11.＿＿＿＿＿＿ or posture. For instance, the long neck of the fox extends into the band, and wraps around the wearer's finger gently as if it's part of the finger. The glittery 12.＿＿＿＿＿＿ of the sapphire zircon adds an aura of 13.＿＿＿＿＿＿ to the owl, since owls are the symbol of 14.＿＿＿＿＿. Our ring sand pendants 15.＿＿＿＿＿＿ both daily and formal attire. Each piece can be custom made, including the colors and types of 16.＿＿＿＿＿＿. Or we can adjust the rings into earrings, pendants into brooches for you.

032

▶▶ 參考答案

Unit 3　東京國際珠寶展

1. pendants
2. minimalist
3. sterling
4. geometric
5. glamour
6. accentuates
7. animal
8. emerald
9. sapphire
10. exhibits
11. expression
12. refraction
13. sophistication
14. wisdom
15. complement
16. gemstones

Part 1 新制閱讀 part 6 答題強化

Part 2 核心文法和單字考點

Part 3 精選模擬試題

033

005

巴黎家具家飾展
Maison & Object in Paris

▶ 影子跟讀「短段落」練習　🎧 MP3 005

此篇為「**影子跟讀短段落練習**」，規劃了由聽「**短段落**」的 shadowing 練習，強化考生定位和聆聽數個句子的專注力，除了強化聽力外亦大幅提升答閱讀 Part 5 和 Part 6 的答題能力，現在就一起動身，開始聽「**短段落**」！

A furniture designer is explaining the functions of a unique chair in Maison & Object in Paris. This multi-functional and multi-sided chair might seem avantgarde at first sight. It is made of staggered panels of pastel tones. You might even feel a little puzzled regarding how to use it. What we have in mind for the design is to create a sustainable chair that caters to users of different age groups, and accompanies children as they grow up.

一位家具設計師正在巴黎家具家飾展解釋一個獨特椅子的功能。這個多功能及多邊椅子可能看來頗前衛。它以柔和色的嵌板互相交錯製作。你甚至可能對如何使用感到有點困惑。我們設計時考慮的是創造一把能持續使用，迎合不同年齡的使用者，而且能陪伴小孩成長的椅子。

The chair is very lightweight and all of the edges are con-

cealed by rubber strips for safety. As I speak, feel free to flip it – you might be surprised by how versatile it is! The panels are polished and of various shapes and sizes. The small circular one here can be used as a stool for young children, and the large semicircular one is for adults. If you flip over and have the rectangular panel face upward, it serves as a side table or coffee table. As for the five short rectangular panels between the circular and semicircular ones, they serve as shelves.

這個椅子很輕，而且為了安全，所有邊角都以橡膠條包覆。我一邊說，你們可以轉一下椅子—你可能會對它的多功能感覺驚訝！這些嵌板都經過拋光處理，有各種形狀和尺寸。這個小的圓形嵌板能當小朋友的凳子，大的半圓形嵌板可給成人使用。如果你把它翻轉過來，讓長方形嵌板朝上，它能當邊桌或咖啡桌使用。至於圓形和半圓形嵌板之間的五片短的矩形嵌板則能當作架子。

涵蓋各豐富主題
鞏固基礎實力
道地表達句強化翻譯、口譯等英語能力

· 藉由零碎時間反覆聽誦，無形中便能回想到主題中的字句、甚至隨著時間，更能朗朗上口，猶如勢如破竹般的提升口說、翻譯和口譯實力。

文法單字強化 ❶：

· 每題例句除了附中譯和解析外，獨家錄音，考生能藉由音檔，於零碎時間反覆聽誦，潛移默化中記憶無數常考句型和佳句，大幅提升英文閱讀和寫作實力。

Marketing
UNIT 7 用社群媒體網站打廣告 🎧 MP3 018

❼ To attract the attention of younger consumers, the company ------ advertised on social media websites rather than the newspaper.
(A) do (B) is (C) have (D) should have

中譯 (D) 那間公司本該用社群媒體網站打廣告來吸引年輕消費者，而非報紙。

速解 看到整個句子目光直接鎖定「the company ----- advertised」，空格前為單數名詞，後有主要動詞，空格內應填符合語意且可用在單數形名詞前的助動詞，故選(D) should have。選項(A) do 與選項(C) have 用在非第三人稱單數動詞上，不可選。選項(B) is 為單數形，但形成被動語態，語意不合，不選。

進階 本題重點為主詞動詞一致以及假設語氣。本題的「should have + 過去分詞」是用來表示與過去事實相反的一種假設，含「本來應該...」的意思，而本題空格後的主要動詞為過去分詞，且想表達的句意為「本來應該使用社群媒體」，故應選擇(D) should have。此外，本句主詞為單數形，**should 不論單複數名詞皆可共用**，故有達到主詞動詞一致。其他選項與句主詞或是本句語意皆不合，不選。

098

Unit 8 提升認知度

Marketing
UNIT 8 提升認知度 🎧 MP3 018

❽ Companies encourage celebrities and athletes to use their products because it will lead to ------- awareness and increased revenue.
(A) more (B) many (C) a couple of (D) several

中譯 (A) 各家公司鼓勵明星與運動員使用他們的產品，因為可以提升認知度與增加收益。

速解 看到整個句子目光直接鎖定「----- awareness」，空格後為不可數名詞，空格內應填可搭配不可數名詞的形容詞，即選項(A) more。選項(B) many、(C) a couple of 與選項(D)several，都只能接可數名詞，故不可選。

進階 本題重點為正確的量詞。從句子結構可判斷 awareness 為名詞、空格須填修飾名詞的形容詞。選項皆為量詞，也就是限定程度與數量的形容詞，而名詞的可數與不可數決定可使用的量詞。選項(B)到(D)的量詞都只能放在可數名詞前（如 many celebrities, a couple of celebrities, several celebrities），而選項(A) more **則可數與不可數名詞都可使用**（如 more awareness 或 more celebrities）。而本題中的 awareness 屬於不可數名詞，故只能使用選項(A) more。

099

Computers and the Internet
電腦與網路的普及 🎧 MP3 019

UNIT 23

㉓Computer and Internet use are becoming increasingly commonplace not only in schools ----- also in homes.
(A) but　(B) or　(C) nor　(D) and

中譯▶ (A) 使用電腦與網路已不只在學校越來越平常，在家裡也是如此。

速解▶ 看到整個句子目光直接鎖定「**not only in schools ----- also in homes**」，空格前後有相關連接詞的一部份 **not only... also**，空格應填能完整此相關連接詞的字詞，故填選項(A) **but** 以形成連接詞 **not only...but also**。選項(B) **or**、選項(C) **nor** 與選項(D) **and** 都是別的相關連接詞的一部份，不可選。

進階▶ 本考題重點為相關連接詞。相關連接詞用來連接相同類型的字詞或字句。本句是藉由相關連接詞 **not only...but also** 來連接 **in schools** 與 **in homes** 來表達「不但在學校也在家裡」很常見。藉常見的相關連接詞即可判斷其他選項不正確，其他常見的連接詞如 **both and** 表「A 和 B 都~」，有 **or** 或 **whether or**「不論 A 或 B」與 **either or**「不是 A 就是 B」，而 **neither nor** 則表示「既不 A 也不 B」。

114

Unit 24 網路連線速度

Computers and the Internet
網路連線速度 🎧 MP3 019

UNIT 24

㉔Internet connection speed depends on the use and number of users, but eight megabits per second is usually -------.
(A) satisfy　(B) satisfied　(C) satisfaction　(D) satisfactory

中譯▶ (D) 網路連線速度根據使用內容以及使用人數不同，但通常每秒 8MB 就夠了。

速解▶ 看到整個句子目光直接鎖定「**eight megabits per second is usually -----**」，空格前為副詞與名詞片語，空格應填形容詞，即選項(D) **satisfactory**。選項(A) **satisfy** 為動詞、選項(B) **satisfied** 為過去分詞、選項(C) **satisfaction** 為名詞，皆不選。

進階▶ 本題重點為正確搭配的詞性。不同詞性會有固定搭配的詞性，如形容詞可能搭配名詞，副詞可能搭配動詞等。本題空格前為副詞 **usually**，空格可能填形容詞、動詞或副詞，但因前方有名詞片語 **eight megabits per second**，而空格的詞需能修飾此名詞片語，故不選其它詞性，而需選擇形容詞 **satisfactory**。選項(A)-fy 結尾，為常見的動詞結尾，選項(B)的 -ed 可能為過去分詞或過去式動詞，因此 **satisfied** 也可作形容詞，但和 **satisfactory** 不同的是，**satisfied** 表達的是「感到滿足」，選項(C)的 -ion 結尾可判斷此為名詞。

115

Part 1 新制閱讀 part 6 答題強化

Part 2 核心文法和單字考點

Part 3 精選模擬試題

文法單字強化 ❷：

· 規劃**「速解」**和**「進階」**的學習模式，同時滿足兩種類型的考生，注重快速答題跟備考時間較短者，可以選擇速解模式，時間較充裕且重確實理解者，可選擇進階模式，慢慢研究相關考點，應試時更無往不利。

模擬試題規劃 ❶：

· 先演練一整回的 Part 5 文法單字題模擬試題，共 30 題檢視本身的實力和程度，亦可以限時作答，提升臨場感，將這個部分的答題時間壓縮得越短越好，這樣後面才有更充裕的時間答剩下較需要花時間的題型。

READING TEST 1
In this section, you must demonstrate your ability to read and comprehend English. You will be given a variety of texts and asked to answer questions about these texts. This section is divided into three parts and will take 75 minutes to complete.

Do not mark the answers in your test book. Use the answer sheet that is separately.

PART 5
Directions: In each question, you will be asked to review a statement that is missing a word or phrase. Four answer choices will be provided for each statement. Select the best answer and mark the corresponding letter (A), (B), (C), or (D) on the answer sheet.

101. Please be aware that all personal ------- sent from the office computers is subject to review by the management staff.
(A) corresponding
(B) correspondingly
(C) correspondent
(D) correspondence

102. ------- who worked overtime on the weekend to finish the project were given Monday morning off as compensation.
(A) Them
(B) That
(C) Their
(D) Those

103. A monthly newsletter highlighting the achievements of the company will especially be sent out to keep the newcomers better ------- as well as positive on duty.
(A) informative
(B) information
(C) informed
(D) informing

104. Though the company considers the orientation the most efficient method in adjusting rookies to our firm in the very short time, many people find the intensive training schedule rather -------.
(A) exhausting
(B) exhausted
(C) exhaustingly
(D) exhaustion

105. After all applications are received, the city council ------- a meeting to choose new marketing contractors for the new outlet plaza.
(A) held
(B) holds
(C) hold
(D) will hold

106. Concern about the future of many marine animals ------- to a rapid reduction in trading of marine products recently, especially those made from international conserved ones.
(A) leads

Part1 新制閱讀 part 6 答題強化

Part 2 核心文法和單字考點

Part 3 精選模擬試題

模擬試題規劃 ❷：

· 每回模擬試題均附錄音，考生在前述的學習模式並融會貫通後，進行第三階段的練習強化，記誦佳句，一次記誦 30 句 Part 5 佳句，此時的練習更能有效將學習點內建成長期記憶，學習效果更卓越。

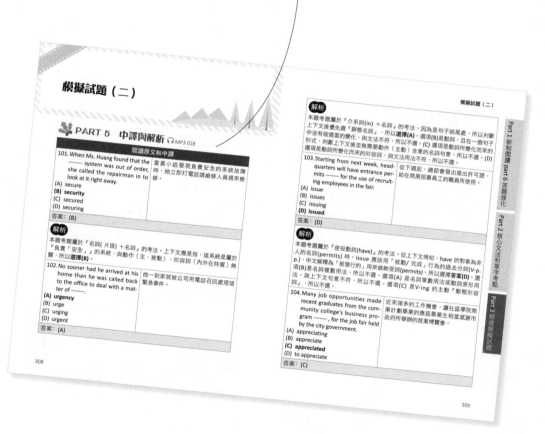

模擬試題（二）

🌿 PART 5 中譯與解析 🎧 MP3 028

閱讀原文和中譯	
101. When Ms. Huang found that the ------- system was out of order, she called the repairman in to look at it right away. (A) secure **(B) security** (C) secured (D) securing	當黃小姐發現負責安全的系統故障時，她立即打電話請維修人員過來檢修。
答案：(B)	

解析

本題考題屬於『名詞(片語) ＋名詞』的考法。上下文應是指，這系統是屬於『負責「安全」』的系統，與動作（主、被動）、形容詞（內外在特質）無關，所以**選擇(B)**。

102. No sooner had he arrived at his home than he was called back to the office to deal with a matter of -------. **(A) urgency** (B) urge (C) urging (D) urgent	他一到家就被公司用電話召回處理這緊急事件。
答案：(A)	

解析

本題考題屬於『介系詞(in) ＋名詞』的考法。因為是句子結尾處，所以判斷上下文後優先選『靜態名詞』，所以**選擇(A)**。選項(B)是動詞，且在一個句子中沒有做適當的變化，與文法不符，所以不選。(C) 選項是動詞所變化而來的形式，判斷上下文後並無需要動作（主動）含意的名詞句意，所以不選。選項是動詞所變化而來的形容詞，與文法用法不符，所以不選。(D)

103. Starting from next week, headquarters will have entrance permits ------- for the use of recruiting employees in the fair. (A) issue (B) issues (C) issuing **(D) issued**	從下週起，總部會發出進出許可證，給在商展招募員工的職員所使用。
答案：(D)	

解析

本題考題屬於『使役動詞(have)』的考法。從上下文得知，have 的對象為非人的名詞(permits) 時，issue 應該用「被動/ 完成」行為的過去分詞(V-p.p.)，中文解釋為「被發行的」用來修飾受詞(permits)，所以選擇**答案(D)**。選項(B)是名詞複數用法，所以不選。選項(A) 是名詞單數用法或動詞原形用法，與上下文句意不符，所以不選。選項(C) 是V-ing 的主動『動態形容詞』，所以不選。

104. Many job opportunities made recent graduates from the community college's business program -------, for the job fair held by the city government. (A) appreciating (B) appreciate **(C) appreciated** (D) to appreciate	近來諸多的工作機會，讓社區學院商業計劃畢業的應屆畢業生相當感謝市政府所舉辦的就業博覽會。
答案：(C)	

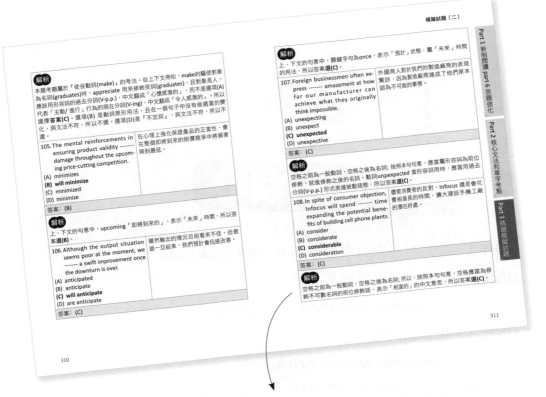

解析
本題考題屬於『使役動詞(make)』的考法。從上下文得知，make的驅使對象為名詞(graduates)時，appreciate 用來修飾受詞(graduates)，且對象是人，應該用形容詞的過去分詞(V-p.p.)，中文翻成「心懷感激的」，而不是選項(A)代表「主動/ 進行」行為的現在分詞(V-ing)，中文翻成「令人感激的」。所以選擇**答案(C)**。選項(B) 是動詞原形用法，與文法不符，所以不選。選項(D)是「不定詞」，與文法不符，所以不選。

105. The mental reinforcements in ensuring product validity ------ damage throughout the upcoming price-cutting competition.
(A) minimizes
(B) will minimize
(C) minimized
(D) minimize

在心理上強化保護產品的正當性，會在整個即將到來的削價競爭中將損害降到最低。

答案：(B)

解析
上、下文的句意中，upcoming「即將到來的」，表示「未來」時間，所以答案選**(B)**。

106. Although the output situation seems poor at the moment, we ------ a swift improvement once the downturn is over.
(A) anticipated
(B) anticipate
(C) will anticipate
(D) are anticipate

雖然輸出的情況目前看來不佳，但衰退一旦結束，我們預計會迅速改善。

答案：(C)

解析
上、下文的句意中，關鍵字句為once，表示「預計」狀態，屬「未來」時間的用法，所以答案選**(C)**。

107. Foreign businessmen often express ------ amazement at how far our manufacturer can achieve what they originally think impossible.
(A) unexpecting
(B) unexpect
(C) unexpected
(D) unexpective

外國商人對於我們的製造廠商的表現驚訝，因為製造廠商達成了他們原本認為不可能的事情。

答案：(C)

解析
空格之前為一般動詞，空格之後為名詞；按照本句句意，應當屬形容詞為前位修飾，就進修飾之後的名詞。動詞unexpected 當作形容詞用時，應當用過去分詞(V-p.p.) 形式表達被動語態，所以答案選**(C)**。

108. In spite of consumer objection, Infocus will spend ------ time expanding the potential benefits of building cell phone plants.
(A) consider
(B) considerate
(C) considerable
(D) consideration

儘管消費者的反對，Infocus 還是會花費相當長的時間，擴大建設手機工廠的潛在好處。

答案：(C)

解析
空格之前為一般動詞，空格之後為名詞；所以，按照本句句意，空格應當為修飾不可數名詞的前位修飾語、表示「相當的」的中文意思，所以答案選**(C)**。

模擬試題規劃 ❸：
· 在答題完後觀看解析，確實理解答錯的部分，如果答對也可以檢視是否是猜對的，更小心應對考試。再搭配解析觀看完後，也別忘了記誦相關選項中所列出的英文單字，更全面的備考新制多益考試。

目次 CONTENTS

Part 1 新制閱讀part 6答題強化

Part 2　核心文法和單字考點

合約和行銷 ⸻ *092*

1　未經正式接納的合約
2　收到合約終止通知
3　談判聘僱契約
4　嘗試與製造商和解
5　服裝市場中的消費者趨勢
6　最熱銷的智慧型手機
7　用社群媒體網站打廣告
8　提升認知度

會議和電腦與網路 ⸻ *108*

17　參加商業會議
18　主辦的國際商務會議
19　繳交計畫書
20　與會者都須繳交報名費
21　提供的免費線上課程
22　透過社交媒體互動
23　電腦與網路的普及
24　網路連線速度

保固和商業規劃 ⸻ *100*

9　保固期限內
10　三年的損傷保固
11　產品被下架
12　保固期限會延長
13　寫公司概況與目標
14　具備特殊的行銷策略
15　仔細研究市場與競爭對手
16　負責團隊的責任

辦公室科技和程序 ⸻ *116*

25　組織辦公科技
26　用智慧型手機做信用卡付款
27　更新辦公室科技
28　善用辦公室科技
29　遵循辦公室的流程
30　研讀公司手冊
31　緊急出口與急救工具
32　仔細閱讀手冊

Part 3　精選模擬試題

雙效強化聽讀實力，補足單靠閱讀和寫試題的盲點，聽讀是相輔相成的，先運用聽力強化專注力，並接續完成填空練習，迅速記憶更多高階字彙，不費吹灰之力就能攻略聽讀考試。

PART 1

UNIT ❶

紐約秋冬女鞋展
the New York Shoe Expo

▶▶ 影子跟讀「短段落」練習 🎧 MP3 001

　　此篇為「**影子跟讀短段落練習**」，規劃了由聽「**短段落**」的 shadowing 練習，強化考生定位和聆聽數個句子的專注力，除了強化聽力外亦大幅提升答閱讀 Part 5 和 Part 6 的答題能力，現在就一起動身，開始聽「**短段落**」！

　　The publicist for footwear designer, Mina Huang, is introducing the major fall and winter trends of the designer's eponymous brand in a press conference in the New York Shoe Expo held by FFANY (Fashion Footwear Association of New York). As a trend-setter in the women's footwear industry, Mina Huang brings you the trendiest footwear styles for fall and winter 2017.

　　鞋類設計師 Mina Huang 的公關人員正在紐約鞋類博覽會的記者會介紹設計師同名品牌的主要秋冬流行趨勢；紐約鞋類博覽會是由紐約時尚鞋類協會舉辦。身為女性鞋類產業的潮流創造者，Mina Huang 為您帶來 2017 年秋冬最潮的鞋類時尚。

　　Luxury is the key, as you might have noticed from the array of posh and polished shoes on display. Consumers will easily find the right pairs for a variety of occasions, be it casual or formal.

For party goers, Mina Huang's high-heel ankle boots, knee-high boots, or thigh-high boots will make you the center of the spotlight, as some of these boots are made with embossed leather, and others are bejeweled or embellished with fur. On casual occasions, consumers can choose from clogs and moccasins covered by floral print overlays. All of Mina Huang's shoes are made with supreme sheepskin and non-skid soles, so they not only dazzle people with their unique design, but also fit like a glove because of the soft texture.

從展出的這一系列奢華雅致女鞋，您可能已經注意到，奢華是重點。消費者很容易就找到適合各種場合的鞋類，不管是休閒或正式場合。Mina Huang 的高跟踝靴、及膝靴或大腿靴能讓參加派對的人成為焦點，因為這些靴子有的以印花皮革製成，有的以珠寶或軟毛裝飾。在休閒場合，消費者可以選擇以花卉圖案裝飾片覆蓋的圓頭無跟厚底鞋及莫卡辛軟皮鞋。所有 Mina Huang 的鞋子都是以最高級的羊皮及防滑鞋根製作，所以它們不只精緻的設計讓人讚嘆不已，也因柔軟的質感，穿著感覺非常舒適。

此部分為**聽、讀雙效「填空」練習**，現在就一起動身，開始聽「短段落」，提升常考字彙、語感等答題能力！

The 1.＿＿＿＿＿＿＿ for footwear designer, Mina Huang, is introducing the major fall and winter 2.＿＿＿＿＿＿＿ of the designer's 3.＿＿＿＿＿＿＿ brand in a press conference in the New York Shoe Expo held by FFANY (Fashion Footwear Association of New York). As a 4.＿＿＿＿＿＿＿ in the women's footwear 5.＿＿＿＿＿＿＿, ... 6.＿＿＿＿＿＿＿ is the key, as you might have noticed from the array of posh and polished shoes on 7.＿＿＿＿＿＿＿. 8.＿＿＿＿＿＿＿ will easily find the right pairs for a variety of 9.＿＿＿＿＿＿＿, be it casual or formal. For party goers, Mina Huang's high-heel ankle boots, knee-high boots, or thigh-high boots will make you the center of the 10.＿＿＿＿＿＿＿, as some of these boots are made with 11.＿＿＿＿＿＿＿ leather, and others are bejeweled or 12.＿＿＿＿＿＿＿ with fur. On casual occasions, consumers can choose from clogs and moccasins covered by 13.＿＿＿＿＿＿＿ print overlays. All of Mina Huang's shoes are made with 14.＿＿＿＿＿＿＿ sheepskin and non-skid soles, so they not only 15.＿＿＿＿＿＿＿ people with their 16.＿＿＿＿＿＿＿ design, but also fit like a glove because of the soft texture.

▶▶ **參考答案**

1. publicist	2. trends
3. eponymous	4. trendsetter
5. industry	6. Luxury
7. display	8. Consumers
9. occasions	10. spotlight
11. embossed	12. embellished
13. floral	14. supreme
15. dazzle	16. unique

智慧型手機周邊商品展
Smartphone Accessory Exhibition

▶▶ 影子跟讀「短段落」練習 🎧 MP3 002

　　此篇為**「影子跟讀短段落練習」**，規劃了由聽**「短段落」**的 shadowing 練習，強化考生定位和聆聽數個句子的專注力，除了強化聽力外亦大幅提升答閱讀 Part 5 和 Part 6 的答題能力，現在就一起動身，開始聽**「短段落」**！

　　一位主修工業設計系的學生正在介紹他設計的雙重功能手機套。大家好，我很榮幸能向你們呈現這個雙重功能手機套。首先，我想提一下是什麼啟發了我的設計。我注意到很多人喜歡一邊慢跑，一邊聽音樂。如果因為電池沒電，音樂停了，那是很掃興的事。或者你可能有這種經驗，你在手機上聊天，但不幸地因電池沒電而被迫中斷談話。嗯，有了這個雙重功能手機套，你可以放心這個尷尬的狀況不會再發生。

　　A student who majors in Industrial Design is giving a presentation on his dual function cell phone case. Hello, everyone, I'm proud to present to you the dual function cell phone case. First, I'd like to fill you in on what inspired my design. I noticed lots of people like to go jogging and listen to music at the same time, and it's quite a bummer if the music stops because the battery dies. Or you might have had the experience in which your phone conversation unfortunately got cut off because your battery was dead. Well, with this dual function phone case, you can rest assured that the awkward situation won't happen again.

這手機套整合了一個藍芽喇叭和內建 5000mAh 鋰聚合電池的行動電源。因為流線型的設計，大部份的人不會注意到它有額外功能。歡迎拿拿看—你會發現他真的很輕。這個手機套是以耐久的橡膠製作，表面有霧面處理，也有防刮及防震處理，TPU 防撞邊框提供穩定的手持手感。有三個顏色可選擇，黑色、紅色及迷彩色，只跟 iPhone 7 相容。

The case integrates a Bluetooth speaker and a portable charger with a built-in 5000mAh lithium polymer battery. Because of the streamlined design, most people wouldn't notice it embodies extra functions. Feel free to hold it— you'll find it's really light. The case is made of durable rubber with matte finish, which is anti-scratch and shockproof, and the TPU bumper frame offers a firm grip. It is available in three colors, black, red, and camouflage, and is compatible with iPhone 7 only.

此部分為**聽、讀雙效「填空」練習**，現在就一起動身，開始聽「短段落」，提升常考字彙、語感等答題能力！

First, I'd like to fill you in on what 1.＿＿＿＿＿＿ my design. I noticed lots of people like to go jogging and listen to music at the same time, and it's quite a 2.＿＿＿＿＿＿ if the music stops because the 3.＿＿＿＿＿＿ dies. Or you might have had the experience in which your phone 4.＿＿＿＿＿＿ unfortunately got cut off because your battery was dead. Well, with this 5.＿＿＿＿＿＿ function phone case, you can rest 6.＿＿＿＿＿＿ that the 7.＿＿＿＿＿＿ situation won't happen again. The case 8.＿＿＿＿＿＿ a 9.＿＿＿＿＿＿ speaker and a 10.＿＿＿＿＿＿ charger with a built-in 5000mAh lithium polymer battery. Because of the 11.＿＿＿＿＿＿ design, most people wouldn't notice it 12.＿＿＿＿＿＿ extra functions. Feel free to hold it— you'll find it's really light. The case is made of 13.＿＿＿＿＿＿ rubber with matte finish, which is anti-scratch and 14.＿＿＿＿＿＿, and the TPU bumper frame offers a firm grip. It is 15.＿＿＿＿＿＿ in three colors, black, red, and 16.＿＿＿＿＿＿, and is compatible with iPhone 7 only.

▶▶ **參考答案**

1.　inspired	2.　bummer
3.　battery	4.　conversation
5.　dual	6.　assured
7.　awkward	8.　integrates
9.　Bluetooth	10. portable
11. streamlined	12. embodies
13. durable	14. shockproof
15. available	16. camouflage

Part 1 新制閱讀 part 6 答題強化

Part 2 核心文法和單字考點

Part 3 精選模擬試題

東京國際珠寶展
International Jewelry Tokyo

▶▶ 影子跟讀「短段落」練習 🎧 MP3 003

　　此篇為「**影子跟讀短段落練習**」，規劃了由聽「**短段落**」的 shadowing 練習，強化考生定位和聆聽數個句子的專注力，除了強化聽力外亦大幅提升答閱讀 Part 5 和 Part 6 的答題能力，現在就一起動身，開始聽「**短段落**」！

　　A jewelry designer from Taiwan is introducing her latest series in IJT (International Jewelry Tokyo). All of the pendants and rings in the minimalist animal series are hand carved and made of the fine sterling silver. The minimalist and geometric style does not reduce the glitz and glamour, but rather accentuates the zircons embedded as these animals' eyes.

　　一位來自台灣的珠寶設計師正在東京國際珠寶展介紹她的最新系列。所有這一極簡風動物系列的垂飾及戒指都是由手工雕刻，以最高品質的 925 銀製作。極簡風和幾何風格並不會減少耀眼的光采及魅力，反而強調了鑲嵌為動物眼睛的鋯石。

　　The colors of zircons vary from one animal to another. Let me take the fox and the owl rings for example. Their eyes are emerald and sapphire blue zircon inlays respectively. Since every piece is hand carved, each exhibits a unique facial expression or posture. For instance, the long neck of the fox extends into the band, and wraps around the wearer's finger gently as if it's part of the finger. The glittery refraction of the sapphire zircon adds an aura of sophistication to the owl, since owls are the symbol of wisdom. Our ring sand pendants complement both daily and formal attire. Each piece can be custom made, including the colors and types of gemstones. Or we can adjust the rings into earrings, pendants into brooches for you.

　　每個動物造型搭配的鋯石顏色都不同。以狐狸和貓頭鷹戒指來說，它們的眼睛分別由祖母綠和藍寶鋯石鑲嵌。因為每件珠寶都是手工雕刻，每件都展現獨特的表情及姿態。例如，狐狸的脖子延伸至指環，溫柔地圍繞手指好像它是手指的一部分。因為貓頭鷹是智慧的象徵，藍寶鋯石耀眼的折射增加了貓頭鷹優雅的氣息。我們的戒指及垂飾能搭配平日和正式服裝。每件可訂做，包括寶石的顏色和種類。或者我們能為您將戒指調整成耳環，垂飾調整成胸針。

此部分為**聽、讀雙效「填空」練習**，現在就一起動身，開始聽「短段落」，提升常考字彙、語感等答題能力！

All of the 1._____ and rings in the 2._____ animal series are hand carved and made of the fine 3._____ silver. The minimalist and 4._____ style does not reduce the glitz and 5._____, but rather 6._____ the zircons embedded as these animals' eyes. The colors of zircons vary from one 7._____ to another. Let me take the fox and the owl rings for example. Their eyes are 8._____ and 9._____ blue zircon inlays respectively. Since every piece is hand carved, each 10._____ a unique facial 11._____ or posture. For instance, the long neck of the fox extends into the band, and wraps around the wearer's finger gently as if it's part of the finger. The glittery 12._____ of the sapphire zircon adds an aura of 13._____ to the owl, since owls are the symbol of 14._____. Our ring sand pendants 15._____ both daily and formal attire. Each piece can be custom made, including the colors and types of 16._____. Or we can adjust the rings into earrings, pendants into brooches for you.

▶▶▶ 參考答案

1. pendants	2. minimalist
3. sterling	4. geometric
5. glamour	6. accentuates
7. animal	8. emerald
9. sapphire	10. exhibits
11. expression	12. refraction
13. sophistication	14. wisdom
15. complement	16. gemstones

拉斯維加斯消費電子展
the Consumer Electronics Show in Las Vegas

▶▶ **影子跟讀「短段落」練習** 🎧 MP3 004

　　此篇為**「影子跟讀短段落練習」**，規劃了由聽**「短段落」**的 shadowing 練習，強化考生定位和聆聽數個句子的專注力，除了強化聽力外亦大幅提升答閱讀 Part 5 和 Part 6 的答題能力，現在就一起動身，開始聽**「短段落」**！

　　A home robot is being unveiled in the Consumer Electronics Show (CES) in Las Vegas. I'm thrilled to unveil the incredibly cute robot, Kimmy, to all of you. It might look like a toy, with the height of 45 centimeters and weight of merely 4 kilograms, but it's a highly intelligent home robot. Once familiarized with its amicable attributes, users will become used to the presence of Kimmy as if it is a family member.

　　一台家用機器人在拉斯維加斯消費者電子展初次亮相。我很興奮能向各位揭幕這台非常可愛的家用機器人，Kimmy。它的高度是 45 公分，重量只有 4 公斤，看起來可能很像玩具，但是它是高度智能的家用機器人，一旦熟悉它友善的特性，使用者馬上會習慣 Kimmy 的存在，好像它是家人一般。

　　Kimmy is voice-controlled, and can individualize its sounds

and tones in response to different family members, while show-ing various facial expressions on the rectangular screen, which serves as its head. Speaking of family members, Kimmy can cali-brate for the needs of the elderly, such as speaking at a louder volume, reminding them to take medications and recording their blood pressure, etc. The screen is also equipped with a camera, so it can be utilized as a surveillance camera when users are away from home. Kimmy also comes with wi-fi connectivity, a microphone, and 2 Bluetooth speakers. The built-in sensors allow it to avoid collision with people and objects.

Kimmy 具備聲控功能，而且能因應不同家人個別調整它的聲音及語調，同時在這個矩形螢幕顯示各種表情，螢幕也是它的頭部。提到家人，Kimmy 能為了長輩的需求做出校正，例如提高音量說話，提醒他們吃藥及記錄他們的血壓等等。它的螢幕也配備相機，所以當使用者不在家時，它能當作監視器。Kimmy 也有 wi-fi 連接功能、一個麥克風及兩個藍芽喇叭。內建的感應器讓它避免碰撞到人和物體。

此部分為**聽、讀雙效「填空」練習**，現在就一起動身，開始聽「短段落」，提升常考字彙、語感等答題能力！

I'm 1.＿＿＿＿＿＿ to unveil the 2.＿＿＿＿＿＿ cute robot, Kimmy, to all of you. It might look like a toy, with the 3.＿＿＿＿＿＿＿＿ of 45 centimeters and 4.＿＿＿＿＿＿ of merely 4 kilograms, but it's a highly 5.＿＿＿＿＿＿ home robot. Once 6.＿＿＿＿＿＿ with its 7.＿＿＿＿＿＿ attributes, users will become used to the presence of Kimmy as if it is a family member. Kimmy is 8.＿＿＿＿＿＿, and can 9.＿＿＿＿＿＿ its sounds and tones in response to different family members, while showing various facial expressions on the rectangular screen, which serves as its head. Speaking of family members, Kimmy can 10.＿＿＿＿＿＿ for the needs of the elderly, such as speaking at a louder 11.＿＿＿＿＿＿, reminding them to take medications and recording their blood 12.＿＿＿＿＿＿, etc. The screen is also equipped with a camera, so it can be utilized as a 13.＿＿＿＿＿＿ camera when users are away from home. Kimmy also comes with wi-fi 14.＿＿＿＿＿＿, a 15.＿＿＿＿＿＿, and 2 Bluetooth speakers. The built-in sensors allow it to avoid 16.＿＿＿＿＿＿ with people and objects.

▶▶ 參考答案

1. thrilled	2. incredibly
3. height	4. weight
5. intelligent	6. familiarized
7. amicable	8. voice-controlled
9. individualize	10. calibrate
11. volume	12. pressure
13. surveillance	14. connectivity
15. microphone	16. collision

Part 1 新制閱讀 part 6 答題強化

Part 2 核心文法和單字考點

Part 3 精選模擬試題

巴黎家具家飾展
Maison & Object in Paris

▶ 影子跟讀「短段落」練習 🎧 MP3 005

此篇為**「影子跟讀短段落練習」**，規劃了由聽**「短段落」**的 shadowing 練習，強化考生定位和聆聽數個句子的專注力，除了強化聽力外亦大幅提升答閱讀 Part 5 和 Part 6 的答題能力，現在就一起動身，開始聽**「短段落」**！

A furniture designer is explaining the functions of a unique chair in Maison & Object in Paris. This multi-functional and multi-sided chair might seem avantgarde at first sight. It is made of staggered panels of pastel tones. You might even feel a little puzzled regarding how to use it. What we have in mind for the design is to create a sustainable chair that caters to users of different age groups, and accompanies children as they grow up.

一位家具設計師正在巴黎家具家飾展解釋一個獨特椅子的功能。這個多功能及多邊椅子可能第一眼看來頗前衛。它以柔和色的嵌板互相交錯製作。你甚至可能對如何使用感到有點困惑。我們設計時考慮的是創造一把能持續使用，迎合不同年齡的使用者，而且能陪伴小孩成長的椅子。

The chair is very lightweight and all of the edges are concealed by rubber strips for safety. As I speak, feel free to flip it — you might be surprised by how versatile it is! The panels are polished and of various shapes and sizes. The small circular one here can be used as a stool for young children, and the large semicircular one is for adults. If you flip over and have the rectangular panel face upward, it serves as a side table or coffee table. As for the five short rectangular panels between the circular and semicircular ones, they serve as shelves.

　　這個椅子很輕，而且為了安全，所有邊角都以橡膠條包覆。我一邊說，你們可以轉一下椅子一你可能會對它的多功能感覺驚訝！這些嵌板都經過拋光處理，有各種形狀和尺寸。這個小的圓形嵌板能當小朋友的凳子，大的半圓形嵌板可給成人使用。如果你把它翻轉過來，讓長方形嵌板朝上，它能當邊桌或咖啡桌使用。至於圓形和半圓形嵌板之間的五片短的矩形嵌板則能當作架子。

此部分為**聽、讀雙效「填空」練習**，現在就一起動身，開始聽「短段落」，提升常考字彙、語感等答題能力！

A 1.＿＿＿＿＿＿ designer is explaining the functions of a unique chair in Maison & Object in 2.＿＿＿＿＿＿. This 3.＿＿＿＿＿＿ and multisided chair might seem 4.＿＿＿＿＿＿ at first sight. It is made of 5.＿＿＿＿＿＿ panels of pastel 6.＿＿＿＿＿＿. You might even feel a little 7.＿＿＿＿＿＿ regarding how to use it. What we have in mind for the design is to create a 8.＿＿＿＿＿＿ chair that caters to users of 9.＿＿＿＿＿＿ age groups, and 10.＿＿＿＿＿＿ children as they grow up. The chair is very 11.＿＿＿＿＿＿ and all of the edges are 12.＿＿＿＿＿＿ by rubber strips for 13.＿＿＿＿＿＿. As I speak, feel free to flip it – you might be surprised by how 14.＿＿＿＿＿＿ it is! The panels are 15.＿＿＿＿＿＿ and of various shapes and sizes. The small circular one here can be used as a stool for young children, and the large semicircular one is for adults. If you flip over and have the 16.＿＿＿＿＿＿ panel face upward, it serves as a side table or coffee table. As for the five short rectangular panels between the circular and semicircular ones, they serve as shelves.

▶▶ 參考答案

1.　furniture	2.　Paris
3.　multi-functional	4.　avantgarde
5.　staggered	6.　tones
7.　puzzled	8.　sustainable
9.　different	10. accompanies
11. lightweight	12. concealed
13. safety	14. versatile
15. polished	16. rectangular

Part 1 新制閱讀 part 6 答題強化

Part 2 核心文法和單字考點

Part 3 精選模擬試題

上海國際智能家居展覽會
Shanghai Smart Home Technology

▶▶ 影子跟讀「短段落」練習 🎧 MP3 006

　　此篇為「**影子跟讀短段落練習**」，規劃了由聽「**短段落**」的 shadowing 練習，強化考生定位和聆聽數個句子的專注力，除了強化聽力外亦大幅提升答閱讀 Part 5 和 Part 6 的答題能力，現在就一起動身，開始聽「**短段落**」！

　　A presenter is explaining how a smart home functions. While the connections between home security systems and your smart phones are not uncommon, smart homes will eventually encompass devices of all areas, and those devices will communicate with one another. They will help you manage your household, so you can focus on more crucial parts of your life.

　　一位演講者正在解釋智慧屋如何運作。住宅保全系統和你的智慧型手機連結已經很普遍，而未來智慧屋會涵蓋所有領域的裝置，那些裝置還會彼此溝通。它們會協助你管理好家裡，這樣你就能更專注在人生重要的部分。

　　Earlier when I said "devices of all areas ", I mean areas from automatic temperature control to tiny gadgets, such as smart fridges that track your food and sensors in bins that detect the kinds of trash. The more these devices talk to one another, the more they will understand your lifestyle and personal preference whereby they adjust their operations. With this intricate web of communication, your house will become a living entity that responds to your lifestyle. Now let me walk you through a scenario, and you'll have a sense of home automation. Picture this: On your way home in a self-driving car on a scorching hot day, you give a voice command to your smartphone, demanding a home air conditioner to be switched on, and catch a glimpse of what your children are doing from the home surveillance app ....

早些當我說所有領域的裝置，我是指從自動調溫到小器具，例如智慧冰箱能追蹤你的食物，和垃圾桶內的感應器能偵測垃圾的種類。這些裝置彼此溝通越多，它們越能理解你的生活型態及個人偏好，並依此調整它們的運作。有這個複雜的溝通網路，你的房子將變成能呼應你生活型態的生命體。現在讓我描繪一個場景，你們就會有家庭自動化的概念。想像一下，在炎熱的夏天，你坐自動駕駛車回家的途中，你對智慧型手機下一個口語指令，要求打開冷氣，順便從監視 app 看一下你的孩子正在做甚麼...。

此部分為**聽、讀雙效「填空」練習**，現在就一起動身，開始聽「短段落」，提升常考字彙、語感等答題能力！

They will help you 1._____ your 2._____, so you can focus on more 3._____ parts of your life. Earlier when I said "devices of all areas", I mean areas from 4._____ 5._____ control to tiny 6._____, such as smart fridges that track your food and 7._____ in bins that 8._____ the kinds of trash. The more these devices talk to one another, the more they will understand your 9._____ and personal 10._____ whereby they adjust their operations. With this 11._____ web of communication, your house will become a living 12._____ that 13._____ to your lifestyle. Now let me walk you through a 14._____, and you'll have a sense of home automation. Picture this: On your way home in a self-driving car on a 15._____ hot day, you give a voice command to your 16._____, demanding a home air conditioner to be switched on, and catch a glimpse of what your children are doing from the home surveillance app ....

▶▶ 參考答案

1.	manage	2.	household
3.	crucial	4.	automatic
5.	temperature	6.	gadgets
7.	sensors	8.	detect
9.	lifestyle	10.	preference
11.	intricate	12.	entity
13.	responds	14.	scenario
15.	scorching	16.	smartphone

Part 1　新制閱讀 part 6 答題強化

Part 2　核心文法和單字考點

Part 3　精選模擬試題

德國建築設計展
German Architecture and Design Exhibition

▶ 影子跟讀「短段落」練習 🎧 MP3 007

此篇為「**影子跟讀短段落練習**」，規劃了由聽「**短段落**」的 shadowing 練習，強化考生定位和聆聽數個句子的專注力，除了強化聽力外亦大幅提升答閱讀 Part 5 和 Part 6 的答題能力，現在就一起動身，開始聽「**短段落**」！

An architect is illustrating the latest design concept called biodesign. What kind of image springs to your mind when you hear the word "biodesign"? Obviously, it is a design method that utilizes biological formation. Though it's a relatively new concept among architects in the west, in fact centuries ago, people in India already began using tree roots as bridges. It might take 10 to 15 years for root bridges to fully form their shapes, yet they might last hundreds of years, and thus a highly sustainable and environmentally friendly construction.

一位建築師正在闡述仿生設計這個最新的設計觀念。當你聽到仿生設計時，什麼樣的形象躍入腦海裡？明顯地，它是利用生物形塑的設計方法。雖然在西方建築圈是相當新的觀念，事實上幾個世紀前，印度人已經利用樹根形塑成橋梁。樹根橋可能得花十到十五年長成形狀，但是它們能維持數百年，因此是高度永續及環保的建設。

Compared with the root bridges, western architects are probing into more refined ways to develop building materials. Imagine that instead of employing construction workers to build your house, your house will not only grow itself, but also adjust itself automatically in response to climatic changes. I'm referring to bricks made from concrete synthesized with microorganisms. How do the bricks grow? A special mineral solution is mixed with the concrete to facilitate the microorganisms to grow and harden the concrete. During the growing process, the bricks emit no greenhouse gases, and can be shaped in response to weather conditions.

和樹根橋相比，西方建築師正在探索更細微的發展建材的方法。想像一下，與其雇用建築工人蓋房子，未來你的房子不但會自己成長，也會因應氣候變化自動調整。我指的是以微生物複合水泥製作的磚塊，這些磚塊是如何成長？一種特殊的礦物質溶液和水泥混合，促進微生物成長並硬化水泥。在成長過程，磚塊不會排放溫室氣體，而且可因應天氣情況被塑形。

此部分為**聽、讀雙效「填空」練習**，現在就一起動身，開始聽「短段落」，提升常考字彙、語感等答題能力！

Obviously, it is a design method that utilizes 1.＿＿＿＿＿＿ 2.＿＿＿＿＿＿＿. Though it's a relatively new concept among 3.＿＿＿＿＿＿ in the west, in fact centuries ago, people in India already began using tree roots as 4.＿＿＿＿＿＿. It might take 10 to 15 years for root bridges to fully form their shapes, yet they might last 5.＿＿＿＿＿＿ of years, and thus a highly 6.＿＿＿＿＿＿ and environmentally friendly 7.＿＿＿＿＿＿. Compared with the root bridges, 8.＿＿＿＿＿＿ architects are probing into more refined ways to develop building 9.＿＿＿＿＿＿. Imagine that instead of 10.＿＿＿＿＿＿ construction workers to build your house, your house will not only grow itself, but also adjust itself 11.＿＿＿＿＿＿ in response to climatic changes. I'm referring to bricks made from 12.＿＿＿＿＿＿ 13.＿＿＿＿＿＿ with 14.＿＿＿＿＿＿. How do the bricks grow? A special mineral 15.＿＿＿＿＿＿ is mixed with the concrete to facilitate the microorganisms to grow and harden the concrete. During the growing process, the bricks emit no greenhouse gases, and can be shaped in 16.＿＿＿＿＿＿ to weather conditions.

▶▶ 參考答案

1. biological	2. formation
3. architects	4. bridges
5. hundreds	6. sustainable
7. construction	8. western
9. materials	10. employing
11. automatically	12. concrete
13. synthesized	14. microorganisms
15. solution	16. response

UNIT 8

華山文創園區綠建築展
Green Building Exhibition, Huashan Creative Park

▶ 影子跟讀「短段落」練習 🎧 MP3 008

　　此篇為**「影子跟讀短段落練習」**，規劃了由聽**「短段落」**的 shadowing 練習，強化考生定位和聆聽數個句子的專注力，除了強化聽力外亦大幅提升答閱讀 Part 5 和 Part 6 的答題能力，現在就一起動身，開始聽**「短段落」**！

　　A docent working in the Green Building Exhibition in Huashan Creative Park is explaining the concept of green building to a group of visitors. Believe it or not, lots of people still have some misconceptions about green buildings. For example, some think the concept involves merely planting more trees around the house, while others view it as a system composed of expensive high-tech devices.

　　一位在華山文創園區綠建築展工作的導覽員正在向一群訪客解釋綠建築的概念。信不信由你，許多人對綠建築仍有一些誤解。例如，有些人以為這概念只牽涉到在房子周圍多種樹，而有些人將它視為由昂貴的高科技裝置組合成的一套系統。

　　Well, designing green buildings involves many more elements than the ones I just described. Luckily, green buildings are quite affordable, and if you transform your residence into one, keep these three ways in mind. First, begin with small steps to achieve sustainability. For instance, using energy efficient appliances and natural ventilation, as well as lighting. Secondly, to save water, install flow restrictors and sensor taps in bathrooms. Such installation is already very common in public lavatories. Another way to save water is to reduce water pressure. Thirdly, consider installing solar panels. Solar power is one of the prime renewable energies.

嗯，設計綠建築牽涉到的元素比我剛剛描述的多很多。幸運的是，綠建築變容易負擔得起。而且如果你計畫將住宅轉換成綠建築，記住這三個方式。首先，要達到永續目標，從小步驟做起。例如，使用節能家電及自然的空調系統及採光。第二，為了達到省水的目標，在浴室裝設節水閥及自動感應水龍頭。這種裝置在公共廁所已經很普遍。另一個省水的方式是減少水壓。第三，考慮裝設太陽能板。太陽能是最主要的可替代能源之一。

此部分為**聽、讀雙效「填空」練習**，現在就一起動身，開始聽「短段落」，提升常考字彙、語感等答題能力！

A 1.＿＿＿＿＿＿＿ working in the Green Building Exhibition in Huashan Creative Park is explaining the 2.＿＿＿＿＿＿＿ of green building to a group of visitors. Believe it or not, lots of people still have some 3.＿＿＿＿＿＿＿ about green buildings. For example, some think the concept involves merely planting more trees around the house, while others view it as a 4.＿＿＿＿＿＿ composed of 5.＿＿＿＿＿＿＿ high-tech devices. Well, designing green buildings involves many more 6.＿＿＿＿＿＿＿ than the ones I just 7.＿＿＿＿＿＿＿. Luckily, green buildings are quite 8.＿＿＿＿＿＿＿, and if you 9.＿＿＿＿＿＿＿ your 10.＿＿＿＿＿＿＿ into one, keep these three ways in mind. First, begin with small steps to achieve 11.＿＿＿＿＿＿＿. For instance, using energy 12.＿＿＿＿＿＿＿ appliances and natural 13.＿＿＿＿＿＿＿, as well as lighting. Secondly, to save water, install flow 14.＿＿＿＿＿＿＿ and sensor taps in bathrooms. Such installation is already very common in public 15.＿＿＿＿＿＿＿. Another way to save water is to reduce water pressure. Thirdly, consider installing solar panels. Solar power is one of the prime 16.＿＿＿＿＿＿＿ energies.

▶▶ 參考答案

1. docent	2. concept
3. misconceptions	4. system
5. expensive	6. elements
7. described	8. affordable
9. transform	10. residence
11. sustainability	12. efficient
13. ventilation	14. restrictors
15. lavatories	16. renewable

阿拉伯杜拜醫療儀器展覽
Arab Health

▶▶ **影子跟讀「短段落」練習** 🎧 MP3 009

　　此篇為**「影子跟讀短段落練習」**，規劃了由聽**「短段落」**的 shadowing 練習，強化考生定位和聆聽數個句子的專注力，除了強化聽力外亦大幅提升答閱讀 Part 5 和 Part 6 的答題能力，現在就一起動身，開始聽**「短段落」**！

　　A wearable assistive device for the elderly is being presented in Arab Health. Ladies and gentlemen, I'm honored to unveil the amazing wearable assistive device that will greatly enhance the living quality of the aging population. This device aims to increase the muscle power so that daily movements, such as getting up, walking, and sitting down, don't generate fatigue on the wearer. How does the device achieve that? Basically, these diamond shaped sensors are embedded with artificial intelligence technology that records the wearer's muscle movement, and adds strength when needed.

　　在阿拉伯杜拜醫療儀器展覽中，一項穿戴式輔具正在被介紹。先生女士，很榮幸能發表這個很棒的穿戴式輔具，這個輔具將大幅改善老化人口的生活品質。這個輔具主要的目的是加強肌力，讓日常活動，如起身、走路和坐下，不會造成穿戴者的疲憊。這要如何辦到

呢？基本上，這些菱形的感應器有內嵌人工智慧科技，能記錄穿戴者的肌肉動作，並在需要時加強肌力。

At first glance, you might not associate this device with the lifestyle of assisted living. That's exactly what our team had in mind when we designed this device. We hoped to design a device that blends in with everyday life, and tone down the rehabilitative look. As you might have noticed, the one-piece clothing with sensors is very lightweight, and when the elderly put it on, the feel is not much different from wearing an undergarment. The clothing is made from elastic fabric, and in the lumbar area, there is a stronger band of fabric to offer extra support.

光看第一眼，你可能不會將這個輔具和照護生活型態聯想在一起。那就是我們團隊當初在設計這輔具時，所考慮到的。我們希望設計出能融入日常生活的輔具，並讓復健商品的外觀看來柔和一些。你可能注意到，這附帶感應器的一件式服裝非常輕，當長輩穿上時，感受跟穿內衣差不多。服裝是由彈性布料製作而成，在腰部的部分，有加強布料能提供額外支撐。

此部分為**聽、讀雙效「填空」練習**，現在就一起動身，開始聽「短段落」，提升常考字彙、語感等答題能力！

Ladies and gentlemen, I'm honored to unveil the amazing 1._____ assistive device that will greatly 2._____ the living quality of the aging 3._____. This device aims to increase the 4._____ power so that daily 5._____, such as getting up, walking, and sitting down, don't generate 6._____ on the wearer. How does the device achieve that? Basically, these 7._____ shaped sensors are embedded with 8._____ intelligence technology that records the wearer's muscle movement, and adds 9._____ when needed. At first glance, you might not 10._____ this device with the lifestyle of assisted living. We hoped to design a device that 11._____ in with everyday life, and tone down the 12._____ look. As you might have noticed, the one-piece clothing with sensors is very 13._____, and when the 14._____ put it on, the feel is not much different from wearing an 15._____. The clothing is made from 16._____ fabric, and in the lumbar area, there is a stronger band of fabric to offer extra support.

▶▶ 參考答案

1. wearable	2. enhance
3. population	4. muscle
5. movements	6. fatigue
7. diamond	8. artificial
9. strength	10. associate
11. blends	12. rehabilitative
13. lightweight	14. elderly
15. undergarment	16. elastic

Part 1 新制閱讀 part 6 答題強化

Part 2 核心文法和單字考點

Part 3 精選模擬試題

UNIT ❿

美國地熱能協會地熱能博覽會

GEA GeoExpo

▶▶ **影子跟讀「短段落」練習** 🎧 MP3 010

　　此篇為**「影子跟讀短段落練習」**，規劃了由聽**「短段落」**的 shadowing 練習，強化考生定位和聆聽數個句子的專注力，除了強化聽力外亦大幅提升答閱讀 Part 5 和 Part 6 的答題能力，現在就一起動身，開始聽**「短段落」**！

　　A speaker at GEA GeoExpo is talking about the benefits of geothermal heat pumps. What are the main benefits of installing a geothermal heat pump? The first that comes to mind is the cost. Although it costs more for installation at the beginning, in the long run, it will decrease your ventilation bill by up to 30% or 40%. In fact, it is estimated that heat pumps use merely about one sixth of electricity compared with traditional heating and cooling systems.

　　美國地熱能協會地熱能博覽會的一位演講者正在談論地熱能熱泵的優點。安裝地熱能熱泵主要的優點有哪些？第一個想到的是成本。雖然最初安裝成本比較貴，長遠來看，熱泵能降低 **30%** 至 **40%** 的空調費用。事實上，據估計，和傳統的空調系統比較的話，熱泵只使用電量的六分之一。

The second advantage is low maintenance. Since the apparatus is buried a few feet underground, it is not exposed to the effects of weather or vandalism. We might even say that the maintenance is negligible. In other words, geothermal heat pumps are extremely durable; according to some research, they can keep functioning effectively for 25 to 50 years. On top of these advantages, it is also highly eco-friendly; no greenhouse gases are released during operation. Besides, it generates little noise. In fact, the noise is as little as that of a refrigerator.

第二個優點是少量維修。因為這裝置是埋在地底數英呎深，不會受到天氣或人為破壞的影響。我們甚至能說只需要極少的維修。也就是說，地熱能熱泵極端地耐用。根據一些研究，它們能持續有效率地運作長達 25 至 50 年。除了這些優點，熱泵非常地環保。運作中不會產生任何溫室氣體。此外，它運作時幾乎沒有噪音，事實上，音量和一台電冰箱的音量一樣低。

此部分為**聽、讀雙效「填空」練習**，現在就一起動身，開始聽「短段落」，提升常考字彙、語感等答題能力！

What are the main 1.＿＿＿＿＿＿ of 2.＿＿＿＿＿＿a geothermal heat pump? The first that comes to mind is the cost. Although it costs more for 3.＿＿＿＿＿＿ at the beginning, in the long run, it will 4.＿＿＿＿＿＿ your ventilation bill by up to 30% or 40%. In fact, it is 5.＿＿＿＿＿＿ that heat pumps use merely about one sixth of electricity compared with 6.＿＿＿＿＿＿ heating and cooling systems. The second advantage is low 7.＿＿＿＿＿＿. Since the 8.＿＿＿＿＿＿ is buried a few feet 9.＿＿＿＿＿＿, it is not exposed to the effects of weather or 10.＿＿＿＿＿＿. We might even say that the maintenance is 11.＿＿＿＿＿＿. In other words, geothermal heat pumps are extremely 12.＿＿＿＿＿＿; according to some research, they can keep functioning 13.＿＿＿＿＿＿ for 25 to 50 years. On top of these advantages, it is also highly eco-friendly; no greenhouse gases are 14.＿＿＿＿＿＿ during operation. Besides, it 15.＿＿＿＿＿＿ little noise. In fact, the noise is as little as that of a 16.＿＿＿＿＿＿.

▶▶ 參考答案

1. benefits	2. installing
3. installation	4. decrease
5. estimated	6. traditional
7. maintenance	8. apparatus
9. underground	10. vandalism
11. negligible	12. durable
13. effectively	14. released
15. generates	16. refrigerator

Part 1 新制閱讀 part 6 答題強化

Part 2 核心文法和單字考點

Part 3 精選模擬試題

亞洲永續能源科技展
SETA (Sustainable Energy and Technology Asia)

▶▶ 影子跟讀「短段落」練習 🎧 MP3 011

此篇為「**影子跟讀短段落練習**」，規劃了由聽「**短段落**」的 shadowing 練習，強化考生定位和聆聽數個句子的專注力，除了強化聽力外亦大幅提升答閱讀 Part 5 和 Part 6 的答題能力，現在就一起動身，開始聽「**短段落**」！

A speaker from a renewable energy startup is addressing the advantages of wind turbine generator and unveiling a new product. With the rapid growth of wind farms all over the world since the 1980s, the advantages of wind turbine generators in terms of cost, environmental friendliness, and electricity yield have been widely proven. For instance, during operation, wind turbine generators emit no air pollutants.

一位替代能源新興公司的演講者正針對風力渦輪發電機的優點發表演說，並介紹一項新產品。自從 1980 年代起，風力發電廠在世界各地快速興起，風力渦輪發電機的優點，如成本、環保及電力產量，已經被廣泛證實。例如，在運作過程中風力渦輪發電機不會散發任何氣體汙染物質。

Moreover, in areas with stable wind, the energy source is unlimited, and during off-peak seasons, electricity from wind farms can be utilized to produce hydrogen gas, which is then stored, further generating electricity when needed. However, compared with solar panels, rooftop wind turbine generators have not been so popularized in residential areas. With the aforementioned advantages in mind, our company designed this small scale wind turbine generator. We have overcome the major obstacle of rooftop wind turbines, that is, noise. With these specifically designed blades, it is almost silent when functioning. Theoretically, combined with solar panels, the rooftop wind turbine would allow a household to be self-sufficient, off-grid.

此外，在風力穩定的地區，這種能源是取之不盡的，在非高峰期，風力發電廠產生的電力能被利用製造氫氣，將氫氣儲存後，需要時能再產生電力。然而，和太陽能板比較，屋頂型風力渦輪發電機在住宅區還不是很普及。考慮到上述優點，我們公司設計了這個小型風力渦輪發電機。我們已經克服屋頂型風力渦輪發電機主要的障礙，就是噪音。有了這些特殊設計的葉片，它運作時幾乎是無聲的。理論上，和太陽能板一起使用時，屋頂型風力渦輪發電機能讓一戶家庭的電力完全自給。

此部分為**聽、讀雙效「填空」練習**，現在就一起動身，開始聽「短段落」，提升常考字彙、語感等答題能力！

A speaker from a 1.＿＿＿＿＿＿＿ energy 2.＿＿＿＿＿＿＿ is addressing the advantages of wind 3.＿＿＿＿＿＿＿ generator and 4.＿＿＿＿＿＿＿ a new product. With the rapid growth of wind farms all over the world since the 1980s, the 5.＿＿＿＿＿＿ of wind turbine generators in terms of cost, 6.＿＿＿＿＿＿＿ friendliness, and 7.＿＿＿＿＿＿＿ yield have been widely proven. For instance, during 8.＿＿＿＿＿＿＿, wind turbine generators emit no air 9.＿＿＿＿＿＿＿. Moreover, in areas with 10.＿＿＿＿＿＿＿ wind, the energy source is 11.＿＿＿＿＿＿＿, and during off-peak seasons, electricity from wind farms can be 12.＿＿＿＿＿＿＿ to produce hydrogen gas, which is then stored, further generating electricity when needed. However, compared with solar 13.＿＿＿＿＿＿＿, rooftop wind turbine generators have not been so 14.＿＿＿＿＿＿＿ in 15.＿＿＿＿＿＿＿ areas. We have overcome the major obstacle of rooftop wind turbines, that is, noise. With these specifically designed blades, it is almost 16.＿＿＿＿＿＿＿ when functioning. Theoretically, combined with solar panels, the rooftop wind turbine would allow a household to be self-sufficient, off-grid.

▶▶ 參考答案

1. renewable	2. startup
3. turbine	4. unveiling
5. advantages	6. environmental
7. electricity	8. operation
9. pollutants	10. stable
11. unlimited	12. utilized
13. panels	14. popularized
15. residential	16. silent

Part 1 新制閱讀 part 6 答題強化

Part 2 核心文法和單字考點

Part 3 精選模擬試題

東京車展
Tokyo Motor Show

▶▶ 影子跟讀「短段落」練習 🎧 MP3 012

此篇為**「影子跟讀短段落練習」**，規劃了由聽**「短段落」**的 shadowing 練習，強化考生定位和聆聽數個句子的專注力，除了強化聽力外亦大幅提升答閱讀 Part 5 和 Part 6 的答題能力，現在就一起動身，開始聽**「短段落」**！

A product development manager is introducing a new fuel cell car. How exciting it is to unveil our latest hydrogen fuel cell car. This stunning car with the metallic silver exterior and suede lining interior is a sure eye-catcher. This car showcases the combination of futuristic style and the latest green technology. Before I go into further details, let me talk a little about the theme of the show, eco-friendly innovation, which, in my opinion, is best embodied by the fuel cell.

一位產品研發經理正在介紹一台新的燃料電池汽車。真興奮能介紹我們最新的氫燃料電池汽車。這台令人驚豔的車有金屬銀的外觀及絨面革內裝，能吸引眾人目光。這台車展現了未來風格和最新綠能科技的結合。在進入更多細節前，我想稍微談一下這次展覽的主題，環保創新，我認為燃料電池最能體現這個主題。

Fuel cells are absolutely clean power generators. By harnessing hydrogen, fuel cells can generate electricity almost endlessly, and emit only vapor when functioning. A single tank of hydrogen can keep the car traveling up to 350 miles before it needs to be refueled. Besides, it takes no more than 5 minutes to refuel. Our fuel cell engine delivers 130 horsepower. We are also displaying the hydrogen generating station. In a few minutes, I will be more than glad to explain how it works if you have further questions.

燃料電池是毫無汙染的發電機。藉由利用氫氣，燃料電池幾乎能無止盡地產生電力，而且運作時只會產生水蒸氣。一槽氫氣能讓這台車行駛達 350 英里，然後再補充氫能源。此外，充滿氫能源的時間不到五分鐘。我們的燃料電池引擎能傳達 130 馬力。我們也展出製氫站。幾分鐘後，如果你們有更多問題，我很樂意向你們解釋製氫站如何運作。

　　此部分為**聽、讀雙效「填空」練習**，現在就一起動身，開始聽「短段落」，提升常考字彙、語感等答題能力！

　　How exciting it is to unveil our latest 1.＿＿＿＿＿＿ fuel cell car. This 2.＿＿＿＿＿＿ car with the 3.＿＿＿＿＿＿ silver 4.＿＿＿＿＿＿ and suede lining interior is a sure eye-catcher. This car showcases the combination of 5.＿＿＿＿＿＿ style and the latest green technology. Before I go into further details, let me talk a little about the theme of the show, 6.＿＿＿＿＿＿ innovation, which, in my opinion, is best 7.＿＿＿＿＿＿ by the fuel cell. Fuel cells are absolutely clean power 8.＿＿＿＿＿＿. By harnessing hydrogen, fuel cells can generate 9.＿＿＿＿＿＿ almost 10.＿＿＿＿＿＿, and emit only vapor when functioning. A single tank of hydrogen can keep the car traveling up to 350 miles before it needs to be 11.＿＿＿＿＿＿. Besides, it takes no more than 5 minutes to refuel. Our fuel cell 12.＿＿＿＿＿＿ delivers 130 13.＿＿＿＿＿＿. We are also 14.＿＿＿＿＿＿ the hydrogen generating 15.＿＿＿＿＿＿. In a few minutes, I will be more than glad to 16.＿＿＿＿＿＿ how it works if you have further questions.

▶▶ 參考答案

1. hydrogen	2. stunning
3. metallic	4. exterior
5. futuristic	6. eco-friendly
7. embodied	8. generators
9. electricity	10. endlessly
11. refueled	12. engine
13. horsepower	14. displaying
15. station	16. explain

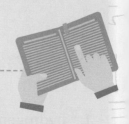

UNIT 13

國際食品加工及製藥機械展
International Food Processing & Pharmaceutical Machinery Show

▶ 影子跟讀「短段落」練習 🎧 MP3 013

此篇為「**影子跟讀短段落練習**」，規劃了由聽「**短段落**」的 shadowing 練習，強化考生定位和聆聽數個句子的專注力，除了強化聽力外亦大幅提升答閱讀 Part 5 和 Part 6 的答題能力，現在就一起動身，開始聽「**短段落**」！

A presenter is illustrating the highlights of International Food Processing and Pharmaceutical Machinery Show in the opening ceremony. Good morning, distinguished guests and media friends! Welcome to our show. The show is a hub for food processing and pharmaceutical machinery from all over the world. Buyers will have access to the machines of outstanding quality and cutting-edge designs. Certainly, from the wide spectrum of machines, they can procure the products of interest at the most competitive prices.

一位演講者正在開幕典禮中描述國際食品加工及製藥機械展的焦點。早安，各位嘉賓及媒體朋友們！歡迎來到這場展覽。這場展覽是來自世界各地食品加工及製藥機械的集中地。買家們能接觸到高品質及最尖端設計的機械。當然，從各種多樣化的機械中，買家們能以最具競爭性的價格購買到有興趣的產品。

In total, there are 284 exhibitors from 38 countries, and there are 5 pavilions, which are China, the USA, Latin American nations, Japan and Taiwan. The food processing machinery includes packaging handling, meat tempering, vegetable processing, beverage preparation, refrigeration, and bakery equipment, as well as turnkey systems. The pharmaceutical machinery ranges from processing, packaging, and laboratory equipment, which is further divided into detailed categories, such as pulverizer, drying machines, filling and sealing machines, coater, granulator, etc.

這次總共有來自 38 個國家的 284 家參展者，共有五個展館，分別是中國、美國、拉丁美洲國家、日本及台灣。食品加工機械包括包裝處理、肉類處理、蔬菜加工、飲料製作、冷藏及烘培設備，也有啟鑰系統。製藥機械則涵蓋加工、包裝及實驗設備，更細分為磨粉機、乾燥機、填充和密封機、塗料器、製粒機等等。

此部分為**聽、讀雙效「填空」練習**，現在就一起動身，開始聽「短段落」，提升常考字彙、語感等答題能力！

Good morning, 1.＿＿＿＿＿＿ guests and media friends! Welcome to our show. The show is a 2.＿＿＿＿＿＿ for food 3.＿＿＿＿＿＿ and 4.＿＿＿＿＿＿ machinery from all over the world. Buyers will have 5.＿＿＿＿＿＿ to the machines of 6.＿＿＿＿＿＿ quality and cutting-edge designs. Certainly, from the wide spectrum of 7.＿＿＿＿＿＿, they can 8.＿＿＿＿＿＿ the products of interest at the most 9.＿＿＿＿＿＿ prices. In total, there are 284 exhibitors from 38 countries, and there are 5 10.＿＿＿＿＿＿, which are China, the USA, Latin American nations, Japan and Taiwan. The food processing machinery includes 11.＿＿＿＿＿＿, handling, meat 12.＿＿＿＿＿＿, vegetable processing, beverage preparation, 13.＿＿＿＿＿＿, and bakery equipment, as well as turnkey systems. The 14.＿＿＿＿＿＿ machinery ranges from processing, packaging, and 15.＿＿＿＿＿＿ equipment, which is further divided into detailed categories, such as 16.＿＿＿＿＿＿, drying machines, filling and sealing machines, coater, granulator, etc.

▶▶ 參考答案

1. distinguished	2. hub
3. processing	4. pharmaceutical
5. access	6. outstanding
7. machines	8. procure
9. competitive	10. pavilions
11. packaging	12. tempering
13. refrigeration	14. pharmaceutical
15. laboratory	16. pulverizer

Part 1 新制閱讀 part 6 答題強化

Part 2 核心文法和單字考點

Part 3 精選模擬試題

UNIT ⑭

印尼雅加達家庭用品暨家飾展
Indonesia Housewares Fair Jakarta

▶ 影子跟讀「短段落」練習 🎧 MP3 014

此篇為**「影子跟讀短段落練習」**，規劃了由聽**「短段落」**的 shadowing 練習，強化考生定位和聆聽數個句子的專注力，除了強化聽力外亦大幅提升答閱讀 Part 5 和 Part 6 的答題能力，現在就一起動身，開始聽**「短段落」**！

The curator of Housewares Fair Jakarta is outlining the highlights of the fair. Housewares Fair Jakarta is not only the one - stop fair for international manufacturers to enter the Indonesian market, but also the best gateway to the rest of the ASEAN countries. Visitors will be exposed to a spectrum of products, including of illuminations, glassware, porcelain, giftware, home textiles, decorative accessories, and kitchen appliances, etc.

雅加達家庭用品暨家飾展的策展人正簡短描述這場展覽的重點。雅加達家庭用品暨家飾展對各國製造商而言，不只是進入印尼市場的一站式展覽，也是打入其他東協國家的最佳途徑。訪客將能接觸到多樣化的產品，包括照明設備、玻璃器皿、瓷器、禮品、家用紡織品、飾品、廚房家電等等。

It is expected that 362 exhibitors from 58 nations and 450

buyers will participate in the fair. The uniqueness of the fair is fortified by the keynote speeches on marketing strategies in the ASEAN nations and the latest trends of urbanization in Indonesia. We are also delighted to unveil the first concurrent exhibition, the NEXT Interior Design and Furnishings Exhibition, where promising young designers from Indonesia and globally will display their creative designs that cater to the metropolitan lifestyle in Indonesia.

預計有來自 58 個國家的 362 家廠商及 450 位買家參與這次展覽。針對東協國家的行銷策略和印尼都化會最新趨勢的演講,加強了這次展覽的特殊性。我們也很高興宣布第一次的同場展覽,NEXT 室內設計和陳設展。來自印尼和全球的新銳年輕設計師將展出針對印尼都會化生活型態的創意設計。

　　此部分為**聽、讀雙效「填空」練習**，現在就一起動身，開始聽「短段落」，提升常考字彙、語感等答題能力！

　　Housewares Fair Jakarta is not only the one - stop fair for 1._____ manufacturers to enter the 2._____ market, but also the best 3._____ to the rest of the ASEAN countries. Visitors will be 4._____ to a 5._____ of products, including illuminations, glassware, 6._____, giftware, home textiles, 7._____ accessories, and kitchen 8._____, etc. It is expected that 362 exhibitors from 58 nations and 450 buyers will participate in the fair. The 9._____ of the fair is 10._____ by the keynote speeches on marketing strategies in the ASEAN nations and the latest trends of 11._____ in Indonesia. We are also delighted to 12._____ the first 13._____ exhibition, the NEXT 14._____ Design and Furnishings Exhibition, where promising young designers from Indonesia and 15._____ will display their creative designs that cater to the 16._____ lifestyle in Indonesia.

▶▶ 參考答案

1. international	2. Indonesian
3. gateway	4. exposed
5. spectrum	6. porcelain
7. decorative	8. appliances
9. uniqueness	10. fortified
11. urbanization	12. unveil
13. concurrent	14. Interior
15. globally	16. metropolitan

Part 1 新制閱讀 part 6 答題強化

Part 2 核心文法和單字考點

Part 3 精選模擬試題

UNIT ⑮

芝加哥家庭用品展

The International Home & Housewares Show Chicago

▶▶ 影子跟讀「短段落」練習 🎧 MP3 015

　　此篇為**「影子跟讀短段落練習」**，規劃了由聽**「短段落」**的 shadowing 練習，強化考生定位和聆聽數個句子的專注力，除了強化聽力外亦大幅提升答閱讀 Part 5 和 Part 6 的答題能力，現在就一起動身，開始聽**「短段落」**！

　　A reporter from Best TV is covering the characteristics of the International Home & Housewares Show in Chicago. The International Home & Housewares Show in Chicago bridges top retailers and distributors in the U.S. with global buyers. On average, the show accommodated at least 2200 exhibitors and more than 60,000 visitors.

　　來自倍斯特電視台的記者正在報導芝加哥家庭用品展的特色。芝加哥家庭用品展將全球買家與美國頂級的零售商和經銷商聯結。平均來說，這場展覽容納至少 2200 家參展廠商及超過 60,000 訪客。

　　Often referred to as the largest trade show in the U.S., the show not only encompasses an array of household products, from decorations, lighting, and brewer accessories to healthcare and energy conservation products, but also has established its leadership status in household technological innovations. For instance, since 2016, the Smart Home Pavilion has been in the public eye, and showcased the latest technologies on how to transform an average home into an intelligent one. Also highly praised is the E-Marketing Center, where consultants who specialize in marketing strategies in the social media offer free consultations. Besides, the show offers a promising stage for aspiring young designers through the Student Designer Competition.

　　這場展覽常被稱為美國最大的貿易展，不只居家產品包羅萬象，有家飾品、照明設備、釀造器具、健康照護及節能產品，也已經建立它在居家科技創新的領導地位。例如，自從 2016，智慧屋展館一直受到大眾注目，展出如何將普通的家轉換為智慧屋的最新科技。電子行銷中心也備受稱讚，這裡有社群媒體行銷專長的顧問提供免費諮詢。此外，透過學生設計競賽，展覽提供給有抱負的年輕設計師一個充滿前景的舞台。

▶▶ 聽、讀雙效「填空」練習 🎧 MP3 015

此部分為**聽、讀雙效「填空」練習**，現在就一起動身，開始聽「短段落」，提升常考字彙、語感等答題能力！

The International Home & Housewares Show in Chicago bridges top retailers and distributors in the U.S. with 1._____ _____ buyers. On average, the show 2._____ at least 2200 3._____ and more than 60,000 visitors. Often referred to as the largest trade show in the U.S., the show not only 4._____ an array of 5._____ products, from decorations, lighting, and brewer 6._____ to 7._____ _____ and energy 8._____ products, but also has established its leadership status in household technological 9.____ _____. For instance, since 2016, the Smart Home Pavilion has been in the public eye, and 10._____ the latest technologies on how to 11._____ an average home into an 12._____ one. Also highly 13._____ is the E-Marketing Center, where 14._____ who specialize in marketing 15._____ in the social media offer free consultations. Besides, the show offers a 16._____ stage for aspiring young designers through the Student Designer Competition.

▶▶ 參考答案

1. global	2. accommodated
3. exhibitors	4. encompasses
5. household	6. accessories
7. healthcare	8. conservation
9. innovations	10. showcased
11. transform	12. intelligent
13. praised	14. consultants
15. strategies	16. promising

美國手工藝品展
The Craft & Hobby World Fair

▶ 影子跟讀「短段落」練習 🎧 MP3 016

此篇為**「影子跟讀短段落練習」**，規劃了由聽**「短段落」**的 shadowing 練習，強化考生定位和聆聽數個句子的專注力，除了強化聽力外亦大幅提升答閱讀 Part 5 和 Part 6 的答題能力，現在就一起動身，開始聽**「短段落」**！

The organizer of the Craft & Hobby World Fair is illustrating the highlights of the fair. The fair gathers designers, craftsmen, retailers, distributors, buyers and suppliers. Attendees will not only familiarize themselves with traditional American crafts, but also interact with prominent craftsmen from around the globe. I'm pleased to announce a new sector, the upcycling sector, which is highly informative on sustainable lifestyle. The fair has received accolades for diverse products in the paper and textile sectors, from origami paper, blotters, and wrappers to quilting, crochet, and patchwork, to name just a few.

美國手工藝品展的籌備人員正在描述展覽的焦點。這次展覽集結設計師、工藝師、零售商、經銷商、買家和供應商。與會者不但能熟悉美國傳統工藝品，也能和來自世界各地傑出的工藝師互動。很高興宣佈一個新展區，升級再造區，這個展區提供永續生活型態的豐富資

訊。此展覽以紙類區和紡織類區豐富的商品受到讚賞，這些商品有摺紙，記事簿，包裝紙，縫被工藝、鉤針編織及補綴藝品，而這只是稍微列舉。

Besides, the jewelry sector has seen unabated boom according to our statistics of visitors and orders. Another new addition is the exhibitors from Japan, Korea, and Taiwan, as well as ASEAN nations. We feel honored to have invited eminent designers and craftsmen from the above countries to give speeches on their specialties.

此外，根據訪客和訂單的統計數字，珠寶區一直維持盛況。另一個新加入的元素是來自日本，韓國和，台灣及東協國家的參展者，我們很榮幸能邀請到來自以上國家的傑出設計師和工藝家進行關於他們專長的演講。

▶▶ 聽、讀雙效「填空」練習 🎧 MP3 016

　　此部分為**聽、讀雙效「填空」練習**，現在就一起動身，開始聽「短段落」，提升常考字彙、語感等答題能力！

　　The 1.＿＿＿＿＿＿＿ of the Craft & Hobby World Fair is illustrating the 2.＿＿＿＿＿＿＿ of the fair. The fair gathers designers, 3.＿＿＿＿＿＿＿, retailers, 4.＿＿＿＿＿＿＿, buyers and suppliers. Attendees will not only 5.＿＿＿＿＿＿ themselves with 6.＿＿＿＿＿＿＿ American crafts, but also interact with 7.＿＿＿＿＿＿ craftsmen from around the globe. I'm pleased to announce a new sector, the upcycling sector, which is highly 8.＿＿＿＿＿＿ on 9.＿＿＿＿＿＿＿ lifestyle. The fair has received 10.＿＿＿＿＿＿ for 11.＿＿＿＿＿＿＿ products in the paper and 12.＿＿＿＿＿＿ sectors, from 13.＿＿＿＿＿＿ paper, blotters, and wrappers to quilting, crochet, and patchwork, to name just a few. Besides, the jewelry sector has seen 14.＿＿＿＿＿＿ boom according to our 15.＿＿＿＿＿＿ of visitors and orders. Another new addition is the exhibitors from Japan, Korea, and Taiwan, as well as ASEAN nations. We feel honored to have invited 16.＿＿＿＿＿＿ designers and craftsmen from the above countries to give speeches on their specialties.

▶▶ 參考答案

1. organizer	2. highlights
3. craftsmen	4. distributors
5. familiarize	6. traditional
7. prominent	8. informative
9. sustainable	10. accolades
11. diverse	12. textile
13. origami	14. unabated
15. statistics	16. eminent

Part 1 新制閱讀 part 6 答題強化

Part 2 核心文法和單字考點

Part 3 精選模擬試題

香港玩具展
Hong Kong Toys & Games Fair

▶▶ 影子跟讀「短段落」練習 🎧 MP3 017

　　此篇為「**影子跟讀短段落練習**」，規劃了由聽「**短段落**」的 shadowing 練習，強化考生定位和聆聽數個句子的專注力，除了強化聽力外亦大幅提升答閱讀 Part 5 和 Part 6 的答題能力，現在就一起動身，開始聽「**短段落**」！

　　A staffer at the booth of ABC Toy Company is talking to an interested visitor about the company's products. Hello, I see you are looking at our fidget toys. May I guide you through the types of these toys? Over here are our flagship products, hand spinners, which come in three shapes. The shape that is the most popular with beginners is the tri-spinner. This one I am holding is made of copper with ceramic center bearing.

　　一位 ABC 玩具公司攤位的職員正在對一位感興趣的訪客講解公司產品。嗨，我注意到您正在看我們的舒壓玩具。我能向您介紹這些玩具的種類嗎？這邊有我們的主打商品，指尖陀螺。共有三種形狀。最受初學者歡迎的是三角指尖陀螺。我手上這個是銅器製作，中間有陶製軸承。

Besides, we have quad spinners and oval spinners, made of stainless steel and aluminum respectively. All of our hand spinners are CNC machined and manufactured with SLA and laser molding technologies. The other toys that you might find interesting and stress-relieving are these fidget cubes. They are six-sided with six variants. For instance, on this side, there is the button for those who enjoy clicking.

此外，我們有四方形和橢圓形的指尖陀螺，分別以不銹鋼和鋁製作。所有的指尖陀螺都經過 CNC 加工，並以光固化成形法（SLA）及雷射鑄模科技製作。其他您可能會覺得有趣而且紓壓的玩具有這些紓壓骰子。這些骰子的六面有六種不同形式。例如，這一面有按鈕，適合喜歡玩按壓的人。

▶▶ 聽、讀雙效「填空」練習 🎧 MP3 017

　　此部分為**聽、讀雙效「填空」練習**，現在就一起動身，開始聽「短段落」，提升常考字彙、語感等答題能力！

　　A staffer at the booth of ABC Toy Company is talking to an 1._____ visitor about the company's 2._____. Hello, I see you are looking at our 3._____ toys. May I guide you through the types of these toys? Over here are our 4._____ products, hand 5._____, which come in three shapes. The shape that is the most 6._____ with beginners is the tri-spinner. This one I am holding is made of 7._____ with 8._____ center bearing.

　　Besides, we have quad spinners and oval spinners, made of 9._____ steel and 10._____ 11._____. All of our hand spinners are CNC machined and 12._____ with SLA and laser molding 13._____. The other toys that you might find interesting and 14._____ are these fidget cubes. They are six-sided with six 15._____. For instance, on this side, there is the 16._____ for those who enjoy clicking.

▶▶ 參考答案

1. interested	2. products
3. fidget	4. flagship
5. spinners	6. popular
7. copper	8. ceramic
9. stainless	10. aluminum
11. respectively	12. manufactured
13. technologies	14. stress-relieving
15. variants	16. button

先完成試題，再觀看解析，解析中包含速解和進階兩種學習模式，可擇一學習或循序漸進掌握解題攻略和相關考點，最後搭配獨家錄音，記誦佳句累積寫作字彙語庫和閱讀高分實力。

PART 2

Contracts
未經正式接納的合約 🎧 MP3 018

❶ A contract without formal acceptance is usually not considered to be ------- binding to either party.
(A) legal　(B) lawful　(C) legally　(D) law

中譯 ▶ (C) 未經正式接納的合約在正常情況下通常不對任何一方有法律約束力。

速解 ▶ 看到整個句子目光直接鎖定「**considered as ----- binding**」，空格後為 **binding**，形容詞 binding 前必須接副詞，許多副詞皆以 -ly 結尾，如本題選項(C) legally。選項(A) legal 與(B) lawful 皆為形容詞，因此不可選。選項(D) law 為名詞，同樣不可選。

進階 ▶ 本題重點為詞性的搭配。考生可先藉由「A contract... is... considered (to be)」的結構，to be 後沒有冠詞等，推測 binding 為形容詞。考生也須了解形容詞會搭配副詞，**藉由副詞來修飾形容詞本身，通常置於形容詞前方**，如本題選項(C) legally，用來修飾形容詞 binding，表示是在「法律上」具有約束力。選項中的 legal 與 lawful 有常見的形容詞結尾 -al 與 -ful，可判斷為形容詞。而 law 為名詞，以上皆無法修飾句中的形容詞 binding，都不選。前後，都可能需要填入副詞。副詞可能出現在動詞前後（如 rapidly increased 或 increased rapidly）。副詞也可能在前修飾其他副詞（如 dropped unusually quickly）。副詞也可能修飾整個句子（如 Consequently, the case has been overturned.）。

Contracts
收到合約終止通知 🎧 MP3 018

❷The renewal of the contract is ------- unless a six-month termination notice is received.
(A) automatic
(B) automation
(C) automatically
(D) automaton

中譯▶ (A) 除非提前六個月收到合約終止通知，否則合約會自動續約。

速解▶ 看到整個句子目光直接鎖定「**The renewal... is -----**」，空格前為 **is**，是一種聯繫動詞，後多接形容詞，故應選用來修飾主詞的形容詞(A)automatic。選項(B) automation 與(D) automaton 皆為名詞，常見的名詞結尾如 tion, sion, ness, ment，空格前無冠詞或形容詞，推測空格非名詞。選項(C) automatically 為副詞，空格後無動詞或形容詞，不可選。

進階▶ 本題考的重點同樣為詞性的搭配。考生可只注意主詞中的重點字 **the renewal**，忽略後續僅作限定或形容的字（**of the contract**），並注意 be 動詞 is。Be 動詞是連綴動詞的一種，不表示動作，而用來連繫主詞與後面的詞（補語），多接形容詞，如 She is pretty. 或 I am smart. 等。Be 動詞後也可能是名詞（如 They are students.）。但選項中的 automation 與 automaton 雖為名詞，在語意上與本句不合，不可選。選項中的 automatically 為副詞，無法修飾名詞 the renewal，故不選。

Contracts
談判聘僱契約
UNIT 3 🎧 MP3 018

❸------- an employment contract may sound intimidating, especially for a new graduate.
(A) Negotiate　　　　(B) Negotiation
(C) Negotiating　　　(D) Negotiated

中譯▶ (C)（與雇主）談判聘僱契約可能聽起來很恐怖，尤其對職場新鮮人來說。

....

速解▶ 看到整個句子目光直接鎖定「- - - - - a n...contract...sound」，空格在主詞位置，應選原形動詞改為動名詞的選項(C) negotiating，才可作主詞。選項(A) negotiate 與(D) negotiated 分別為原形動詞與過去分詞，不可置於主詞位置。選項(B) negotiation 為名詞，後不接冠詞，故不可選。

....

進階▶ 本題為動名詞作主詞的概念。原形動詞（以及選項中的過去分詞）不可作主詞，故不選(A)或(D)。動詞須改為動名詞（Ving）才可當作主詞，仍帶有動作的含意。在本題目中，negotiating 連同後面名詞 an employment contract 一併作為主詞，主要動詞則為 sound（連綴動詞），後接補語 intimidating，到此已為一完整句子。**名詞也可接名詞作為主詞，為複合名詞的一種**，中間可能有空格或連字號，也可能不留空格（如 benefits package、fund-raiser 或 marketplace），但名詞與名詞間不會有冠詞，因此本題空格不可選(B)。

Contracts
嘗試與製造商和解 🎧 MP3 018

❹During mediation last week, the company attempted -------
with the manufacturer but failed.
(A) to settle　(B) settling　(C) settled　(D) settle

中譯 (A) 在上周的調停中，這家公司曾嘗試與製造商和解，但並沒有成功。

速解 看到整個句子目光直接鎖定「**attempted -----**」，空格前為動詞 **attempted**，attempt 後的動詞必須是不定詞，即(A) to settle。選項(B) settling 為動名詞，選項(C) settled 為過去分詞，選項(D) settle 為原形動詞，都不可接在動詞 attempt 後，故不可選。

進階 本題重點為動名詞與不定詞的概念。本題應先注意一個句子不可以有兩個動詞，若要有兩個動詞，須透過適當的連接詞（如 and, so, that, if, although 等）連接兩個子句或其他文法概念。當句子有連續兩個動詞時，第二個動詞必須改為動名詞（Ving）或不定詞（to V.），故(C)與(D)不可選，而使用動名詞或不定詞會因第一個動詞不同，本題空格前為動詞 attempted，後方不選其他動詞形態，必須使用不定詞，故選(A)。

Marketing
服裝市場中的消費者趨勢 🎧 MP3 018

❺ She interviewed young adults in Tokyo to do an ------- of consumer trends in the fashion market.
(A) analyze　(B) analysis　(C) analyses　(D) analyzing

中譯 (B) 她訪問東京的年輕人以分析流行服裝市場中的消費者趨勢。

速解 看到整個句子目光直接鎖定「**do an ----- of**」，空格前為 **an**，後面一定要接名詞，且必須是**以母音開頭的單數名詞**，即是選項(B) analysis。選項(A) 與(D)皆為動詞，不可選。選項(C)analyses 為 analysis 的複數形，因此不可選。

進階 本題句型被稱為「複合句」，因為它含有一個從屬子句以及一個獨立子句。獨立子句必須含有一個主詞與一個動詞。根據英語的 S-V-O 句型，動詞後面通常跟著受詞（ 名詞、代名詞或片語），因此在動詞 do 後，可預期會是個受詞，如名詞 analysis。此外，名詞前可能直接是冠詞（a、an 或 the）或是接著冠詞與形容詞，因此，如果空格前為冠詞，則空格內可能為名詞或形容詞。因為空格後為介係詞 of，而不是名詞，空格內則不可能是形容詞。冠詞 an 後須是母音開頭的單數名詞，因此，本題才會選擇兩個條件都符合的 analysis。

Marketing
最熱銷的智慧型手機 🎧 MP3 018

❻ The best-selling smartphone ------- the market has an attractive design, useful features, and cutting-edge functions.
(A) on　(B) in　(C) from　　(D) of

中譯 (A) 市場上最熱銷的智慧型手機有迷人的設計、實用的特色與最尖端的功能。

速解 看到整個句子目光直接鎖定「----- the market」，片語「on the market」最符合句意， 用來表示「開始販賣的、已經可以買到的」，故填選項(A) on。選項(B) in 合成的「in the market」表「特定地點」。選項(C) from 指來源。選項(D) of 組成的「of the market」表市場的一部份。與本題語意不合，皆不選。

進階 本題重點為介系詞。介系詞通常出現在名詞前，表示名詞與其他字的關係，本題中 on 在 market 前表示 best-selling smartphone 與 market 的關係。本題空格前後為名詞，且語意不明確，可知缺少介系詞。而判斷正確答案可藉由帶入選項以確定關係是否清楚合理。此外，也可熟悉介系詞的用法與含意或熟記常用的介系詞片語，如本題的 on the market 屬慣用語，指「市場上可以買得的」。

Part 1 新制閱讀 part 6 答題強化

Part 2 核心文法和單字考點

Part 3 精選模擬試題

Marketing
用社群媒體網站打廣告 🎧 MP3 018

❼ To attract the attention of younger consumers, the company ------- advertised on social media websites rather than the newspaper.
(A) do　(B) is　(C) have　(D) should have

中譯▶ (D) 那間公司本該用社群媒體網站打廣告來吸引年輕消費者，而非報紙。

速解▶ 看到整個句子目光直接鎖定「**the company ----- advertised**」，空格前為單數名詞，後有主要動詞，空格內應填符合語意且可用在單數形名詞的助動詞，故選(D) should have。選項(A) do 與選項(C) have 用在非第三人稱單數名詞上，不可選。選項(B) is 為單數形，但形成被動語態，語意不合，不選。

進階▶ 本題重點為主詞動詞一致以及假設語氣。本題的「should have + 過去分詞」是用來表示與過去事實相反的一種假設，含「本來應該…」的意思，而本題空格後的主要動詞為過去分詞，且想表達的句意為「本來應該使用社群媒體」，故應選擇(D) should have。此外，本句主詞為單數形，**should 不論單複數名詞皆可共用**，故有達到主詞動詞一致。其他選項與子句主詞或是本句語意皆不合，不選。

Marketing
提升認知度 🎧 MP3 018

❽Companies encourage celebrities and athletes to use their products because it will lead to ------- awareness and increased revenue.
(A) more　(B) many　(C) a couple of　(D) several

中譯▶ (A) 各家公司鼓勵明星與運動員使用他們的產品，因為可以提升認知度與增加收益。

速解▶ 看到整個句子目光直接鎖定「----- awareness」，空格後為不可數名詞，空格內應填可搭配不可數名詞的形容詞， 即選項(A) more。選項(B) many、(C) a couple of 與選項(D)several，都只能接可數名詞，故不可選。

進階▶ 本題重點為正確的量詞。從句子結構可判斷 awareness 為名詞、空格須填修飾名詞的形容詞。選項皆為量詞，也就是限定程度與數量的形容詞，而名詞的可數與不可數決定可使用的量詞。選項(B)到(D)的量詞都只能放在可數名詞前（如 many celebrities, a couple of celebrities, several celebrities），而選項(A) **more 則可數與不可數名詞都可使用**（如 more awareness 或 more celebrities）。而本題中的 awareness 屬於不可數名詞，故只能使用選項(A) more。

Warranties
保固期限內 🎧 MP3 018

UNIT 9

❾ She argued with the ------- when she found out that accidental damage was not covered by the basic warranty.
(A) manage　(B) manageably　(C) manager　(D) manageable

中譯 (C) 當她發現意外損壞不含在基本保固內時和經理吵了一架。

速解 看到整個句子目光直接鎖定「**She argued with the -----**」，空格前方有主詞與動詞，空格內應填受詞，即選項(C) manager。選項(A) manage 為動詞，選項(B) manageably 為副詞，選項(D) manageable 為形容詞，與本句不合，不可選。

進階 本題重點為正確詞性。由句子結構可判斷有主詞與動詞，且空格前為介系詞 with 與定冠詞 the，後無名詞，故空格應填入名詞當作受詞。解題時可先判斷空格內應填的詞性。選項(A)為動詞，選項(B)有副詞常見詞尾 -ly，故可判斷為副詞，選項(D)有形容詞常見詞尾 -able，為形容詞，而選項(A)前可接冠詞或數量詞、可改為複數形、可加上形容詞，且有名詞常見詞尾 -er，故可判斷為名詞，故本題填入(A)的 manager。

Warranties
三年的損傷保固 🎧 MP3 018

❿ My car has the ------- warranty of all because it covers damages for three years and includes roadside assistance.

(A) reliablest　　　　(B) most reliable

(C) more reliable　　　(D) most reliablest

中譯▶ (B) 我的車的保固最可靠，因為它包含三年的損傷保固與道路救援。

速解▶ 看到整個句子目光直接鎖定「**My car has the ----- warranty of all**」，空格後為名詞，且後有 **of all**，空格內應填形容詞最高級，即選項(B)most reliable。選項(A) reliablest 為錯誤的最高級形，選項(C)more reliable 為比較級，選項(D) most reliablest 為錯誤形，皆不可選。

進階▶ 本題重點為形容詞最高級。本題已有主詞與動詞，且空格後有名詞，空格前應填形容詞，又空格前有 the，而不見比較級常出現的字眼，如「as + 形容詞」或「形容詞 + than」，且從 of all 明顯可看出比較的東西超過兩件（如所有的保固之中），故形容詞須使用最高級。最高級可能是形容詞尾加 **-est** 或形容詞前加 **the most**，當單字為單一音節時（與部分雙音節）可直接加 **-est**，但部分雙音節與全部三個音節以上的單字則在前加 **the most**。選項中的 reliable 有四個音節，應使用 the most，故選(B)。

Warranties
產品被下架 🎧 MP3 018

UNIT 11

⓫ The number of units sent back for replacement ------- more than we expected so the product was pulled off the market.
(A) is (B) are (C) was (D) were

中譯 ▸ (C) 送回更換的產品量比我們想像的多,所以產品被下架了。

....

速解 ▸ 看到整個句子目光直接鎖定「**The number of ----- more than we expected**」,空格前為 **the number of**,且整句為過去式,空格應填過去式的單數動詞,即選項(C) was。選項(A) is 為現在式的單數動詞,選項(B) are 為現在式的複數動詞,而選項(D) were 為過去式複數動詞,皆不可選。

....

進階 ▸ 本題考的重點是 the number of 的用法。片語 **the number of** 表達數量,後接複數名詞(如 the number of students),但卻須視為單數,故後方使用單數動詞。本句主詞為 the number of 接上複數名詞 units,加上修飾語 sent back for replacement,句中無主要動詞,空格中應填入單數主要動詞,故不選為複數動詞的選項(B)與選項(D)。又從句子中的 expected 等可判斷句子談論過去事件,故選擇過去式的選項(C) was,而非現在式的選項(A)。

Warranties
保固期限會延長 🎧 MP3 018

⓬ If the item is not repaired ------- the end of the warranty period, the warranty period will be extended.
(A) by　(B) on　(C) in　(D) until

中譯▶ (A) 如果這個產品在保固期間的尾聲還沒修好的話，保固期限會被延長。

速解▶ 看到整個句子目光直接鎖定「----- **the end of the warranty period**」，空格後為截止的時間 **the end of...**，空格應填適當的介系詞，即選項(A)by。選項(B) on 可表某日，選項(C) in 與較長的時間共用，選項(D) until 表「直到」，皆不選。

進階▶ 本題考的重點是時間介系詞用法。介系詞 **by** 可表示「不晚於」，會**用來表達某個截止的時間點**（如 by Monday）。本句空格後為 the end of 與其他選項的介系詞都不符，只能使用 **by** 來表示「保固時間截止前」。介系詞 **on** 可和表某日的詞共用（如 on Monday 或 on April 25），介系詞 **in** 則可和月份、季節或年份等較長的時間共用（如 in summer 或 in 2020），而介系詞 **until** 則表示直到某個時間點，以上語意都不合，不選。

103

Business Planning
寫公司概況與目標

UNIT 13 🎧 MP3 018

⓭ The ------- step of creating a business plan is writing a summary about your company profile and goals.
(A) initial　(B) infant　(C) intuition　(D) concluding

中譯 (A) 做營運計畫的第一步就是寫公司概況與目標。

速解 看到整個句子目光直接鎖定「**the ----- step**」，空格前後為冠詞 **the** 與名詞 **step**，空格內應填可修飾名詞 **step** 的形容詞，即選項(A) initial。選項(B) infant 與(C) intuition 為名詞，不可選。選項(D) concluding 可能是動詞或形容詞，在本句必須解讀為形容詞，但語意不合，同樣不可選。

進階 本題重點為正確詞性。首先應判斷空格中應填的詞性，因為空格前是 the 且後方是名詞，可推斷空格中應填形容詞。判斷形容詞的方法，可試著將單字套入 more + 形容詞或 most + 形容詞的結構，或是加在動詞 seems 的後面（如 seems initial/ seems concluding），由此可知選項(B)與(C)非形容詞，不可選。選項(A)與(D)皆可能為形容詞，故須判斷語意。理論上，撰寫公司概要與目標需在建立營運計畫的一開始，故空格中的字詞的語意應該表達「一開始」的概念，及選項(A) initial。選項(D) concluding 則為相反詞。

Business Planning
具備特殊的行銷策略 🎧 MP3 018

❹ She made ------- business a success through unique marketing strategies that gave her a competitive advantage over other businesses.
(A) she　(B) her　(C) hers　(D) herself

中譯 ▶ (B) 她事業有成來自於其具備了特殊的行銷策略，這也使她擁有其他企業所沒有的競爭優勢。

速解 ▶ 看到整個句子目光直接鎖定「**She made ----- business**」，空格後為名詞 **business**，空格中可能是**人稱代名詞所有格**，即(B) her。選項(A) she 為人稱代名詞主格，選項(C) hers 為所有格代名詞，選項(D) herself 為反身代名詞，以上皆與本句不符，皆不可選。

進階 ▶ 本題考的重點是代名詞。本句已有主詞、動詞與受詞 business，而空格在受詞前，基本上需填入形容詞，而人稱代名詞所有格也是形容詞的一種，用來表述某物的歸屬，故本題應該選擇是人稱代名詞所有格的(B) her，來表示「她的事業」。選項(A)為人稱代名詞主格，應做主詞用。選項(C) hers 為所有格代名詞，不可與名詞共用，而是用來替代所有格＋名詞（例 hers = her business）。選項(D)為反身代名詞，皆以 -self（-selves）結尾出現，必須做受詞用。以上都與所有格的要求不符，不可選。

Business Planning
UNIT 15 仔細研究市場與競爭對手 🎧 MP3 018

⓯ Thoroughly research the market and competitors, ------- you will be able to increase your business success rate.
(A) and   (B) or   (C) but   (D) while

中譯 ▶ (A) 仔細研究市場與競爭對手,你就可以增加你事業的成功率。

速解 ▶ 看到整個句子目光直接鎖定「**research...increase success**」,這些字眼顯示空格前後意思無對立關係,且似乎同樣重要,故選(A) and。選項(B) or 表示有兩樣選擇,選項(C) but 表對立關係,選項(D) while 表動作同時進行,皆不可選。

進階 ▶ 本考題重點為連接詞。空格前後為兩個完整的子句,空格內需填入連接詞來顯現兩子句的關係。對等連接詞是用來連接兩個相同重要性的子句,包含 but, or, so, and, yet, for, nor,根據兩子句的語意關係必須使用不同連接詞。本題兩子句皆著重在創立事業,且兩者語意關係相符(研究會使你成功,而成功建立在研究上),除了選項(A)以外的連接詞皆不符合語意,故只能選擇(A) and。

Business Planning
負責團隊的責任 🎧 MP3 018

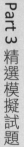

⑯ If you clearly identify the responsibilities of your management team, your employees ------- well together.

(A) will work　(B) would not work　(C) worked　(D) work

中譯 ▶ (A) 若你能清楚地辨識你負責團隊的責任，你的員工就能合作無間。

速解 ▶ 看到整個句子目光直接鎖定「**your employees ----- well**」，由 **if** 帶領的條件句是現在簡單式時，另一個子句的結果句可能會是現在式或未來式，選項(B) would not work 與(C) worked 不可選。當講述的是事實，結果句會使用現在式，若講述的是未來的結果，則會使用未來式，本句解釋的是未來會達到的結果，故不選(D) work，而選(A) will work。

進階 ▶ 本考題重點為假設語氣，由 if 帶領的條件句加上一句結果句所組成，條件句可能是與事實相符或不相符的設定，當條件句是與事實相符的設定條件時，if 句會使用現在簡單式，而結果句可能會是現在式或未來式，使用現在式時表示一定會發生的結果、不變的習慣或事實等，使用未來式時，表示不真實但很可能發生的狀況、還沒發生但很可能會發生的狀況。本題中「假設責任清楚的辨識出來」那麼很容易可以想像「員工能合作無間」，是個未來很可能發生的結果，只能選擇(A) will work。

Conferences
參加商業會議 🎧 MP3 018

⑰ Attending business conferences is a good way to ------- with people who have the same interests.
(A) connecting　(B) connected　(C) connection　(D) connect

中譯 (D) 參加商業會議是個與有相同興趣的人聯繫的好方法。

速解 看到整個句子目光直接鎖定「**to ----- with**」，空格前有 **to**，後面應該接原形動詞，即選項(D)connect。選項(A) connecting 為現在分詞，選項(B)connected 過去分詞，選項(C) connection 為名詞，皆不可選。

進階 本考題重點為不定詞。雖然 to 這個字通常當作介系詞使用，但也常常用在不定詞的結構中（**to** +動詞原式），即此結構中的動詞不可加上任何字尾（**to** 在某些特定動詞的使用中可省略，如「特殊動詞＋受詞＋原形動詞」）。本題的空格前為 **to**，且語意要表達的不是去某地，而是與人連結，故應為不定詞結構，空格內不填其他詞性或動詞形態，而需填入原形動詞(D) connect。

Conferences
主辦的國際商務會議 　🎧 MP3 018

⓲ The office is empty because all our employees ------- to host the international business conference next month.

(A) prepares

(B) are preparing

(C) is preparing

(D) preparing

Part 1 新制閱讀 part 6 答題強化

中譯▶ (B) 全部的員工都在準備下個月我們主辦的國際商務會議，所以辦公室是空的。

速解▶ 看到整個句子目光直接鎖定「**employees ----- to host**」，從屬子句中無動詞，故空格應填入與主詞相符的動詞，即選項(B) are preparing。選項(A) prepares 與(C) is preparing 為須用在單數名詞後的單數形動詞，與本題主詞不符，不可選，選項(D) preparing 缺少 be 動詞，故不可選。

進階▶ 本考題重點為主動詞一致性。本句含從屬連接詞 because 連接的主要子句與從屬子句，兩個子句都各自會有一個主詞與一個動詞，故本句的 employees 後面應該接動詞。而主詞與動詞必須要一致，即動詞可能因主詞不同而有變化，選項(A)與(C)都與複數形的 employees 不符，不可選用。另外，**本題應使用現在進行式，目的是強調進行中但很快就會結束的動作**，也就是 am/are/is + Ving，結構中有兩個元素，故不選只有 Ving 的(D)而選(B) are preparing。

Part 2 核心文法和單字考點

Part 3 精選模擬試題

Conferences
繳交計畫書
🎧 MP3 018

❶⓽ I will ------- a proposal describing the purpose and content of my presentation for the conference.

(A) submission   (B) submittingly   (C) submittable   (D) submit

---

中譯 ▶ (D) 我會繳交計畫書，描述我會議報告的目的與內容。

速解 ▶ 看到整個句子目光直接鎖定「**I will ----- a proposal**」，空格前為助動詞 **will**，必須與主要動詞共用，故空格應填動詞，即選項(D) submit。選項(A) submission 為名詞，選項(B) submittingly 為副詞，選項(C) submittable 為形容詞，皆不可選。

進階 ▶ 本考題重點為詞性。根據英語 SVO 句型結構與句中的 will 可知空格中為動詞。助動詞 will 其中一個功能是可被用來表示未來，結構為 will + 動詞原形，故本題選擇原形動詞的(D) submit。另外，可藉字尾判斷選項的詞性，如選項(A)結尾 -ion 為常見的名詞結尾，選項(B)結尾的 -ly 為常見的副詞結尾，選項(C)的 -able 則是常見的形容詞結尾，由字尾可判斷這些選項都非本題答案（動詞較無常見的結尾，較常見的有 -en, -ify, ize 等）。

Conferences
與會者都須繳交報名費

🎧 MP3 018

⑳ ------- participant is required to pay the conference registration fee which includes meals and conference materials.

(A) A lot of　(B) Every　(C) Many　(D) Both

中譯 (B) 每位與會者都須繳交報名費，報名費含餐點與會議資料。

速解 看到整個句子目光直接鎖定「----- **participant**」，空格後為單數可數名詞 **participant**，空格應填相符的字詞，即選項(B)Every。選項(A) A lot of、選項(C) Many 與選項(D)Both 須搭配複數的可數名詞，皆不可選。

進階 本考題重點為不定數量形容詞（量詞）。有某些形容詞後面只能接單數名詞或複數名詞。選項(C) Many 與選項(D) Both 後方必須接複數可數名詞，選項(A) A lot of 後面的名詞可是不可數名詞（則不可改複數）或是可數名詞（必須改為複數），選項(B) Every 後方必須接單數可數名詞。句中的 participant 為單數，且為可數名詞因為它可改為複數形，根據前述形容詞的解説，只有選項(A)與(B)後方可接單數名詞，但使用 a lot of 時若為可數名詞必須改為複數，與題中 participant 不和，故選後方可接單數可數名詞的(A) Every。

Computers and the Internet
提供的免費線上課程 🎧 MP3 019

㉑ Students ------- free online courses provided by well-known universities to increase their skills and qualifications.
(A) are often taking　　(B) often are taking
(C) often taking are　　(D) are taking often

中譯 (A) 學生經常上名校提供的免費線上課程，以增加技能與條件。

速解 看到整個句子目光直接鎖定「**Student ----- free online courses**」，空格前後有主詞和受詞，空格應填動詞，且應符合正確語序，故填選項(A) are often taking。選項(B) often are taking、選項(C) often taking are 與選項(D) are taking often 語序皆不正確或不常見，不可選。

進階 本考題重點為語序（word order）。句中 Students 是主詞，而 free online courses 是直接受詞，選項中的 are 是 be 動詞，taking 是主要動詞，而 often 是副詞。根據句型結構，副詞需置於主詞與主要動詞之間，而有 be 動詞時，副詞應置於 be 動詞之後。故本題應該選擇副詞置於 be 動詞與主要動詞之間的(A) are often taking。

Computers and the Internet
透過社交媒體互動 🎧 MP3 019

㉒ Users can interact and collaborate ------- people from all over the world through social media tools.

(A) to　(B) at　(C) with　(D) for

中譯 (C) 使用者可透過社交媒體與世界各地的人互動與合作。

速解 看到整個句子目光直接鎖定「**collaborate ----- people**」，空格前後有動詞和受詞，空格應填代表「一起」的介系詞，故填選項(C) with。選項(A) to 指向某物移動，選項(B) at 指特定時間或地方，選項(D) for 表原因或時間等，與本句意不符，皆不可選。

進階 本考題重點為介系詞。動詞 collaborate 後常接的介系詞可能有 with，表人或團體共同合作，也可能接 on 把重點放在合作本身，或加 in 並接 Ving。由此可判斷選項中只有 (C) 是常與 collaborate 共用的介係詞。另外，也可藉由介系詞所帶來的意義來判斷該使用的詞。介系詞 to 是用來指移向某地、某人或某物，也可用來指一個限度、關係或是一段時間；介系詞 at 是用來指特定的時間、地點或活動；介系詞 for 則用來表示用處、原因或是時間。而本題該使用的 with 則表一起合作或是同意的狀態，與本句語意最相符。

Computers and the Internet
電腦與網路的普及

UNIT 23

🎧 MP3 019

㉓ Computer and Internet use are becoming increasingly commonplace not only in schools ------- also in homes.
(A) but   (B) or   (C) nor   (D) and

中譯 (A) 使用電腦與網路已不只在學校越來越平常，在家裡也是如此。

速解 看到整個句子目光直接鎖定「**not only in schools ----- also in homes**」，空格前後有相關連接詞的一部份 **not only... also**，空格應填能完整此相關連接詞的字詞，故填選項(A) but 以形成連接詞 not only...but also。選項(B) or、選項(C) nor 與選項(D) and 都是別的相關連接詞的一部份，不可選。

進階 本考題重點為相關連接詞。相關連接詞用來連接相同類型的字詞或子句。本句是藉由相關連接詞 not only...but also 來連接 in schools 與 in homes 來表達「不但在學校也在家裡」很常見。藉常見的相關連接詞即可判斷其他選項不正確，其他常見的連接詞如 both and 表「A 和 B 都～」，有 or 的 whether or「不論 A 或 B」與 either or「不是 A 就是 B」，而 neither nor 則表示「既不 A 也不 B」。

Computers and the Internet
網路連線速度 🎧 MP3 019

㉔ Internet connection speed depends on the use and number of users, but eight megabits per second is usually -------.
(A) satisfy　(B) satisfied　(C) satisfaction　(D) satisfactory

中譯▶ (D) 網路連線速度根據使用內容以及使用人數不同，但通常每秒 8MB 就夠了。

速解▶ 看到整個句子目光直接鎖定「**eight megabits per second is usually -----**」，空格前為副詞與名詞片語，空格應填形容詞，即選項(D) satisfactory。選項(A) satisfy 為動詞，選項(B) satisfied 為過去分詞，選項(C) satisfaction 為名詞，皆不可選。

進階▶ 本考題重點為正確詞性。不同詞性會有固定搭配的詞性，如形容詞可能搭配名詞，副詞可能搭配動詞等。本題空格前為副詞 usually，空格可能填形容詞、動詞或副詞，但因前方有名詞片語 eight megabits per second，而空格的詞需能修飾此名詞片語，故不選其它詞性，而需選擇形容詞 satisfactory。選項(A)-fy 結尾，為常見的動詞結尾，選項(B)的 -ed 可能為過去分詞或過去式動詞，因此 satisfied 也可作形容詞，但和 satisfactory 不同的是，satisfied 表達的是「感到滿足」，選項(C)的 -ion 結尾可判斷此為名詞。

Office Technology
組織辦公科技 🎧 MP3 019

㉕ ------- helps workers to communicate with clients, manage payment information, and analyze sales data.
(A) Organizational office technology
(B) Organizational office technologies
(C) An organizational office technology
(D) An organizational office technologies

中譯 ▶ **(A)** 組織辦公科技協助員工與客戶聯繫、管理收付款資訊以及分析銷售資料。

速解 ▶ 看到整個句子目光直接鎖定「**----- helps workers**」，空格後有單數形動詞，空格應填單數名詞，故不可選有 technologies 的選項(B)或選項(D)。此外，在此 technology 為不可數名詞，不可有定冠詞 an，應填入選項(A)。

進階 ▶ 本考題重點為主動詞一致以及詞義。根據主詞動詞一致的要求，當主要動詞是第三人稱單數時（動詞尾加上 -s），主詞必須是單數名詞，故含複數名詞的選項(B)與(D)皆不可選，此外選項(D)更有單數不定冠詞 an 加上複數名詞的錯誤。此外 technology 為不可數名詞，基本上不使用 an 或是複數形，若加上複數是為特別強調不同類的科技，故含有 an 的選項(C)也不可選。正確答案應填入符合主動詞一致且沒有違反冠詞規定的選項(A)Organizational office technology。

Office Technology
用智慧型手機做信用卡付款 🎧 MP3 019

Part 1 新制閱讀 part 6 答題強化

㉖ He has been ------- his smartphone to make credit card transactions ever since he first started his business.
(A) uses　(B) used　(C) using　(D) usen

中譯 ▶ (C) 他從開始創業之後就一直使用智慧型手機做信用卡付款。

速解 ▶ 看到整個句子目光直接鎖定「**He has been -----**」，空格前有 **has been**，空格應填現在分詞形的動詞，組成現在完成進行式，即選項 (C) **using**。選項(A) **uses**、選項(B) **used** 與選項(D) **usen** 都不可用在 has been 之後，故以上皆不可選。

進階 ▶ 本考題重點為現在完成進行式。現在完成進行式的結構為 have/has + been + Ving，用來**表達過去開始且一直延續到現在的動作**，本題中 making transactions 與空格前 has been 結合的動作便是指「從創業開始便一直延續到現在」。選項(A) **uses** 為現在簡單式的動詞，表達時常或固定發生的事物，選項(B) **used** 為過去簡單式的動詞，指已發生過的事，選項(D) **usen** 為過去分詞動詞的錯誤寫法，正確應作 used，以上皆與想表達的時態及題中 has been 不符。

Part 2 核心文法和單字考點

Part 3 精選模擬試題

Office Technology
UNIT 27
更新辦公室科技 🎧 MP3 019

❷ Companies regularly upgrade their office technology to increase their ------- and attract future employees.
(A) productive   (B) productivity
(C) productize   (D) productively

中譯▶ (B) 企業經常更新辦公室科技來增加他們的生產力並吸引未來的員工。

速解▶ 看到整個句子目光直接鎖定「**increase their -----**」，空格前為所有格 **their**，空格應填名詞，即選項(B) productivity。選項(A) productive 為形容詞、選項(C)為動詞，而選項(D) productively 為副詞，皆不可選。

進階▶ 本考題重點為詞性。句中的 their 是所有格，是用來表現擁有某物或某物的歸屬，置於形容詞與名詞之前，本句空格後沒有名詞，故空格中不可能是形容詞，應填名詞，從字尾 -ity 可判斷出選項(B)為名詞，故應選(B)。從字尾也可判斷其他選項的詞性。選項(A)的結尾為常見的形容詞結尾-ive，為形容詞；選項(C)的結尾 -ize 表動詞；選項(C)的結尾是 -ly，表副詞。以上都與本句不符。

Office Technology
善用辦公室科技 🎧 MP3 019

UNIT 28

28 Employees who know how to use office technology are usually ------- than employees who do not.

(A) accurater　　　　(B) most accurate

(C) more accurater　(D) more accurate

中譯▶ (D) 懂得善用辦公室科技的員工通常會比不懂的員工更精確。

速解▶ 看到整個句子目光直接鎖定「**usually ----- than**」，空格後有 **than**，表示比較級，空格應填比較級形容詞，故填選項(D) **more accurate**。選項(A) accurater 與選項(C) more accurater 為錯誤的比較級形容詞，選項(B) most accurate 為最高級形容詞，皆不可選。

進階▶ 本考題重點為形容詞。句中比較兩樣東西 employees who... 以及 employees who do not，加上題目中的 than，表示中間應使用比較級形容詞。當形容詞只有一或兩個音節時，比較級為形容詞加上 -er；若形容詞為三個音節以上時（以及部份雙音節單字），比較級為形容詞前加上 more。本題的 accurate 有三個音節，故比較級應為 more accurate，即選項(D)。

Office Procedures
UNIT 29 遵循辦公室的流程 🎧 MP3 019

29 It would be wise to follow office procedures ------- customers want to file a complaint.
(A) whenever　(B) although　(C) because　(D) unless

中譯 (A) 當有客戶抱怨的時候，最好遵循辦公室的流程。

速解 看到整個句子目光直接鎖定「**follow office procedures ----- customers want to**」，空格前後有兩個子句，空格應填符合語意的連接詞，即選項(A) whenever。選項(B) although、選項(C) because 與選項(D)unless 皆是連接詞，但語意與本句不符，故不可選。

進階 本考題重點為連接詞。兩個子句需要以連接詞串連，而選項中皆為從屬連接詞，用來連接獨立子句與從屬子句，表達兩者的關係。藉瞭解各從屬連接詞的語意，可判斷應使用的連接詞。選項(A) whenever 表示「每當」，選項(B) although 表示「雖然、即使」，選項(C) because 表「因為」，選項(D) unless 表「除非」，只有選項(A)才能有邏輯的表達兩個子句的關係，將兩句串成有意義的句子，故選(A)。

Office Procedures
研讀公司手冊 🎧 MP3 019

㉚ New employees should read the company manual and become familiar with the rules ------- their first day of work.
(A) in　(B) at　(C) before　(D) until

中譯 ▶ (C) 新進員工在開始上班之前應研讀公司手冊並熟悉公司規範。

速解 ▶ 看到整個句子目光直接鎖定「**----- their first day of work**」，空格後有 **first day of work**，空格應填在文法與語意上都相符的介系詞，即選項(C) before。選項(A) in 表一段時間，選項(B) at 表特定時間，選項(D) until 表直到一個特定時間，皆不符合本句，故不可選。

進階 ▶ 本考題重點為介系詞。介系詞可用來表達時間關係。選項中的 in 後通常皆月份、季節、年份、（非特定）一段時間等，「first day of work」較確切，無法與 in 共用。介系詞 at 則接 night 或一個特定的時間點，而 until 則指到一個特定時間，皆與句中的時間語意或邏輯不符，不可選。選項中的 **before 則指在某個時間之前**。本句中該做的事情應在上班第一天前完成是符合邏輯的，故選(C)。

Office Procedures
緊急出口與急救工具 🎧 MP3 019

㉛ Everyone ------- to know about the emergency exits and safety tools in case a dangerous situation occurs.

(A) need　(B) needs　(C) are needing　(D) have needed

中譯 (B) 每個人都應該要知道緊急出口與急救工具，以防緊急狀況發生。

速解 看到整個句子目光直接鎖定「**Everyone ----- to know**」，空格前有單數形的主詞，空格應填單數動詞，即選項(B) needs。選項(A) need、選項(C) are needing 與選項(D)have needed 皆為複數形的動詞，不可選。

進階 本考題重點為主詞動詞一致。大部分主詞為一般名詞，單複數形容易辨認（ 如 people, computers 等）。不定代名詞也可做主詞，某些代名詞為單數形，包含 anyone, anything, none, nothing, neither, either, what, whatever, whoever, somebody, something, someone, each, everyone, everything, everybody。句中的 **everyone** 為單數形的不定代名詞，故需使用單數形動詞 **needs**。其他選項皆為複數形動詞，需分別改為 needs、is needing 與 has needed 才為單數形動詞。

Office Procedures
仔細閱讀手冊 🎧MP3 019

UNIT 32

㉜ Please read the manual ------- because it provides important information about the dress code and holidays.
(A) care　(B) careful　(C) carefully　(D) carer

中譯 ▶ (C) 請仔細閱讀手冊，因為手冊提供了服裝要求與節日相關的重要資訊。

速解 ▶ 看到整個句子目光直接鎖定「**read... -----**」，空格前有動詞，空格應填入副詞來修飾動詞，即選項(C) carefully。選項(A) care 為動詞，選項(B) careful 為形容詞，選項(D) carer 為名詞，詞性皆不符，不可選。

進階 ▶ 本考題重點為詞性。本句為祈使句，主詞為省略的 you，動詞為 read，受詞為 manual，其後需要副詞來修飾，即有副詞結尾 - ly 的（C）carefully。此外，副詞可置於句首、句尾或句中（句子或子句），置於句後的副詞包含說明動作如何發生的情狀副詞，即選項(C) carefully。利用字尾可判斷其他選項非副詞。選項(B)的結尾為-ful，為形容詞，應修飾名詞而非動詞。選項(D)-er 結尾表名詞，而選項(A)為動詞，皆不可用來修飾動詞，不可選。

Electronics
監視攝影機 🎧 MP3 019

UNIT 33

㉝ Security cameras are installed at every entrance and exit to ensure ------- safety of employees.
(A)(no article)　(B) the　(C) an　(D) a

中譯 ▶ (B) 在每個出入口都裝有監視攝影機來確保員工的安全。

速解 ▶ 看到整個句子目光直接鎖定「**ensure ----- safety of employees**」，空格前為動詞，空格後為名詞，空格內可能為冠詞。然而 safety 為不可數名詞，選項(C) a 與選項(D) an 不可選。不可數名詞前有時不需冠詞，然而此處指的是由介係詞片語所限定的特定一群人，需加上定冠詞 the，故不選(A)而選(B) the。

進階 ▶ 本考題重點為冠詞。要判斷正確的冠詞時，記得 a 與 an 只能與單數可數名詞共用，句中的名詞 safety 為不可數名詞，不可使用。而定冠詞 the 後可接可數或不可數名詞，用來指特定的人事物。有時名詞前不須使用冠詞，特別是指整體事物、抽象事物或一些特定字詞（如城市、國家、疾病等），然而當介係詞片語用來修飾名詞時，時常會限定這個名詞，如本句的 safety of employees「員工的安全」，已被限定，故應使用定冠詞 the。

Electronics
電腦、高速網路與檔案櫃　🎧 MP3 019

㉞ A computer, high-speed internet access, and a file cabinet ------ to set up an efficient home office.

(A) needed　(B) am needed　(C) is needed　(D) are needed

中譯▶ (D) 想設立一個有效率的家庭辦公室，你需要一台電腦、高速網路與檔案櫃。

速解▶ 看到整個句子目光直接鎖定「**A computer, high-speed internet access, and a file cabinet ------**」，空格前為主詞，空格內應填被動語態的動詞，故選(D) are needed。選項(A) needed 為主動語態的過去是動詞，而選項(B) am needed 與選項(C) is needed 與主詞不一致，同樣不可選。

進階▶ 本考題重點為動詞形態。本題中主詞「A computer, high-speed internet access, and a file cabinet」與動詞 need 的關係為被動關係，動詞應使用被動語態，即 be + 過去分詞，故不可選(A) needed。被動語態結構中的 be 應隨主詞作改變，須與主詞一致。選項(B)裡的 am 用在主詞為 I 時，選項(C)的 is 與第三人稱單數的主詞共用，選項(D)的 are 與複數主詞共用。本題主詞中有三樣東西，為複數，故需使用 are needed。

Electronics
UNIT 35 手機電腦的修護生意 🎧 MP3 019

35 ------- decided to invest her money into starting a small cellphone and laptop repair business at home.
(A) Hers　(B) She　(C) Her　(D) Herself

中譯 (B) 她決定投入資金在家創立一個小型的手機電腦修護生意。

速解 看到整個句子目光直接鎖定「----- **decided to invest her money**」，句中無主詞，且空格後有 **her**，空格內應填正確的主詞，即選項(B) She。選項(A) Hers 為所有格代名詞，選項(C) Her 為人稱代名詞所有格，選項(D) Herself 為反身代名詞，皆與本句不符，不可選。

進階 本考題重點為代名詞。本句有主要動詞 decided，無主詞，空格需填入主詞，故須從選項中挑選能做主詞且符合語意的代名詞，因此應該選擇人稱代名詞主格的選項(B) She。選項(A)的所有格代名詞也可當主詞，但代表的是之前提過的人事物（如 hers = her books），但與本句並不符。選項(C)為人稱代名詞受格或所有格，當所有格的時候必須加上名詞才可當主詞（如 Her father decided...）。選項(D) Herself 為反身代名詞，不可當主詞。故皆不可選。

Electronics
碎紙機處理機密文件

🎧 MP3 019

36 Paper shredders are the ------- way to get rid of private documents and protect company information.

(A) quickest　(B) most quickest　(C) most quick　(D) quicker

中譯 ▶ (A) 碎紙機是消除機密文件、保護公司資訊的最快方法。

速解 ▶ 看到整個句子目光直接鎖定「**Paper shredders are the -----**」，空格前為 **the**，空格內應填形容詞的最高級，即選項(A) quickest。選項(B) most quickest 使用兩個最高級形，選項(C) most quick 為錯誤的最高級形，選項(D) quicker 為形容詞比較級，皆不可選。

進階 ▶ 本考題重點為形容詞最高級。本句有主詞與動詞，且空格前有 the，後有名詞 way，可知缺少形容詞，且由 the 可得知應為最高級，且因為比較的事物為三件以上（即方法有很多），也確認需使用最高級，故不可選(D)。而選項中的形容詞 quick 為單音節字詞，最高級應直接在字尾加上 -est 而不是加上 most，故不選(C)而選(A)。而選項(B)中最高級的 most 與最高級的 -est 不可共用。

Correspondence
將信件寄給客人 🎧 MP3 019

㊲ Please send out the correspondence ------- our customers to inform them about our new policies.
(A) of　(B) to　(C) from　(D) about

中譯▶ (B) 請將這份信件寄給我們的客人，告知他們新的政策。

速解▶ 看到整個句子目光直接鎖定「**send out the correspondence ----- our customers**」，空格前 **correspondence**，後方為對象 **our customers**，空格應填表「從一地移動到另一地」的介系詞，即選項 (B) to。選項(A) of、選項(C) from 與選項(D) about 皆與本句語意不合，不可選。

進階▶ 本題考的重點是介系詞。從本句語意可看出通信信件會向著某個方向寄出。而選項中的介系詞 to 可用來表達「朝向某個方向、某地或某人」，因此句子 please send out the correspondence to our customers 表示通信會向著客戶的方向寄出。其他選項中的介系詞 of 用來表達「關聯」。介系詞 from 則可表達「開端或是某人／某物離開的地方」，與介系詞 to 相反。介系詞 about 則表「主題」。

Correspondence
抱怨某個職員的行為 🎧 MP3 019

38 Correspondences can be used to send a ------- about an employee's actions or company's services.

(A) complaint　(B) complain　(C) complaining　(D) complainer

中譯 (A) 信件能被用來抱怨某個職員的行為或公司的服務。

速解 看到整個句子目光直接鎖定「**correspondence can be used to send a -----**」，空格前為不定冠詞 **a** ， 空格應填適當的單數名詞， 即選項(A)complaint。選項(B) complain 為動詞， 選項(C) complaining 為現在分詞或動名詞，選項(D) complainer 表「人」名詞，皆不選。

進階 本題考的重點是詞性辨別。不定冠詞 **a** 用在單數可數名詞前，且此單數名詞須為子音開頭，用來引出初次提及的人事物。本題空格前為不定冠詞 a，後方應使用子音開頭的單數名詞，選項(B)與(D)為動詞，故不選，即便 complaining 作為動名詞解（意表「抱怨」這件事或動作），語意不通，且動名詞前通常不使用冠詞，選項(D)為表「抱怨者」的名詞，雖為子音開頭的單數名詞，語意上也不合，不選，故本題應使用選項(A)。

Correspondence
寄道歉函給客戶

🎧 MP3 019

39 An apology letter was mailed to customers after private information was accidentally leaked on ------- May 17th.
(A) a　(B) an　(C) the　(D)(no article)

中譯 (D) 在五月十七日個人資訊意外流出後，道歉函便被寄給客戶。

···

速解 看到整個句子目光直接鎖定「**leaked on ----- May 17th**」，空格前為動詞與介系詞，後為日期，空格不應填入任何冠詞，即選項(D)(no article)。選項(A) a 與選項(B) an 為不定冠詞，選項(C) the 為定冠詞，皆不可選。

···

進階 本題考的重點是冠詞使用時機。基本上名詞，尤其單數可數名詞前必須使用冠詞，但有些情況下不可使用冠詞，例如月份、星期、日期、假日或季節等（月份如 May、星期如 Monday、假日如 Christmas、季節如 autumn）。本句空格後是特定的一個日期 May 17th，這時候為符合文法規則不應使用冠詞，故本題不選擇用來引出第一次出現的人事物的不定冠詞的(A)或(B)，也不選擇表特定人事物的選項(C)，而應選擇(D)。

Correspondence
書寫職場商業信件 🎧 MP3 019

UNIT 40

❹ Writing business letters is important for ------- employees information about projects and assignments.
(A) giving　(B) gave　(C) give　(D) have given

中譯▶ (A) 書寫職場商業信件對給予員工關於專案和任務的相關訊息來說很重要。

速解▶ 看到整個句子目光直接鎖定「**important for -----**」，空格前 **for**，後方為子句 **employees information about...**，空格應填動名詞，即選項(A) giving。選項(B) gave 為過去動詞，選項(C) give 為原形動詞，選項(D) have given 為現在完成式動詞，皆不可選。

進階▶ 本題考的重點是動詞形態。介系詞後方需使用名詞、代名詞或動名詞，若介系詞後方需使用動詞，則須改為動名詞，即原形動詞加上 -ing。本句以主詞 writing business letter 開頭，接上動詞 is、形容詞 important 與介系詞 for，空格前為介系詞 for，後方的動詞用作介系詞的受詞，應改為動名詞，故不選過去動詞的 gave、原形動詞的 give 或現在完成式的 have given，應填入動名詞作受詞的選項(A) giving。

Part 1 新制閱讀 part 6 答題強化

Part 2 核心文法和單字考點

Part 3 精選模擬試題

131

Job Advertising and Recruiting

UNIT
41

招募有能力又適合的應試者 🎧 MP3 020

❹1 Recruiting ------- capable and suitable candidates is critical to the success of an organization.

(A) a   (B) an   (C) the   (D)(no article)

中譯▶ (D) 招募有能力又適合的應試者對一個組織的成功與否是個重要的關鍵。

......

速解▶ 看到整個句子目光直接鎖定「**Recruiting ----- capable and suitable candidates**」，空格後為名詞，空格應不填入冠詞，即選項(D)(no article)。選項(A) a 與選項(B) an 為不定冠詞，選項(C) the 為定冠詞，皆不可選。

......

進階▶ 本題考的重點是冠詞的使用。冠詞用來引出第一次提及的名詞或特定的名詞。本句空格前為動詞改動名詞的 Recruiting，後為形容詞 capable 與 suitable，接上複數可數名詞 candidates，空格可能需使用冠詞引出名詞。當判斷是否使用冠詞或該使用哪個冠詞時，可略過句中形容詞，只需由名詞判斷。空格後為複數可數名詞 candidates，故不可使用引出單數可數名詞的不定冠詞選項(A)或選項(B)（此外，不定冠詞 an 只能用在首音為母音的字詞）。又從句意可判斷 candidates 在此用作總稱（指所有的 candidates），而定冠詞 the 是用來引出特定的單數或複數的可數或不可數名詞，在此不適用，故空格不應填入任何冠詞。

Job Advertising and Recruiting
招募人員受聘審閱履歷　🎧 MP3 020

❷ A recruiter is hired to review resumes, negotiate salaries, -------
match candidates with appropriate positions.
(A) but　(B) and　(C) nor　(D) yet

中譯　(B) 招募人員被聘來審閱履歷、談判薪資以及將人選媒合至適當的位置。

速解　看到整個句子目光直接鎖定「**review resumes, negotiate salaries, ----- match candidates**」，空格前後為對等的片語，空格應填適當的連接詞，即選項(B) and。選項(A) but 表對立，選項(C) nor 表否定，選項(D) yet 表「然而、還沒」等，皆不可選。

進階　本題考的重點是連接詞。對等連接詞用來連接對等的字詞、片語或子句，對等連接詞包含 and, but, or, nor, for, so, yet，各自表達的意思不同，判斷使用哪個連接詞，可先判斷連接的兩個成份為相似或是相對的概念。本句中空格前後為三個片語 review resumes, negotiate salaries 以及 match candidates with appropriate positions，且三個片語表達相似的概念，因為三者皆表達招募人員的工作內容，故不使用表達相對概念的選項(A)與(D)，而選項(C) nor 只用在否定句（如 recruiters don't review resumes nor negotiate salaries），因本題為肯定句，故不選。本題空格應使用(B) and 來連結相似的概念。

Job Advertising and Recruiting
創造特別的求職廣告 🎧 MP3 020

❹ Companies are always trying to create unique job advertisements to set themselves apart ------- other companies.
(A) to   (B) of   (C) for   (D) from

中譯 (D) 公司總是試著創造特別的求職廣告以和其他公司有區分。

......

速解 看到整個句子目光直接鎖定「**set themselves apart ----- other companies**」，空格前為動詞片語 **set apart**，空格應填適當的介系詞，即選項**(D) from**。選項**(A) to** 可表「到達」，選項**(B) of** 可表關係，選項**(C) for** 可表「用來」，皆不選。

......

進階 本題考的重點是介系詞。介系詞用來表明句中字與字的關係。本題空格前為動詞片語 set apart，用來表達「使某人或某物與某人或某物不同、區分...」，空格中應填入介系詞說明 set themselves apart 與 other companies 的關係，而介系詞 from 表達起始點，即是某物或某人離開的地方，本題應使用 from 來表達 unique job advertisement 可使公司與其他公司區分（自其他公司分離）。介系詞 to 用來表達移動的方向，與空格前的 apart 相反，不可選。介系詞 of 則用來表示從屬關係或連結，然而 set themselves apart 並不是 other companies 的一部份，不選。介系詞 for 表達用法、原因或時間，與本題語意不合，不可選。

Job Advertising and Recruiting
討喜的應徵者 🎧 MP3 020

44 Employers want to hire the ------- candidate with intelligence, integrity, and leadership skills.

(A) likeablest　　　(B) most likeable

(C) more likeable　　(D) likeabler

中譯 ▶ (B) 雇主想要聘請有智慧、正直且有領導能力，又最討喜的應徵者。

速解 ▶ 看到整個句子目光直接鎖定「**Employers want to hire the ----- candidate**」，空格前 **the**，空格應填形容詞最高級，即選項(B) most likeable。選項(A) likeablest 為錯誤用法，選項(C) more likeable 為比較級，選項(D) likeabler 為錯誤用法，皆不選。

進階 ▶ 本題考的重點是形容詞形式。形容詞可能有比較級或最高級，比較級用來比較兩樣東西或人，形式上為形容詞加上 -er 或在前方使用 more，而最高級用來表示三者以上的人事物中，「最...的」，使用上為形容詞 -est 或在前方使用 most。本題因為比較的東西多於兩人，且空格前方有 the，故空格內應使用最高級的形容詞形式，故可刪除 more 或 -er 結尾的選項(C)與(D)，又形容詞 likeable 為三個音節的形容詞，故形容詞的最高級不使用 -est 結尾，而需另外在前方加上 most，故不選(A)，應改選(B)。

Job Advertising and Recruiting
接受雇用測驗 🎧 MP3 020

㊺ If a student wants to get a job, he or she ------- to prepare a resume, write a cover letter, and take employment tests.
(A) need　(B) needing　(C) needed　(D) needs

中譯 (D) 若一個學生想找到工作，他（她）必須準備履歷、撰寫應徵函並接受雇用測驗。

速解 看到整個句子目光直接鎖定「**If a student wants to get a job, he or she ----- to prepare**」，空格前方有 **if** 接現在簡單式動詞，且說明的內容永遠成立，空格應填現在簡單式的動詞，即選項**(D) needs**。選項**(A) need** 為原形動詞，選項**(B) needing** 為現在分詞，選項**(C) needed** 為過去式動詞，皆不可選。

進階 本題考的重點是第零類條件句。第零類條件句為一種假設語氣，用來陳述不變的定律、一般事實或科學真理等，表「只要條件吻合，便會成真或發生」，第零類條件句的主要子句以及 if 的從句都會使用現在簡單式。本句以 If 開頭的從屬子句加上一個主要子句（he or she...），而主要子句中的空格前為第三人稱的 he or she，故不選使用在非第三人稱的 (A) need（若為 he and she 才可使用）。另，選項(B)因沒有 be 動詞，不可選。又 if 從屬句中的動詞為現在簡單式的 wants，陳述的內容為一般事實或習慣，故主要子句也應使用現在簡單式，故應選(D)。

Applying and Interviewing
工作機會的增加 🎧 MP3 020

❹❻ In the United States, jobs in leisure, hospitality, health care, social assistance, and finance have been -------.
(A) increase　(B) increasen　(C) increases　(D) increasing

中譯 ▶ (D) 在美國休閒、觀光服務業、醫療保健、社會服務以及財經產業的工作機會一直在增加。

速解 ▶ 看到整個句子目光直接鎖定「**In the United States jobs...have been -----**」，空格前為 **have been**，空格應填現在分詞，即選項(D) increasing。選項(A) increase 為原形動詞，選項(B) increasen 為錯誤用法，而選項(C) increases 為第三人稱單數動詞，皆不可選。

進階 ▶ 本題考的重點是動詞形態。現在完成進行式的結構為 has/have been + Ving（現在分詞），**用來表達從以前到現在發生的狀況或動作，強調動作或狀況的過程或持續狀況等**，通常也暗指「最近」。本句的主要子句中有主詞 jobs in leisure... and finance，後方有助動詞 have，接上完成式的 been，後方動詞應使用現在分詞的 increasing，來表示在這些產業中的工作從過去到現在都在持續增加，故選(D)，而不填選項(A)與(C)。而選項(B)為錯誤用法。

Applying and Interviewing
說服雇主聘用 🎧 MP3 020

❺❼ During the job application process, applicants must persuade employers to hire them ------- clearly stating their qualifications and availability.

(A) for　(B) through　(C) by　(D) to

中譯 (C) 在工作應徵的過程中，應徵者應清楚闡述他們的條件與可上班時間，以說服雇主聘用他們。

....

速解 看到整個句子目光直接鎖定「**persuade employers to hire them ------ clearly stating...**」，空格前方為動作，後方為方式，空格應填適當的介系詞，即選項(C) by。選項(A) for 可表理由，選項(B) through 可表「穿透」，選項(D) to 表「到達」，皆不可選。

....

進階 本題考的重點是正確的介系詞。 如前述，介系詞是用來表達字詞等成分之間的關係，故必須透過語意確定正確的介系詞。本句中的主要子句 applicants must... availability 中空格前方是情況或想達到的目的，而後方是方法或手段，故空格應使用介系詞 by 來表明「藉著某種方法」。介系詞 to 通常用來表達到達的方向或時間、極限等，而介系詞 for 可用來表達用法、原因或持續的一段時間，而介系詞 through 則用來表達穿透或通過、開始到結束，或表達一段時間。

Applying and Interviewing
提供晉升機會　🎧 MP3 020

❹ Employees are searching for companies that encourage -------
and provide career advancement opportunities.
(A) diversified　(B) diversity　(C) diverse　(D) diversely

中譯 (B) 員工都在尋找鼓勵多元化並提供晉升機會的公司。

速解 看到整個句子目光直接鎖定「**companies that encourage -----**」，
空格前為動詞，後為連接詞，空格應填名詞，即選項(B) diversity。
選項(A) diversified 為形容詞，選項(C) diverse 為形容詞，選項(D)
diversely 為副詞，皆不可選。

進階 本題考的重點是及物動詞。及物動詞為後方必須加上受詞的動詞
（如 send, take, open, want 等），後方若無動詞，則句子顯得不完
整。本題空格前的動詞 encourage 便是及物動詞，後方應加受詞，
而名詞才可作為受詞，故本題應使用 -ity 結尾的 diversity。選項(A)
與(C) 皆為形容詞，空格前後並非名詞，故不可選。選項(D)以-ly 結
尾，為副詞，雖然動詞 encourage 後可使用副詞，但在本句中卻與
encourage 語意不合，不可選（與 encourage 可併用的副詞有
passionately 或 supportively 等）。

Applying and Interviewing
面試練習

🎧 MP3 020

❹The student prepared for his job interview by recording practice interviews, **-------** he really wanted a job.
(A) for   (B) but   (C) nor   (D) so

中譯 ▶ (A) 那位學生錄他的面試練習來作應徵工作的準備，因為他真的很想要有工作。

速解 ▶ 看到整個句子目光直接鎖定「**The student prepared for his job interview..., ----- he really wanted a job**」，空格前表結果的子句，空格後為表原因的子句，空格應填適當的連接詞，即選項(A) for。選項(B) but 表「但是」，選項(C) nor 表「也不」，選項(D) so 表「所以」，皆不可選。

進階 ▶ 本題考的重點是連接詞。連接詞用來連接兩個成分，而判斷應該使用哪個連接詞則必須透過連接詞前後成分想表達的語意。本句有兩個子句 the student prepared for his job interview... 以及 he really wanted a job，後方的子句是前方子句動作的原因、理由。而連接詞 for 便是用來引出理由或原因，故本題空格便應填入連接詞 for。連接詞 but 用來連接兩個對立的字詞或子句，連接詞 nor 用來引出另一個否定的概念，而 so 用來引出效力或結果，以上皆與本句語意不合，不可選。

Applying and Interviewing
對候選人的評量

UNIT 50

🎧 MP3 020

50 Everybody was asked to complete ------- evaluation of the candidates based on skill, character, and professionalism.
(A) their　(B) themselves　(C) he or she　(D) his or her

中譯▶ (D) 所有人都被要求根據技能、人格特質與專業來完成他們對候選人的評量。

速解▶ 看到整個句子目光直接鎖定「**Everybody was asked to complete ------ evaluation**」，空格前方為主詞 **everybody**，空格後為名詞，空格應填第三人稱單數、不分性別的代明詞所有格，即選項 (D) his or her。選項(A) their 為複數代名詞所有格，選項(B) themselves 為複數反身代名詞，而選項(C) he or she 為第三人稱單數主格，皆不可選。

進階▶ 本題考的重點是正確的人稱代名詞。人稱代名詞用來代替名詞，在人稱、數量或格位上都會隨著代替的名詞作變化。本句的空格前為動詞 complete，後為名詞 evaluation，空格應入代名詞所有格。又代名詞的人稱、數量等須依所代替的名詞作變化，因此必須確定所替代的名詞為何。在此，代名詞所替代的名詞為 **everyone**，因 **everyone** 需視為單數，且無性別之分，故不選(A)或(B)。又如前述，空格後方為名詞，必須使用所有格，故不選(C)，而應使用選項(D)第三人稱單數、不分性別的人稱代名詞所有格 his or her。

Hiring and Training
員工於聘用後的訓練 🎧 MP3 020

51 After employees are hired, each employee ------- to receive training in safety, personal growth, and career development.
(A) need　(B) needs　(C) needing　(D) have needed

中譯 ▶ (B) 員工被聘用後，每個人都需要接受安全、個人成長以及事業發展上的訓練。

速解 ▶ 看到整個句子目光直接鎖定「**each employee ----- to receive**」，空格前為主詞 **each employee**，後方為 **to**，空格應填適當的動詞，即選項(B) needs。選項(A) need 為原形動詞，選項(C) needing 為現在分詞，選項(D) have needed 為現在完成式動詞，皆不可選。

進階 ▶ 本題考的重點是主詞動詞一致。英文句子中的主要動詞在人稱或數量上須與主詞相配合，例如當時態皆為現在簡單式，主要動詞為 be 動詞時，主詞 he 會使用 is，主詞 they 會使用 are，若主要動詞是一般動詞時，主詞 he 會使用 -s 結尾的動詞，主詞 they 會使用原形動詞。本句的主詞為 **each employee**，當 **each** 接上名詞時，會視為單數主詞，故動詞會使用第三人稱單數動詞，故不使用複數的(A)與(D)，而應使用選項(B)的 needs。而 needing 前方必須要有 be 動詞，在此不可選。

Hiring and Training
科技產品的報告

UNIT **52**

🎧 MP3 020

52 During the training period, employees are asked to submit ------- papers on the effective use of technology.

(A) an　(B) any　(C) every　(D) several

中譯 ▶ (D) 在實習的階段，員工會被要求提交好幾份關於有效率使用科技產品的報告。

速解 ▶ 看到整個句子目光直接鎖定「**submit ----- papers**」，空格前為動詞，後為複數可數名詞，空格應填適當的量詞，即選項(D) several。選項(A) an、選項(B) any 與選項(C) every 都只能使用在單數名詞，皆不可選。

進階 ▶ 本題考的重點是量詞的使用。量詞用在名詞前方，用來表示名詞的量，有些量詞後方只能使用可數名詞（如 many, a few），有些量詞後方只能接不可數名詞（如 much, a little）。選項(A)為不定冠詞，後方必須接單數的可數名詞，而其他選項中的量詞 any 與 every 後方也只能使用單數可數名詞，而選項(D) several 後方只能接上複數可數名詞。本句空格後為名詞 papers，名詞 paper 可能為不可數名詞，也可以是可數名詞，需依意思做判斷，在此作「報告」解釋，為複數可數名詞，前方不能使用選項中的 an, any, every，只能使用選項中的 several，故選(D)。

Hiring and Training
雇主有義務告知員工

🎧 MP3 020

㊾ Employers are required to ------- employees about customer service skills and workplace safety.

(A) inform　(B) informed　(C) information　(D) informational

中譯 (A) 雇主有義務告知員工客戶服務技巧與職業安全。

速解 看到整個句子目光直接鎖定「**employers are required to ----- employees**」，空格前 **to**，後方為名詞 **employees**，空格應填動詞，即選項(A) inform。選項(B) informed 為過去式動詞，選項(C) information 為名詞，選項(D) informational 為形容詞，皆不可選。

進階 本題考的重點是詞性判斷。本句中的動詞 require 可在後方加上受詞後使用不定詞（to + 原形動詞）。本句結構為主詞 employers 接上被動的 are required to，空格後方是受詞 employees，此處 to 後方必須接上原形動詞，故空格內應填入選項(A) inform。選項中的 informed 為 -ed 結尾的過去式動詞，與 to 不合，也可做「消息靈通的」等意思的形容詞，與空格前的 required to 不合，不可選。結尾為 -al 的 informational 為形容詞，而選項中以 -ion 結尾的 information 為名詞，皆不可選。

Hiring and Training
實習生上商業寫作課 🎧 MP3 020

❺❹ Trainees are highly encouraged to take business writing classes so that they can write as ------- as current employees.

(A) most clearly　(B) more clearly　(C) clearly　(D) clealier

中譯▶ (C) 實習生被積極鼓勵上商業寫作課，書寫內容才能如目前員工一樣清楚。

速解▶ 看到整個句子目光直接鎖定「**write as ----- as current employees**」，空格前後有 **as**，空格應填原形形容詞，即選項(C) clearly。選項(A) most clearly 為副詞最高級，選項(B)more clearly 為副詞比較級，而選項(D) clearlier 為錯誤的比較級用法，皆不可選。

進階▶ 本題考的重點是副詞的比較級使用。副詞用來修飾動詞，當比較兩者的動作時，可使用副詞比較級(-er 或 more)，若比較三者以上的動作，可使用最高級(-est 或 most)， 當比較的結果是一樣的話，則會使用「as + 副詞原形 + as」的結構。本題空格出現在 as... as 之間，比較實習生與現任員工的書寫，前方為動詞 write，需使用副詞來修飾動詞，且比較結果相同，故空格應填入原形副詞，即選項(C)，不選最高級的(A)或比較級的(B)，且 clearly 雖為雙音節，但其比較級是直接在前加 more，故不選(D)。

Hiring and Training
探討溝通策略與組織政策 🎧 MP3 020

55 The trainees are meeting ------- upstairs to review communication strategies and organizational policies.

(A) at   (B) above   (C) to   (D)(no preposition)

中譯 ▶ (D) 實習生要在樓上開會，探討溝通策略與組織政策。

速解 ▶ 看到整個句子目光直接鎖定「**The trainees are meeting ----- upstairs**」，後方為地方副詞 **upstairs**，空格不填介系詞，故填選項 (D)(no preposition)。選項(A) at、選項(B) above 與選項(C) to 皆為介系詞，皆不可選。

進階 ▶ 本題考的重點是地方副詞的用法。地方副詞說明動作發生的地方，當用來描述方向時，某些地方副詞前不需要使用介系詞，如 home, upstairs,downstairs, downtown, uptown, inside, outside 等。本句中的空格出現在 upstairs 前，說明他們要碰面、開會的方向、地方，故前方不使用介系詞。選項中的介系詞 at 用來表示某個特定的地方，表「在...」（如 at the room upstairs）。介系詞 above 用來表示「在...之上」（如 Sign your name above the date.）。介系詞 to 用來描述動作的去向（如 I am going to the meeting.），皆不可選。

Salaries and Benefits
有健保與壽險的工作

UNIT 56　🎧 MP3 020

56 Although the salary was not as high, she ------- the job with health care and life insurance.

(A) choose　(B) chosen　(C) choosed　(D) chose

中譯 ▶ (D) 雖然薪水不高，但她選了有健保與壽險的工作。

速解 ▶ 看到整個句子目光直接鎖定「**she ----- the job**」，空格前主詞為第三人稱單數，空格應填適當的動詞，即選項(D) chose。選項(A) choose 為非第三人稱單數動詞，選項 (B) chosen 為過去分詞，選項 (C) choosed 為錯誤用法，皆不可選。

進階 ▶ 本題考的重點是主詞動詞一致。如前述主詞以及主要動詞一定要在人稱與數量等上面相搭配。本句中的主詞為第三人稱單數的 she，空格後為受詞 the job，空格中必須填入能與主詞相符的動詞。選項中只能選擇過去式的動詞 chose 才能與第三人稱單數主詞一致，故選答案(D)。選項(A)為原形動詞，必須與非第三人稱單數的主詞一起用。選項(B)為過去分詞，通常用在完成式或被動語態，空格前並沒有 have/has/had 等詞或 be 動詞，故不可選。而動詞 choose 屬於不規則動詞，動詞三態的變化是 choose-chose-chosen，故選項(C)為錯誤的過去式動詞，同樣不可選。

Salaries and Benefits
提供完整的福利　🎧 MP3 020

57 If the candidates get hired, the company will ------- them a full benefit package in addition to a competitive salary.
(A) offer　(B) offers　(C) offered　(D) offering

中譯 ▶ (A) 如果應徵者被聘用了，公司除了高薪外，還會提供完整的福利。

速解 ▶ 看到整個句子目光直接鎖定「**the company will -----**」，空格前 **will**，空格應填原形動詞，即選項**(A) offer**。選項**(A) offers** 為第三人稱單數動詞、選項**(C) offered** 為過去式動詞，選項**(D) offering** 為現在分詞，皆不可選。

進階 ▶ 本題考的重點是未來式與第一類條件句。未來式用來表達在未來時間發生的動作，其中一個表達方式便是用 will 加上原形動詞。而第一類條件句是 if 子句使用現在簡單式，而主要子句使用未來式 will + 原形動詞，整句表達可能發生的假設情況。本題以 if 子句開頭（If the candidates get hired），其中的動詞為現在簡單式的 get，後方接主要子句 the company will...。依據上述第一類條件句的結構，空格內應使用原形動詞，故選 offer，而不填其他選項。

Salaries and Benefits
期望薪資

UNIT 58

🎧 MP3 020

❺❽ Before accepting a job offer, ------- employees should consider how much their skills are worth and how much money they want.

(A) prospect
(B) prospectable
(C) prospectively
(D) prospective

中譯 (D) 在接受工作邀約之前，潛在員工應該考慮他們技能的價值以及他們希望的薪資。

速解 看到整個句子目光直接鎖定「----- employees」，空格後為名詞，空格應填適當的形容詞，即選項(D) prospective。選項(A)為動詞或名詞，選項(B)為錯誤用法，選項(C)為副詞，皆不可選。

進階 本題考的重點是詞性。形容詞修飾名詞，而副詞修飾動詞或形容詞。本句空格後為複數名詞 employees，需使用形容詞，選項中 -able 結尾以及 -ive 結尾的(B)與(D)可能為形容詞，然而(B)並不是一個真的字詞，只能選(D)，意思為「預期的、盼望的」，表示公司考慮雇用的候選人。選項(A)可作動詞或名詞，作名詞可表「前途或前景」，若要與名詞一起使用，需要介系詞（如 an employee with prospect）。以 -ly 結尾的選項(C)為副詞，在此不可使用。

Salaries and Benefits
其他的福利　🎧 MP3 020

59 ------- progressive companies allow male employees to take time off of work after the birth or adoption of a child.
(A) Every　(B) A few　(C) Any　(D) Each

中譯 (B) 有一些比較先進的公司允許男性員工在孩子出生或是領養孩子之後放假。

速解 看到整個句子目光直接鎖定「**----- progressive companies**」，空格後方為複數可數名詞，空格應填適當的量詞，即選項(B) A few。選項(A) Every、選項(C) Any、選項(D) Each 皆為與單數可數名詞共用的量詞，皆不可選。

進階 本題考的重點是量詞的使用。如前述特定量詞須與可數名詞共用，而某些量詞只能與不可數名詞共用。本題空格後方為形容詞 progressive 加上複數的可數名詞 companies，必須挑選可搭配的量詞。雖然選項中的量詞皆與可數名詞共用，但其中的 every, any, each 後方皆 _____ 必須使用單數名詞（如 every company, any company, each company），因此本題只能填入可以用在複數名詞前的 a few。

Salaries and Benefits
完成重要專案的員工

UNIT 60　🎧 MP3 020

60 Employees who have improved their productivity and completed important projects will have a ------- salary than those who didn't improve.
(A) better　(B) good　(C) most good　(D) more good

中譯▶ (A) 有增進生產力並完成重要專案的員工比起其他沒進步的員工會得到較好的薪水。

速解▶ 看到整個句子目光直接鎖定「**Employees who have improved their productivity...will have a ----- salary**」，空格前後比較兩種員工，空格應形容詞比較級，即選項(A) better。選項(B) good 為形容詞原形，選項(C) most good 與選項(D) more good 為錯誤用法，皆不可選。

進階▶ 本題考的重點是不規則形容詞變化。形容詞比較級用來表達兩樣人事物經比較過後有差異的結果。大部分比較級以 **-er** 結尾，部分雙音節以及所有三音節以上的單字使用 **more**＋形容詞原形，但有少數形容詞會有不規則變化。本句的空格前是有進步且有所為的員工，而後方是沒進步的員工，兩者的比較後，會有薪水上的差異，故應使用比較級來呈現薪水的不同，故原形的選項(B)不可選。又形容詞 **good** 屬於不規則變化的形容詞，選項(C)與選項(D)都不選，應選擇 better。

Promotions, Pensions, and Awards
退休金說明會

MP3 021

(61) If you are interested ------- signing up for a pension plan, please attend the information session on Thursday.

(A) on (B) of (C) in (D) for

中譯 (C) 如果你想要參加退休金計畫，請參加星期四的說明會。

速解 看到整個句子目光直接鎖定「**If you are interested ----- signing up**」，空格前 **interested**，後方為動名詞，空格應填正確的介系詞，即選項(C) in。選項(A) on、選項(B) of 與選項(D) for 皆與空格前的形容詞不合，不可選。

進階 本題考的重點是正確的介系詞。有些形容詞與名詞之間必須要有介系詞才能連接，這些組合的關係很緊密，形成慣用語。遇到這類形容詞時，比起判斷選項中介系詞的語意，反而應該熟悉慣用的組合。本題空格前為形容詞 interested，便是這類形容詞，後方習慣搭配的介系詞為 in，故其他選項皆不可使用。慣用語 interested in 表示「對...有興趣」，介系詞後方必須使用名詞或動名詞作受詞，如本題後方便是使用動名詞 signing 作受詞。

Promotions, Pensions, and Awards
退休金計畫

MP3 021

(62) Employees need to think ------- which type of pension plan would meet their needs after retirement.

(A) of (B) about (C) up (D) for

中譯 (B) 員工需要思考哪種退休金計畫可以符合他們退休後的需求。

速解 看到整個句子目光直接鎖定「**Employees need to think -----**」，空格前為動詞 **think**，表達的語意為思考，空格應填適當的介系詞，即選項(B)about。選項(A) of 、選項(C) up 與選項(D) for 配上 think 的語意與本句不符，皆不可選。

進階 本題考的重點是不同語意的動詞與介系詞的搭配。如前述有些動詞會與介系詞形容緊密的慣用關係，通常某個動詞會只搭配一個特定的介系詞（如 prepare for, agree to, admit to 等），然而有些動詞卻可以搭配不同介系詞，但代表的意思皆不同，遇到這類動詞時，須小心判斷題目想表達的語意。本題空格前是動詞 think，後方可接上不同的介系詞來表達不同的意思，後方必須接上介系詞 about 來表示原公司要想、要思考某樣事。動詞 think 也可與其他選項中的介系詞合用。當 think 與 of 合用時，可表示「想到某人事物」，而 think up 表「想出、發明」，而介系詞 for 也可用在 think 後方，但後方通常為代名詞，可表「自行思考」。

Promotions, Pensions, and Awards
馬上升職

MP3 021

(63) After his presentation, George was immediately promoted because it was clear that he was capable enough to think for-------.

(A) he (B) him (C) himself (D) ourselves

中譯 (C) 完成簡報後，George 馬上被升職，因為很明顯的他懂得獨立思考。

速解 看到整個句子目光直接鎖定「**think for -----**」，空格前為 **think for**，空格應填反身代名詞，即選項(C) himself。選項(A) he 為人稱代名詞主格，選項(B) him 為人稱代名詞受格，選項(D) ourselves 為複數的反身代名詞，皆不可選。

進階 本題考的重點是片語與反身代名詞。本題中的片語 think for 可表「（自己）思考或做決定」，不依賴其他人的指引，後方通常接反身代名詞，即 myself, yourself 等，因此後方不使用為人稱代名詞主格與受格的 he 或 him。本句的主詞為 George，故 think for 後方的反身代名詞應該要與主詞相符，即男性的第三人稱單數，故不使用選項(D)的複數的反身代名詞 ourselves，而應選 himself。

Promotions, Pensions, and Awards
當月優秀員工獎 🎧 MP3 021

UNIT 64

64 Employees will not be able to receive the employee of the month award ------- they excel in sales, customer service, and attendance.
(A) because　(B) rather than　(C) even though　(D) unless

中譯 ▶ (D) 員工除非在銷售、客戶服務以及出席都表現優異，否則不會得到當月優秀員工獎。

速解 ▶ 看到整個句子目光直接鎖定「**Employees will not be able to receive the employee of the month award ----- they excel in sales...**」，空格前後為表條件與結果的兩個子句，空格應填適當的連接詞，即選項(D) unless。選項(A) because 表原因，選項(B) rather than 表偏好，選項(C) even though 表「儘管」，皆不可選。

進階 ▶ 本題考的重點是適當的連接詞。連接詞用來連接兩個字詞或子句，連接詞可分對等連接詞、相關連接詞與從屬連接詞，本句需要的是從屬連接詞來連接。連接詞的題目通常需要透過整句語意判斷適當的連接詞。選項中的 because 是用來引出原因、理由的連接詞，而 rather than 是用來表達選擇，意指「 是...而不是...」，連接詞 even though 表達相對概念，意指「儘管、即使」，連接詞 unless 則表條件，意指「除非」。本句空格後的子句是空格前子句成立的條件，應使用 unless 來表達除非表現優異，否則不會得獎，故選(D)。

Promotions, Pensions, and Awards
得到現金獎勵 🎧 MP3 021

65 After becoming employee of the month, employers can ------- get cash rewards ------- enjoy paid time off.

(A) either...or   (B) neither...nor

(C) as...as   (D) whether...or

中譯 ▶ (A) 在成為當月優秀員工後，員工可以得到現金獎勵或是享受帶薪休假。

速解 ▶ 看到整個句子目光直接鎖定「**employers can----- get cash rewards ----- enjoy paid time off**」，空格前後為兩個選擇，空格應填適當的連接詞，即選項(A) neither...or。選項(B) neither...nor 表「不...也不...」，選項(C) as...as 表「一樣...」，選項(D) whether...or 表「不論...還是...」，皆不可選。

進階 ▶ 本題考的重點是相關連接詞。相關連接詞用來連接兩個相關的語言成分，連接的兩個成份在文法上必須對稱。本句選項中的 either...or 用來表示兩個選擇中的其中一個，連接詞 as... as 用來表達相同的比較結果，連接詞 whether... or 用來連接兩個不重要的可能。而選項中的 either... nor 不可一起使用，故不選。在本題中空格後為兩個選擇 cash reward 以及 paid time off，應使用相關連接詞 either... or 來連接這兩個選擇，表得獎的員工可從兩個選擇中選一個。

Shopping 列出購物清單

MP3 021

(66) When going shopping, creating ------- shopping list will help shoppers to stay focused on shopping effectively.

(A) the (B) a (C) an (D)(no article)

中譯 (B) 去購物時，列出購物清單能讓購物者專注且買起來有效率。

速解 看到整個句子目光直接鎖定「**creating ----- shopping list will help shoppers**」，空格後詞，空格應填不定冠詞，即選項(B) a。選項(A) the 為定冠詞，選項(C) an 為接母音開頭的單數可數名詞，而選項(D)(no article)不可用在單數可數名詞前，故皆不可選。

進階 本題考的重點是冠詞的使用。本句空格後為單數可數名詞 shopping list，單數可數名詞前方一定要有冠詞（不定冠詞 a/an 或定冠詞 the），故選項(D)不可選，又名詞 shopping list 為子音開頭的名詞，前方的不定冠詞使用 a，不使用 an，故選項(C)也不選。此外，在此的 shopping list，並非特定一份 shopping list，而是普遍泛指購物清單，且強調一份清單，所以不選代表特定的定冠詞 the，而使用不定冠詞 a。

Shopping
UNIT 67 採買日常用品　🎧 MP3 021

❻❼ It is better to go grocery shopping after you have ------- a big meal, so you don't buy unnecessary items.
(A) eat　(B) ate　(C) aten　(D) eaten

中譯 (D) 最好在吃完大餐後才去採買日常用品,避免購入不需要的商品。

速解 看到整個句子目光直接鎖定「**after you have ----- a big meal**」,空格前為助動詞 **have**,空格後為受詞 **a big meal**,空格應填過去分詞,即選項(D) eaten。選項(A) eat 為原形動詞,選項(B) ate 為過去式動詞,選項(C) aten 為錯誤用法,皆不可選。

進階 本題考的重點是正確的動詞形態。現在完成式為 have/has 加上過去分詞(p.p.),可用來表示「(已經)完成某事」、「曾經做過某事」或是「已經做某事做一段時間」。本句後方子句中的主詞為 you,空格前為 have,可知道空格應需填入過去分詞,故不選原形動詞 eat 或過去式 ate,而應選過去分詞 eaten。本句以現在完成式表示已先完成的行為,而另一子句的現在簡單式表現在的結果(not buy unnecessary items)。動詞 eat 為不規則變化的動詞,三態為 eat-ate-eaten,選項 (C) aten 為錯誤拼法,不可選。

Shopping
申請稅捐扣除額的發票 🎧 MP3 021

68 Either the accountant or the managers ------- the receipts we need to apply for a tax reduction.
(A) has　(B) hasn't　(C) have　(D) having

中譯 (C) 會計或是經理持有我們需要用來申請稅捐扣除額的發票。

速解 看到整個句子目光直接鎖定「**Either the accountant or the managers ----- the receipts**」，空格前主詞有連接詞 **either…or**，空格前為複數名詞 **managers**，空格應填複數動詞，即選項(C) have。選項(A) has 為第三人稱單數動詞，選項(B) hasn't 為否定的第三人稱單數動詞，選項(D) having 為現在分詞，皆不可選。

進階 本題考的重點是連接詞與動詞的使用。當主詞包含連接詞時，可能依使用的連接詞不同，表達的意思不同，需使用的動詞也會有所不同。當兩個名詞由 or 或 nor 連接時，動詞會跟隨較靠近的名詞做變化。本句的主詞為 either the accountant or the managers，由連接詞 or 連接兩個名詞 accountant 與 managers，因為動詞較靠近複數的 managers，故動詞應使用能相對應的非第三人稱複數動詞，故不選單數的 has 或 hasn't，空格應填 have。而選項中的現在分詞前應該會有 be 動詞，在此若使用則不合文法，故不選。

Ordering Supplies
訂購辦公室耗材 🎧 MP3 021

69 ------- office supplies is a necessary part of every business, and it helps businesses to operate effectively and consistently.
(A) Has ordered   (B) Ordered   (C) Order   (D) Ordering

中譯 (D) 訂購辦公室耗材對每個企業來說都是不可或缺的部分，因為它讓企業更能有效率且一致的運作。

··

速解 看到整個句子目光直接鎖定「**----- office supplies is a necessary part of every business**」，空格在動詞 **is** 前做主詞的一部份，空格應填動名詞，即選項(D) Ordering。選項(A) Has ordered 為現在完成式動詞，選項 (B) Ordered 為過去式動詞，選項(C) Order 為原形動詞，皆不可選。

··

進階 本題考的重點是動名詞作主詞。當動詞作主詞時，須改為動名詞形式。動名詞作用如名詞，可做主詞、受詞或補語。本句的空格後為名詞，後接 be 動詞 is，空格與名詞 office supplies 一起作為主詞，空格中的動詞必需改為動名詞，故選擇(D)。選項(A)、(B)、(C)皆作動詞用，英語句子中不可直接使用兩個動詞，否則不合文法，故其他選項不選。

Ordering Supplies
訂購商業耗材

MP3 021

(70) When ordering business supplies, the first step is to gather ------- about the services and product quality of the vendors.

(A) inform (B) information

(C) informative (D) informational

中譯 (B) 當訂購商業耗材時，第一步是收集各廠商的服務與產品品質相關資訊。

速解 看到整個句子目光直接鎖定「**the first step is to gather ----- about**」，空格前為動詞，後為介系詞，空格應填名詞，即選項(B) information。選項(A) inform 為動詞，選項(C) informative 與選項(D) informational 為形容詞，皆不可選。

進階 本題考的重點是及物動詞的使用。本題空格前為及物動詞 gather，後方必須要有直接受詞，而名詞可作主詞、受詞與補語，故本題應填入名詞作受詞，即 -ation 結尾的名詞 information。而後方介系詞 about 帶領的子句修飾 information，表明資訊的性質。選項(C)以 -ive 結尾，為形容詞，選項(D)以 -al 結尾，同樣為形容詞，皆不選。選項(A)為動詞，同樣不選。

Ordering Supplies
庫存與出貨資訊 🎧 MP3 021

71 Review ------- list carefully before you order because it includes important information about the storage and retrieval.
(A) this　(B) most　(C) those　(D) none of the

中譯 (A) 訂購之前，仔細審閱這張清單。因為這張清單包含庫存與出貨資訊。

速解 看到整個句子目光直接鎖定「**Review ----- list carefully**」，空格前為動詞，後為單數可數名詞，空格應填適當的詞，即選項(A) this。選項(B) most 、選項(C) those 與選項(D) none of the 後須接複數名詞，皆不可選。

進階 本題考的重點是字詞的搭配。限定詞置於名詞前面，用來限定名詞的含意，限定詞包含冠詞、量詞等，這些詞有些後方只能使用可數名詞，有些後方只能使用不可數名詞。本句空格前是動詞 review，後面接名詞 list，又 list 為單數可數名詞，選項的限定詞中，只能使用 this 在前面與 list 搭配，故選(C)。 選項中的 most 以及 none of the 能與可數或不可數名詞共用，但可數名詞必須是複數。而 these 後只能是複數的可數名詞，以上皆與 list 不合，不可選。

Shipping
選擇隔夜送達　🎧 MP3 021

72 When shipping items, you can ship it overnight, within one to three business days, **-------** within two to eight business days.
(A) or　(B) nor　(C) yet　(D) and

中譯　(A) 運送物品時，你可選擇隔夜送達、一到三個工作天送達，或兩到八個工作天送達。

速解　看到整個句子目光直接鎖定「**you can ship it overnight, within one to three business days, ----- within two to eight business days**」，空格前後為三個選擇，空格應填適當的連接詞，即選項(A) or。選項(B) nor 表「也不是」，選項(C) yet 表「還沒或然而」，選項(D) and 為非第三人稱單數的現在簡單式被動語態，皆不可選。

進階　本題考的重點是正確的連接詞。對等連接詞用來連接字詞、片語或子句，連接的成分必須對等，包含 and, but, or, nor, for, so, yet。本句提供三種運送物品的選擇，應使用對等連接詞 or 來連接兩個以上的可能性、方法或選擇。對等連接詞 nor 必須與 not 或是 neither 共用，表達「既不是...也不是...」，連接的成分必須是否定語氣，與本句不和，故不選。連接詞 yet 用來表達相對立的概念，與 but 類似，與本句不符，同樣不選。而 and 用來連接類似的概念，連接的成分皆包含之意，本提示三選一，故不使用 and，而使用 or。

Shipping 航空寄件

MP3 021

(73) Although shipping by air is -------, shipping by sea is more environmentally friendly because of lower CO2 emissions.

(A) quick (B) quicker (C) more quick (D) quickest

中譯 (B) 雖然航空寄件比較快，但船運對環境比較友善，因為二氧化碳排放量較低。

速解 看到整個句子目光直接鎖定「**Although shipping by air is -----, shipping by sea...**」，空格前後有兩個比較的運送方法，空格應填比較級形容詞，即選項(B) quicker。選項(A) quick 為原形形容詞，選項(C) more quick 為錯誤用法，選項(D) quickest 為最高級形容詞，皆不可選。

進階 本題考的重點是形容詞比較級。當比較兩樣東西時，可使用比較級來表示比較的結果，大部分形容詞使用 -er 結尾來表達比較級。本句中有兩個運送的方式 shipping by air 以及 shipping by sea，故不使用原形的形容詞 quick，也不使用最高級的 quickest，必須使用比較級。又形容詞 quick 為規則的形容詞變化，故比較級為 quicker，最高級為 quickest，本題比較級應選擇 quicker，故選項(C)的 more quick 也不選。

Shipping
從世界各地收到貨運

MP3 021

(74) Wednesdays are our busiest days because we receive shipments ------- from all over the world.

(A) hour　(B) hourment　(C) hourize　(D) hourly

中譯 (D) 星期三是我們最忙的一天，因為我們每小時都從世界各地收到貨運。

速解 看到整個句子目光直接鎖定「**we receive shipments -----**」，空格前方有動詞，空格應填副詞，即選項(D) hourly。選項(A) hour 為名詞，選項(B) hourment 與選項(C) hourize 為錯誤用法，皆不可選。

進階 本題考的重點是判斷詞性。英語中不同詞性的詞可能會有特定的搭配規則，例如動詞會與副詞搭配，即若需要修飾動詞，需使用副詞。本句由連接詞 because 連接兩個子句，而主要子句為 we receive shipments...，主要動詞為 receive，後接受詞 shipment 以及副詞 from all over the world，空格內應填入可修飾主要動詞的副詞，選項中 -ly 結尾的 hourly 為副詞，故填入(D)。選項(A)為名詞，而選項(B)雖為名詞 -ment 結尾，但不是真的單字，動詞結尾的 -ize 的選項(C)也不是真的單字，皆不選。

Invoices
檢查發票

MP3 021

(75) Before buying an expensive item, buyers should check the invoice and make sure ------- agree with the payment terms.

(A) he or she (B) it (C) them (D) they

中譯 (D) 在買昂貴的東西之前，買家應該檢查發票，確定同意付款條件。

速解 看到整個句子目光直接鎖定「**buyers should check the invoice and make sure ----- agree**」，空格前為後方為動詞 **agree**，前方為 **buyers**，空格應填相符的代名詞主格，即選項(D) they。選項(A) he or she 與選項(B) it 為第三人稱單數代名詞，而選項(C) them 為複數代名詞受格，皆不可選。

進階 本題考的重點是正確人稱代名詞的判斷。人稱代名詞用來替代先前說過的名詞或是已知的人事物，以避免重複，使用的代名詞必須與替代的名詞在數量與人稱上一致。從本句語意可知空格中缺少的詞是替代 buyers 的代名詞，因為 buyers 為複數的人，故使用的代名詞應是能代替人的複數代名詞，故不選代替第三人稱單數人的選項(A)或代替第三人稱單數事物的選項(B)。又空格中的 buyers 為動作的執行者，應使用主格而不使用受格，故雖然選項(C)與(D)皆為可代替複數名詞的代名詞，但前者是受格（受詞、動詞接受者），後者是主格（主詞、動作主事者），本題空格應填入代表動作執行者的 they。

Invoices
費用付清前 🎧 MP3 021

76 For sellers, invoices are contracts and bills that can be used as a demand -------- payment until it is paid in full
(A) of　(B) for　(C) to　(D) in

中譯▶ (B) 對銷售員來説，發票是在費用付清前能用來收款的合約與帳單。

速解▶ 看到整個句子目光直接鎖定「**demand -----payment**」，空格前的名詞 **demand** 是因為有 **payment**，空格應填適當的介系詞，即選項(B) for。選項(A) of 可表「...的」，選項(C) to 表「朝向」，選項(D) in 表「在...內」，語意皆不合，不選。

進階▶ 本題考的重點是介系詞。介系詞能用來表達它後方受詞與其他字詞的關係。而本空格須填入介系詞表明 demand 與 payment 的關係。介系詞 for 可表達「用意、目的、原因或一段時間」，故本提空格填入介系詞 for 來表達 payment 是 demand 的目的、原因，介系詞 of 用來表明「屬於」的關係或用來説明數量等，介系詞 to 可表達「方向、限度」等，介系詞 in 通常用來表明「時間、地點、形狀、意見或感覺」等，以上語意都與本句不合。

Invoices
視發票為銷售單據

MP3 021

(77) ------- sellers see invoices as sales invoices, buyers see them as purchase invoices.

(A) Until (B) Rather than (C) Although (D) Whenever

中譯 (C) 雖然銷售員視發票為銷售單據，但買家將之視為購買單據。

速解 看到整個句子目光直接鎖定「**----- sellers see invoices..., buyers see them...**」，空格前後比較兩種對應的觀點，空格應填表相對的連接詞，即選項(C) Although。選項(A) Until、選項(B) Rather than 與選項(D)Whenever 與本句語意皆不合，皆不可選。

進階 本題考的重點是連接詞的用法。連接詞是用來連接字詞或子句等。本句需要一個從屬連接詞（又稱附屬連接詞）來連接兩個互相對立的對發票的觀點（as sales invoices 以及 as purchase invoices），選項中的從屬連接詞 although 便可用來連接兩個對立的概念，故空格應填入選項(C)。選項中 until 同樣為連接詞，意指「直到」，用來表達延續到某個時間（如 until 10 o'clock），連接詞 rather than 則表「是...而不是...」，用來表達兩個之中的某一個比較重要(...drank water rather than juice)，而連接詞 whenever 表達「每當、無論何時」（如 Call me whenever you want to.），以上連接詞皆與本句不合，不選。

Inventory
供應鏈中的多個地點 🎧 MP3 021

UNIT 78

78 Inventory management is required for many locations of ------- supply network anywhere to proceed with production.
(A) a　(B) an　(C) the　(D)(no article)

中譯 (A) 存貨管理在任何一個供應鏈中的多個地點都是必要的，如此才能進行製造。

速解 看到整個句子目光直接鎖定「**many locations of ----- supply network**」，空格前為介系詞，後為非特定的名詞，空格應填適當的不定冠詞，即選項(A) a。選項(B) an 為後方接母音開頭單字的不定冠詞，選項(C) the 為定冠詞，選項(D)(no article)與不可數名詞共用，皆不可選。

進階 本題考的重點是冠詞的使用。冠詞可分為定冠詞與不定冠詞，不定冠詞（a, an）用在單數可數名詞前，表未明確指定的名詞，子音開頭的字詞用 a，母音開頭用 an；而定冠詞（the）後方用可數或不可數名詞，表明特定的人事物。另，未指定的不可數名詞則不使用冠詞（如 They have water）。從語意可判斷本句空格後的名詞 supply network 並非特定的一個供應鏈，而是用來普遍指所有的供應鏈，故不選定冠詞 the。又 supply network 屬於可數名詞，既然是單數可數名詞，又未指定，前方必須要有不定冠詞，supply 為子音開頭，故不選 an，應使用 a。

Inventory
明瞭前置時間與季節需求

MP3 021

(79) An inventory should include a record of everything done prior to sale to be aware of lead time and ------- demand.

(A) season (B) seasoning (C) seasonally (D) seasonal

中譯 (D) 存貨盤點報表應包含販售前的一切紀錄，以明瞭前置時間與季節需求。

速解 看到整個句子目光直接鎖定「**----- demand**」，空格後為名詞 **demand**，空格應填形容詞，即選項(D) seasonal。選項(A) season 為名詞，選項(B) seasoning 為名詞，選項(C) seasonally 為副詞，皆不可選。

進階 本題考的重點是詞性搭配。在本句中介系詞 of 解釋了庫存紀錄與前置時間和季節需求的關係，當 of 有如此作用時，後方通常是接名詞，如 the worst part of the movie 或是 the first part of the book，因此可推測空格後的 demand 為名詞，非動詞。因為句中 demand 為名詞，空格則需填入形容詞。可依據字尾判斷以-ly 結尾的選項(C)為副詞，而 -al 結尾的選項(D)為形容詞，故選(D)。而 season 為名詞或動詞，seasoning 為名詞。

Inventory
存貨紀錄

MP3 021

(80) Inventory records may ------- insight into when some items will sell quickly at the highest price.

(A) giving　(B) give　(C) given　(D) gave

中譯 (B) 存貨紀錄可能可以看出哪些時候某些商品可用最高的價錢快速賣出。

速解 看到整個句子目光直接鎖定「**may ----- insight**」，空格前為助動詞，空格後為名詞，空格應填原形動詞，即選項(B) give。選項(A) giving 為現在分詞，選項(C) given 為過去分詞，而選項(D) gave 為過去式動詞，皆不可選。

進階 本題考的重點是動詞形態。助動詞是用來幫助主要動詞形成不同時態、語氣或語態等，後方必須使用不加 to 的原形動詞。本題中的空格前為情態助動詞 may，用來表達可能性、潛在性，後方必須使用原形動詞，選項(A)為現在分詞、選項(C)為過去分詞、選項(D)為過去式動詞，皆不符，不可選，應使用原形動詞的選項(B)。

Banking
銀行負擔金融債務

MP3 022

(81) Most banks only have a portion ------- the assets needed to cover their financial obligations.

(A) from (B) for (C) of (D) to

中譯 (C) 大部分的銀行只需資產的一部分來負擔金融債務。

速解 看到整個句子目光直接鎖定「**a portion ----- the assets**」，空格前後為兩個名詞，空格應填適當的介系詞，即選項(C) of。選項(A) from 表「從」，選項(B) for 表「為了」，選項(D) to 表「到達」，語意不合，皆不可選。

進階 本題考的重點是介系詞。介系詞用來表達字詞、片語等語言成分之間的關係，本句空格前為 a portion，後方也是名詞 the assets，其中 portion 代表整體 the assets 的一部份，故應使用介系詞 of 來表達「屬於...的」關係，故選(C)。選項中的 from 可用來描述起始點或來源，而介系詞 for 用來表達用途、原因等，介系詞 to 則可表方向或關係，語意與本句皆不合，不選。

Banking
銀行提供額外的服務

MP3 022

(82) Banks accept deposits from customers, raise capital from investors, and then ------- additional services to customers.
(A) provide　(B) provides　(C) is providing　(D) has provided

中譯 (A) 銀行接受客戶的存款、向投資人募資金，然後提供額外的服務給客戶。

速解 看到整個句子目光直接鎖定「**Banks... ----- additional services to customers**」，空格前方主詞為複數名詞，空格應填適當的動詞，即選項(A) provide。選項(B) provides 為第三人稱單數動詞，選項(C) is providing 為第三人稱單數的現在進行式，選項(D) has provided 為第三人稱單數的現在完成式動詞，皆不可選。

進階 本題考的重點是主詞動詞一致。句子中的動詞搭配主詞作變化，當結構如本題一樣，較複雜時，需確認正確的主詞，才能使用正確、相對應的動詞。本句有三個動詞片語 accept deposits...和 raise capital...以及空格後的片語，執行動作的對象都是主詞 banks，因為 banks 是複數可數名詞，動詞也應使用相對應的複數動詞。選項中 provides 為現在簡單式、is providing 為現在進行式，而 has provided 現在完成式，選項(B)、(C)、(D)皆是第三人稱單數的動詞形態，與主詞 banks 不和，故應該使用非第三人稱單數的動詞 provide。

Banking
銀行出借現金 🎧 MP3 022

83 In order to make money, banks tend to lend money at an interest rate ------- than their operating and maintenance costs.

(A) more high　(B) most high　(C) higher　(D) highest

中譯 ▶ (C) 為了賺錢，銀行通常以比營運與維修成本還高的利息出借現金。

速解 ▶ 看到整個句子目光直接鎖定「**an interest rate ----- than their operating and maintenance costs**」，空格前後比較兩種金額，空格應填比較級形容詞，即選項(C) higher。選項(A) more high 與選項(B) most high 為錯誤用法，選項(D) highest 為最高級形容詞，皆不可選。

進階 ▶ 本題考的重點是形容詞比較級。空格前後有兩種比較的金額 an interest rate 還有 their operating and maintenance costs，且空格後方有 than，故空格中應使用形容詞比較級，故不選最高級的(B)與(D)。又形容詞 high 屬單音節的規則變化的形容詞，故比較級應直接加上-er，故不選擇(A)。應特別注意選項中 more high 與 most high 不是 high 的比較級與最高級用法。

Accounting
習慣遠距離工作

UNIT **84**

🎧 MP3 022

84 Working as an accountant for this firm means you have to spend some time ------- working remotely.

(A) get used to
(B) getting used to
(C) to get used to
(D) used to

中譯▶ (B) 在這家事務所當會計表示你必須花時間習慣遠距離工作。

速解▶ 看到整個句子目光直接鎖定「**spend some time ----- working remotely**」，空格前方為 **spend time**，後方為動名詞 **working**，空格應填適當形式的詞，即選項(B) getting used to。選項(A) get used to 與選項(C) to get used to 表「習慣」，前為原形，後為不定詞，而選項(D) used to 表「過去曾經」，皆不可選。

進階▶ 本題考的重點是正確的動詞形態。片語 used to 表「過去曾經做...」，後應接原形動詞（如 She used to like it.）。而 get used to 表「變得習慣」，後方應使用名詞或動名詞。因空格後方為動名詞 working，故空格應使用 get used to，而不使用 used to。動詞 spend 通常加上時間或金錢後，可加上動名詞，表「花費時間／金錢做某事」。本句空格前為 spend some time，故後方應使用動名詞，即 getting used to，而不使用原形或不定詞。

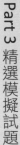

Accounting
簿記員受到的規範 🎧 MP3 022

85 Bookkeepers may have slightly different tasks from accountants, but bookkeepers are regulated as accountants --------.

(A) do　(B) done　(C) be　(D) are

中譯 (D) 簿記員的任務可能與會計有些不同，但簿記員受到的規範和會計是一樣的。

速解 看到整個句子目光直接鎖定「**bookkeepers are regulated as accountants -----**」，空格前為被動語氣的 **are regulated**，空格應填替代的複數 be 動詞，即選項(D) are。選項(A) do 為原形助動詞，選項(B) done 為過去分詞，選項(C) be 為原形 be 動詞，皆不選。

進階 本題考的重點是替代重複部分的用法。英文句子中，當有重複的部分，可省略或以助動詞或 be 動詞替代。**當重複的部分為一般動詞時，會以助動詞替代**，且按照人稱、數量與時態等作變化（如 You don't have to work as late as you did.）；若重複的部分為 be 動詞，則以 be 動詞替代，同樣會按照人稱、數量與時態等變化（如 She is as tall as he is.）。本句的第二個子句原為 bookkeepers are regulated as accountants are regulated，因 are regulated 重複，故第二個部分以 are 替代。

Accounting
在法律範圍內付越少稅
UNIT 86

🎧 MP3 022

❽❻ There are some tricks that allow wealthy individuals to pay ------- tax as legally possible.

(A) as little　(B) as few　(C) as many　(D) as less

中譯 ▶ (A) 有些技巧讓有錢人能在法律範圍內付越少稅越好。

速解 ▶ 看到整個句子目光直接鎖定「**----- tax as**」，空格後有 **as**，且名詞 **tax** 在此做不可數名詞，空格應填 as 加不可數名詞的量詞，即選項 (A) as little。選項(B) as few 與選項(C) as many 後方須接可數名詞，而選項(D) as less 為錯誤用法，皆不可選。

進階 ▶ 本題考的重點是同級比較的用法。當比較的兩樣東西是同樣程度時（A 和 B 一樣...）時，會使用 as...as 的結構，中間可使用形容詞（如 as big as），也可使用形容詞加名詞（如 as many students as...或 as low a currency as...）。本句使用 as + 形容詞 + 名詞 + as 的結構，空格後方的名詞為 tax，可做可數名詞，也可做不可數名詞，但在本句中為單數形，做不可數名詞解釋。選項中的量詞 little、few 與 many 作為形容詞，little 用在不可數名詞，而 few 與 many 與可數名詞共用，故本題應使用與不可數名詞搭配的 as little。而 as...as 表「一樣」，故中間的形容詞必須是原形，而非比較級，故選項(D)為錯誤用法。

Investments
報告給稅務機關
🎧 MP3 022

87 The guideline states that all investment gains and losses are ------- to the taxing authority.

(A) reporting　　　　(B) going to report

(C) to be reported　　(D) to report

中譯 (C) 規範指出所有的投資獲利與損失都要報告給稅務機關。

速解 看到整個句子目光直接鎖定「**all investment gains and losses are -----**」，空格前為 **that** 子句中的主詞，與動詞為被動關係，空格應填適當的動詞形態，即選項(C) to be reported。選項(A) reporting、選項(B) going to report 與選項(D) to report 與空格前的 are 搭配皆屬主動語態，不可選。

進階 本題考的重點是區分主被動語態與 be to 表未來的用法。被動語態用在當主詞為動作的接受者時，且時態皆變化在 be 動詞上（如現在完成式的被動語態為 have/has been p.p.）。而 be to 也可用來表達未來計劃或安排。本句空格在 that 子句中，前方為主詞 all investment gains and losses，選項中的動詞為 report，與主詞的關係應使用被動語態，選項中只能使用(C) to be reported，其中 be reported 表被動，而空格前的 are 與 to 即是前述的未來 be to。其他選項與空格前的 are 形成現在進行式的 are reporting、未來式的 are going to report 以及 be to 未來的 are to report，以上皆是主動語態，語意不合，不可選。

Investments
線上投資 🎧 MP3 022

88 Once -------, you can access your account through the website and invest online.

(A) register
(B) is registered
(C) are registered
(D) registered

中譯 ▶ (D) 你一旦登記完畢，就可以從網站進入你的帳號，並在線上投資。

速解 ▶ 看到整個句子目光直接鎖定「**Once -----,you**」，空格前為附屬連接詞 **once**，且主詞與 **be** 動詞省略，空格應填名詞，即選項(D) registered。選項(A) register 為原形動詞，選項(B) is registered 為第三人稱單數的現在簡單式被動語態，選項(C) are registered 為非第三人稱單數的現在簡單式被動語態，皆不可選。

進階 ▶ 本題考的重點是分詞構句。分詞構句為當兩個子句的主詞相同時，前面的主詞會省略，主動語態的動詞直接改為現在分詞（如 When walking on the street, she bumped into a friend.），若是被動語態，則將主詞與 be 動詞省略，留下過去分詞（如 Given another chance, he worked harder.）。本句的第一個子句沒有主詞，可推測為分詞構句，主詞已被省略，由選項可知 register 在此使用被動語態，被動語態的分詞構句除了省略主詞之外，也應省略 ｂｅ 動詞，即本句原為 once you are registered, ...，移除主詞與 be 動詞後的結果便是 once registered，故空格填 registered。

Investments
UNIT 89 開放型投資公司 🎧 MP3 022

89 An open-end investment company is a company ------- new shares are created for new investors.
(A) which　(B) where　(C) that　(D) who

中譯 (B) 開放型投資公司是創造新股票給新投資者的公司。

速解 看到整個句子目光直接鎖定「**is a company ----- new shares are created for new investors**」，空格前為名詞 **a company**，後方為子句 **new shares are...**，空格應填關係副詞，即選項(B) where。選項(A) which、選項(C) that 與選項(D) who 為關係代名詞，皆不可選。

進階 本題考的重點是區分關係代名詞與關係副詞。關係代名詞用來代替前方的名詞（先行詞）並引導後方的關係子句來修飾此先行詞。既然是代替先行詞，必是關係子句的主詞或受詞（如 The man who is wearing black. 中 who 即是...is wearing black 的主詞）。而關係副詞作為副詞兼連接詞，後方必定是完整子句（如 The place where I saw him. 中 I saw him 為完整句子）。本句中空格後方為一完整子句 new shares are created for new investors，不缺主詞或受詞，故不應使用關係代名詞，不選代替事物的 which、代替人的 who 或可與兩者替換的 that，而應填入關係副詞 where。

Taxes
公開稅務資訊 🎧 MP3 022

90 Before releasing your tax information, you need to sign a ------- authorization.

(A) writing　(B) written　(C) writen　(D) write

中譯 ▶ (B) 在公開你的稅務資訊前，你應該先簽屬書面授權書。

速解 ▶ 看到整個句子目光直接鎖定「**a ----- authorization**」，空格後為 **authorization**，名詞 authorization 與冠詞 a 中間應為形容詞，如選項(B) written。選項(A)同樣可做形容詞，但表主動，因此不可選。選項(D)為動詞，選項(C)為動詞過去分詞的錯誤形式，同樣不可選。

進階 ▶ 本題考的重點為過去與現在分詞作為形容詞。動詞被改為過去分詞（p.p.）或現在分詞（Ving）後，可被用來做形容詞，基本上置於名詞的前方，修飾名詞。當過去分詞做形容詞時，隱含被動的意義，如 an amused crowd（隱含「被逗樂」的意思）。而現在分詞做為形容詞時，則有主動的含意，如 a confusing story（故事不是「被困惑」）。本題授權書是「被寫出來的」，因此應選過去分詞，而非現在分詞，來表示「書面授權」。此外，過去分詞也可能表「已完成」或「感覺、心情」（如 boiled water 與 I'm bored.）。現在分詞則另有「正在進行」或「令人感到」的意思（如 a crying baby 與 The situation is frustrating.）。

Taxes
會計年度報稅 🎧 MP3 022

91 Our company, as many others, ------- a tax return with the IRS every fiscal year, declaring our revenue and capital gains.
(A) File (B) is filing (C) files (D) has filed

中譯 (C) 如同其他很多公司一樣，我們公司每個會計年度都會向 IRS 報稅，申報我們的收入與資本利得。

速解 看到整個句子目光直接鎖定「**Our company ----- a... every year**」，空格前為主詞，後應接動詞，又因後方的時間副詞為 every year，故應選用代表現在簡單式的第三人稱動詞，即 (C) files。選項(A)為原形動詞，用於主詞為非第三人稱單數時，選項(B)為現在進行式的動詞形，選項(D)為現在完成式的動詞形，以上與主詞或與時態不符，皆不可選。

進階 本題考的重點是動詞形態。英語最基本的主要句型之一即是「主詞+動詞」（S.+V.），而本主要子句中只見主詞，不見動詞，表示空格內需填入動詞。在確定本句子缺少主要動詞後，應判斷須使用的時態。現在簡單式，用來表示「習慣」、「現存的狀態」或「不變的事實」，動詞需使用原形動詞，但當主詞為第三人稱單數時，須加上 -s（或 -es 與 -ies）。從句子中的時間副詞 every（fiscal）year，可判斷出表示的是「習慣」（固定會做的事），應使用現在簡單式。加上主詞 our company 為第三人稱單數，需再加上 -s。

Taxes
破產申請

UNIT 92

🎧 MP3 022

92 The business owner ------- for bankruptcy before, so he needs to confirm whether he can file again.

(A) applies　(B) application　(C) would apply　(D) has applied

Part 1 新制閱讀 part 6 答題強化

Part 2 核心文法和單字考點

Part 3 精選模擬試題

中譯 ▶ (D) 業主已申請過破產，需要確認是否可再次申請。

速解 ▶ 看到整個句子目光直接鎖定「**The business owner ----- before**」，空格前為主詞，後應接動詞，又因後方的副詞為 before，故應選用代表現在完成式的第三人稱動詞，即 (D) has applied。選項(A)為現在簡單式的第三人稱單數，選項(C)為助動詞加原形動詞，時態皆不符，不可選。選項(B)為名詞，若填此選項，主要子句無動詞，故不可選。

進階 ▶ 本考題重點為動詞形態。英語最基本的主要句型之一即是「主詞＋動詞（S. + V.），而本主要子句中只見主詞，不見動詞，表示空格內需填入動詞。確定空格應填動詞後，判斷應使用的時態。現在完成式為 have/has +過去分詞（p.p.），第三人稱使用 has，非第三人稱使用 have。現在完成式表達（過去到現在的）「經驗」、「已完成的動作」或「累積一段時間的動作」。從句子中的副詞 before 因單獨出現，表「以前」的意思，即句子想表達的是「經驗」（做過某事），應使用現在完成式。主詞 the business owner 為第三人稱單數，須使用 has + p.p.。

Financial Statements
資產負債表 🎧 MP3 022

93 If the firm ------- heavy losses, its balance sheet would not be as strong as last year.
(A) suffered　(B) has suffered　(C) suffers　(D) suffer

中譯 (A) 假如這間公司損失慘重，今年的資產負債表就會不如去年強勢。

....

速解 看到整個句子目光直接鎖定「**If the firm ----- would**」，空格前是主詞，且前方有 **if**，後方有 **would**，空格應填過去簡單式的動詞形式，即選項(A) suffered。選項(B) has suffered 為現在完成式的動詞形式，選項(C) suffers 為現在式的動詞，選項(D) suffer 為原形動詞，皆不可選。

....

進階 本題重點為條件句（或稱 if 假設語法），且為第二類條件句（second conditional）。第二類條件句為 if 句使用過去簡單式動詞，另一子句（結果句）則使用 would + 原形動詞，表示對現在或未來做不相符或不可能的假設（如 If I were you, we would go home，一般動詞直接改簡單過去式，be 動詞應用 were）。在解本題時，看到 if 即可推測為條件句，從屬子句中看到 would，可判斷為第二類條件句，故 if 引導的主要子句中的動詞應使用過去簡單式的動詞形態，即選項(A)的 suffered。

Financial Statements
資產反映在財報裡

🎧 MP3 022

94 All valuable tangible and intangible assets must ------- in the financial statement.

(A) are reflected　　　(B) be reflected

(C) reflect　　　　　　(D) been reflected

中譯▶ (B) 所有有價值的有形與無形資產都應反映在財務報表裡。

速解▶ 看到整個句子目光直接鎖定「**All... assets -----**」，空格前為主詞，主詞與動詞的關係為被動關係，且空格前方有助動詞 must，應選(B) be reflected。選項(A) are reflected 與選項(D) been reflected 皆為被動語態，但不可置於助動詞後，故不可選。選項(C) reflect 為原形動詞，與本題不符，同樣不可選。

進階▶ 本題重點為動詞形態。忽略前方修飾詞，注意到名詞，且本句並無動詞，表空格須填入動詞。動詞除了要注意時態之外，也要注意主動與被動語態。當主詞是動作的執行者時，需要使用主動語態（如 The government introduced new policies.）。但是當主詞是動作的接受者時，則需要使用被動語態，即是 be 動詞 + 過去分詞（p.p.），be 動詞須隨主詞作變化（如 New policies were introduced last year.），如本題中的 assets 是接受 reflect 動作，故使用被動語態。加上前方有助動詞，後方的動詞必須為原形，所以 be 動詞不作變動。

Financial Statements
本年度的財務報告

🎧 MP3 022

⑨⑤ Today several leading companies ------- their financial statement for the fiscal year.
(A) releases　(B) released　(C) release　(D) were released

中譯 ▶ (B) 今天數個龍頭公司發布了他們本財政年度的財務報告。

速解 ▶ 看到整個句子目光直接鎖定「**Today... leading companies -----**」，空格前為主詞，句子中無主要動詞，故空格中應該填動詞，又時間詞為 today，且語意為主動語態，可推測為過去簡單式的動詞形態的選項(B) released。選項(A) releases 為現在簡單式的第三人稱單數動詞形，選項(C) release 為（現在簡單式的）原形動詞，選項(D) were released 為過去簡單式被動語態的動詞，皆不可選。

進階 ▶ 本題考的重點為動詞形態。考生可忽略前方修飾詞，只注意主詞中的 companies。又主要子句中沒有動詞，表示空格須填入動詞。另需判斷時態，句中的時間副詞為 today，可能會依句子意思，表示過去時間或未來時間。若表達的事情已發生，則動詞須使用簡單過去式（動詞 + ed），若表達的事情尚未發生，則動詞須使用簡單未來式（will/ be going to + 動詞）。本題選項中無未來式選項，又本題主詞與動詞為主動關係，簡單過去不論主詞皆為同形（即不論第一/二/三人稱或單複數皆是 Ved），故選(B) released。

Property and Departments
國際銷售部門接手 🎧MP3 022

96 The International Sales Department ------- when the project reaches its third phase.
(A) will take over　　(B) will be taken over
(C) took over　　　　(D) take over

中譯▶ (A) 待這個計畫進入第三階段時，國際銷售部門便會接手。

速解▶ 看到整個句子目光直接鎖定「**The...department----- when reaches**」，空格前為 **department**，本句缺少主要動詞，且主詞為 the international sales department，故選擇表未來主動的選項(A) will take over。選項(B) will be taken over 為未來被動，因此不可選。選項(C) took over 為過去簡單主動，選項(D) take over 為非第三人稱的現在簡單主動，同樣不可選。

進階▶ 本題重點為動詞形態。本句不見主要動詞，表示空格須填入動詞。表時間的連接詞（如 when, before, as soon as, until）後方須以現在式代替未來式（如 when it reaches 或 as soon as he comes，不可使用未來式 will），來表示相對的未來活動，因此時間是在未來，主要動詞的時態應該選擇未來式，未來式可能是 will 或是 be going to 加上原型動詞，其他能看出需使用未來式的線索尚有如 tomorrow, next year, later, in two days 等。此外，the...department 是要接收 project，而不是被接收，也就是主詞是動詞的執行者，因此動詞的語態應該使用主動語態。時態及語態的配合下，便需填入選項(A) will take over。

Property and Departments
新的收帳政策 🎧 MP3 022

97 By this time next week, the new receivable policy -------.

(A) implemented
(B) will implement
(C) will have been implemented
(D) has been implemented

中譯 ▶ (C) 下周的這個時候，新的應收帳款政策已開始執行。

速解 ▶ 看到整個句子目光直接鎖定「**By this time...policy -----**」，空格前為主詞，後應接被動語態動詞，又因前方的時間副詞為 by...，故應選用代表未來完成式的被動語態，即(C) will have been implemented。選項(A) implemented 為過去形的動詞，選項(B) will implement 為未來式的動詞形，選項(D) has been implemented 為現在完成式的被動動詞形，皆不可選。

進階 ▶ 本題考的重點是動詞形態。本句不見動詞，表示空格內需填入動詞。**未來完成式為「will + have + p.p.」**，用來表達在未來某個時間，某件事情將會被完成，搭配未來完成式的時間詞有 by... 或 before...。由本題的 by this time next week 可看出主要動詞需使用未來完成式。題中的 policy 與動詞為被動關係，因此須使用被動語態（即 be +p.p.）。未來完成式的被動語態，只需將兩者結合後將被動語態的 be 改成過去分詞的 been（will + have + been + p.p.）。因此本題應填入未來完成的被動形態的選項(C) will have been implemented。

Property and Departments
固定資產的報告

UNIT 98

🎧 MP3 022

98 Part of his job is to ensure all reports detailing the fixed assets
------- meet the requirements.
(A) registered　　(B) register　　(C) registering　　(D) to register

中譯▶ (A) 他工作的一部份便是檢閱所有詳述已登記的固定資產的報告，確保這些報告都符合規定。

速解▶ 看到整個句子目光直接鎖定「**the fixed asset -----**」，空格前為名詞，此名詞與選項中動詞為被動關係，應填入表被動的過去分詞，即 (A) registered。選項(B) register 為一般動詞原形或名詞，選項(C) registering 為現在分詞，選項(D) to register 為不定詞，皆不可選。

進階▶ 本考題重點為關係代名詞省略。關係代名詞是代替先前出現的名詞（先行詞），並引導一個子句來修飾這個被代替的名詞。關係代名詞可能是位於主詞或受詞位置，當先行詞是人時，在主詞位置的關係代名詞使用 who，受詞位置使用 whom；先行詞是事物時，在主詞或受詞位置皆使用 which；前述關係代名詞皆可使用 that 替代。關係代名詞位於主詞位置時可連同 be 動詞一起省略，如本題 the fixed assets that/which were registered，經省略後為 the fixed assets registered，故選(A)。

Property and Departments
製造部門的責任 🎧 MP3 022

99 ------- is the responsibility of the Production Department to fix and manage these fixed assets.
(A) There (B) That (C) It (D) Which

中譯▶ (C) 維修與管理這些固定資產是製造部門的責任。

速解▶ 看到整個句子目光直接鎖定「----- is...to fix...」，空格在主詞位置接 **is**，後有真正主詞的不定詞片語，故應選可作為虛主詞的選項(C) It。選項(A) There、(B) That、(D) Which 都可能置於主詞位置，但大部分需要引導子句，且用法與本句皆不符，故不可選。

進階▶ 本考題重點為虛主詞 it 替代不定詞片語。動名詞 Ving 以及不定詞 to + V. 皆可當主詞，尤其當這些子句較複雜時，時常被移到句尾改成不定詞，並使用虛主詞 it 替代。本題真正主詞 **to fix and manage these fixed assets** 在句尾，主詞位置則以 **it** 替代，故空格填入虛主詞 **it**。選項(A) there 也可能置於主詞位置，但並不用來替代真主詞（如 There is a meeting room down the hall.）。選項(B) that 可能引導子句做主詞（如 That we need to be more aggressive is clear to all.），且這種句型更常使用虛主詞 it。選項(D) which 也可能引導子句作為主詞（如 Which place to go needs to be determined now.）。但以上用法皆與本句不符。

Property and Departments
提供完整的解釋 🎧 MP3 022

100 This speaker was able to provide ------- comprehensive explanations on depreciation than the last.
(A) much　(B) most　(C) more　(D) as

中譯 ▶ (C) 這位講者比前一位講者更能針對折舊提供完整的解釋。

速解 ▶ 看到整個句子目光直接鎖定「----- comprehensive...than」，空格後為原形形容詞與 **than**，空格內應填比較級，即(C) more。選項(A) much 可做副詞，用在比較級或最高級前，選項(B) most 為最高級，選項(D) as 為連接詞，表「程度一樣」或「像...一樣」，與本句不符，故不可選。

進階 ▶ 本題重點為比較級。形容詞或副詞可能會有比較級或最高級。形成比較級時，基本上可在字尾直接加上 -er（如 higher 或 faster），當單字為三個音節以上時，則單字不變，另加 more（如 more comprehensive 或 more easily），當兩者在句中比較時，中間需插入 than。題中有 than 且形容詞本身較長，應選(C)。當形成最高級時，字尾直接加上 -est（如 highest 或 fastest），當單字為三個音節以上時，單字不變，另加上 the most（如 the most comprehensive 或 the most easily），不使用 than。當比較結果是一樣時，則可使用 as（如 as high as），同樣不使用 than。故選項(B)與 (D)皆不可選。選項(A)的 much 可置於比較級或最高級的前面做加強，表達「遠為...」（如 His office is much farther away from our house.），本題不選。

191

Board Meetings and Committees
會議中無法得到共識 🎧 MP3 023

101 After hours of negotiation, the board members ------- still not able to reach a consensus in the meeting.

(A) can　(B) did　(C) was　(D) were

中譯 ▶ (D) 經過數個小時的協商，董事們在會議中仍舊無法得到共識。

速解 ▶ 看到整個句子目光直接鎖定「**members----- ...not able to**」，空格前方為複數 **members**，空格後方為 **not able to**，空格內應填選項(D) were。選項(A) can 不可與 able to 同時使用，選項(B) did 後不接 able to，選項(C) was 與主詞不符，故皆不可選。

進階 ▶ 本題重點為助動詞。本句的 be able to 是表達能力的助動詞。able 本身是形容詞，前方須接上 be 動詞，並因主詞做變化。本題主詞為 the board members，是非單數第三人稱，故本題應選擇(D)的 were 而非(C)的 was。助動詞基本上不可單獨使用，必須搭配其他動詞，且須使用原形動詞，故後方有原形動詞 reach。選項(A) can 同樣是表達能力的助動詞，選項(B)也是助動詞，助動詞不可同時使用，在已有 able to 的情況下，知道不可選(A)與(B)。

Board Meetings and Committees
計畫的進度報告

UNIT 102

🎧 MP3 023

102 The board would like ------- updates every six months on the implementation of the plan.
(A) to receive　(B) receiving　(C) received　(D) be received

中譯 ▶ (A) 董事會希望每六個月可以收到計畫實施的進度報告。

速解 ▶ 看到整個句子目光直接鎖定「**would like ----- updates**」，空格前為 **would like**，空格內應填不定詞（to + V.），即 **(A) to receive**。選項 **(B) receiving** 為動名詞/現在分詞，選項 **(C) received** 為過去分詞，選項 **(D) be received** 為被動語態動詞，與本句皆不符，故不可選。

進階 ▶ 本題重點為 would like 的用法。would like 後可接動詞或名詞，本題無主要動詞，因此空格應填入動詞。接在 would like 後的動詞必須是不定詞，故本題填入選項 **(A) to receive**。先前說過句子有兩個動詞時，第二個動詞需要改為不定詞或動名詞，would like 也是相同的概念，當語意是尚未發生時，應該使用不定詞，更能確定本題應選 **(A) to receive**，而不選 **(B)**。選項 **(C)** 因此也不可選。選項 **(D)** 若加上 to，則符合不定詞的要求，但語態則轉為被動。本題主詞與動詞的關係為主動，本題不選。

Board Meetings and Committees
新主席對資深董事過度批評 🎧 MP3 023

103 The new chairman has been overly ------- of some of the senior members.
(A) critic　(B) criticize　(C) criticized　(D) critical

中譯 (D) 新的主席一直對部分資深董事過度批評。

速解 看到整個句子目光直接鎖定「**been overly -----**」，空格前為副詞，且語意為主動，空格內應填形容詞，即(D) critical。選項(A) critic 為名詞，選項(B) criticize 為動詞，選項(C) criticized 為過去分詞，文法以及語意皆與本句不符，故不可選。

進階 本題重點為詞性的搭配。副詞可修飾動詞或形容詞，前方有 been（be 的過去分詞），後方同樣可能為形容詞或被動式的動詞（如 She is worried. 與 He is removed from the team.），本題主詞與動詞的關係為主動，故不可能選過去分詞的選項(C) criticized，所以必須選擇被副詞修飾的形容詞(D)critical。選項(A)的 critic 是名詞，必須由形容詞來修飾，但前方為副詞，故不可選。選項(B) criticize 是原形動詞，英語裡一個句子不可直接使用兩個動詞，且前方是「been」，後方動詞必須改為表示被動語態的 criticized。

Board Meetings and Committees
委員會的提倡 🎧 MP3 023

UNIT 104

104 After the scandal, the committee calls for ensuring support to those with ------- power.
(A) little　(B) few　(C) a little　(D) a few

中譯 (A) 在那件醜聞之後，委員會提倡應確保弱勢族群得到的支持。

速解 看到整個句子目光直接鎖定「**with ----- power**」，空格後為 **power**，空格內應填搭配不可數的量詞（形容詞），且語意為負面的，故選(A) little。選項(B) few 為搭配可數名詞，故不可選。選項(C) a little 可搭配不可數名詞，選項(D) a few 須搭配可數名詞，兩者帶肯定語意，與本句不符，故不可選。

進階 本題重點為量詞。量詞為一種告知數量的形容詞，有些量詞只能用來修飾可數名詞，有些量詞只能用來修飾不可數名詞，本題的 power 屬於不可數名詞，不可使用 few 或 a few，故不可選(B)與(D)。而選項(A)的 little 與選項(C) a little 後面都接不可數名詞，然而 little 指的是「很少、幾乎沒有」，帶有負面的意思，即本題的「those with little power」，表示「幾乎沒有權力的人」；a little 則是「一些、勉強還有一些」，如 There's more to life than a little power.（人生除了一些權力之外還有更重要的東西）。本題修飾的部分含負面語意，故選(A)而不選(C)。另兩個選項的 few 與 a few 也有同樣的差異。

Board Meetings and Committees
委員會開啟秘密調查

MP3 023

(105) Before the scandal was leaked, the committee seemed to ------- a secret investigation.

(A) open (B) have opened (C) opened (D) opens

中譯 (B) 在醜聞流出前，委員會似乎已先開啟秘密調查。

速解 看到整個句子目光直接鎖定「**Before...was...seemed to -----**」，空格前方有另一簡單過去的子句，且直接接著 **seemed to**，空格內應填原形的過去完成式，即(B) have opened。選項(A) open 為原形動詞，不須分辨發生順序時可使用，故本句不可使用。選項(C) opened 為過去式，選項(D)opens 為第三人稱單數的簡單現在式的動詞，皆不可用在 seem to 後方，故不可選。

進階 本題重點為動詞形態。當有兩個過去的動作或事件時，為表示發生順序，先發生的動作會使用過去完成式 had + p.p.，而後發生的動作則使用簡單過去式。本句因為委員會開啟調查的時間是在醜聞流出之前，故開啟的動作應使用過去完成式。空格前為 seemed to，後面應該接上原形動詞，故不可選(C)或(D)，選項(A)的 open 加在 seemed 後面無法表達動作先發生，僅表示當下「看似…」，與本句也不符。在 seemed to 後空格中原本是 had opened 便改為 have opened，故選(B) have opened。

Quality Control
了解控管的政策

UNIT
106

🎧 MP3 023

106 ------- quality control is essential throughout the whole process, all employees should be made aware of the control policy.
(A) Although　(B) Rather than　(C) Since　(D) Whereas

中譯　(C) 既然品質控管對整個程序都很重要，所有的職員都應了解控管的政策。

速解　看到整個句子目光直接鎖定「----- **quality control... essential... should**」，空格後的兩子句有因果關係，空格內應填代表原因的連接詞，即(C) Since。選項(A) Although 為表「雖然」的連接詞，選項(B) Rather than 與選項(D) Whereas 為表對比的連接詞，與本句不符，故不可選。

進階　本題重點為連接詞。連接詞被用來連接兩個單字、片語或句子等，這類考題較需要注意整句前後語意。選項(C) since 表示「既然、因為」，被用來帶出原因。本題第一個子句「品質控管重要」是第二個子句「職員應該了解政策」的原因，故應該選擇(C) Since。選項(A)的 Although 表「雖然、儘管」，當連接的兩子句帶相反意思時使用，作用如 but，但置放的位置會不同。選項(B) Rather than 表示「（不是...）而是」，用來比較並強調某件事的重要性。選項(D) Whereas 表示「然而」，用來連結兩個對比的事件，都與本句不符。

Quality Control
三種品管手法 🎧 MP3 023

107 We use three quality control techniques, ------- ISO 9000 series, statistical process control, and Six Sigma.
(A) namely　(B) such as　(C) nevertheless　(D) as a result

中譯 (A) 我們使用了三種品管手法,即 ISO 9000 系列標準、統計製程管制與六標準差。

速解 看到整個句子目光直接鎖定「**three ...techniques, -----**」,空格後為空格前的例子,且例子全數舉出,空格內應填舉出全數例子的連接副詞,即(A) namely。選項(B) such as 舉例時不全數列出,不可選。選項(C) nevertheless 表「然而」,選項(D) as a result 表「結果」,皆與本句不符,故不可選。

進階 本題重點為舉例的連接副詞。連接副詞基本上同副詞,但也用來連接兩個獨立的子句或引出概念與例子。觀察空格前後,可發現兩者的關係為說明例子的關係,應使用引出例子的詞,選項(A)與(B)皆可引出例子,然而 such as 只能引出部分例子(如...three techniques, such as ISO 9000 series and Six Sigma),namely 才可列舉全數例子,本題空格後有三個例子,故只能選擇 namely。選項(C)的 nevertheless 暗示有兩個對立的概念,選項(D) as a result 表兩個有因果關係的子句,語意皆與本句不符。

Quality Control
品質控制要求

UNIT 108

🎧 MP3 023

108 In accordance with the quality control requirements, all batches ------- be tested before being shipped to customers.
(A) have to   (B) can   (C) could   (D) would

中譯 (A) 根據品質控制要求，所有貨物出貨給客戶前都必須先驗過。

速解 看到整個句子目光鎖定「**requirements, all batches ----- be tested**」，空格前後有主詞與動詞，前方有 **requirements**，空格應填表責任的助動詞，即(A) have to。選項(B) can、(C) could 與(D) would 雖為助動詞，但所表達的語氣皆與本題的 requirements 不符合，故不可選。

進階 本題重點為助動詞。主要子句裡已有主詞 all batches 與主要動詞 be tested，可推斷空格內應填入助動詞。助動詞是用來幫助主要動詞形成各種語氣、時態或否定句等。本題因為 requirements（要求、規定），可知後方的動作為責任、義務，本題選項(A) have to 類似助動詞（為 semi modal verb），可表達「必須...」，與 requirements 符合，故選(A)。選項中 can 與 could 為表示有能力、可能性或請求等的助動詞（例 Can/ Could you help me?），其中 could 可用於過去，或適用於現在且帶有較委婉的口氣，但兩者皆與題中的 requirements 不合。選項中 would 則表示希望、意願或請求（例 Would you help me?），可用於現在或未來，也含有較委婉的語氣，與本題 requirement 同樣不合。

Quality Control
產品於隔天進行檢驗 🎧 MP3 023

109 All products received ------- inspected on the next day.
(A) have been　(B) is　(C) to be　(D) will be

中譯 (D) 所有產品在收到之後，都會在隔天進行檢驗。

速解 看到整個句子目光直接鎖定「----- inspected...next」，空格後為過去分詞與時間副詞 **next day**，空格內應填未來被動式，即(D) **will be**。選項(A) have been 為完成被動式，選項(B) is 為現在簡單式，選項(C) to be 為不定詞，不可選。

進階 本題重點為動詞形態。句子已有主詞 all products received，且有動詞 inspected，空格應填可完成句子時態或語氣等的詞彙。從句中的時間副詞 on the next day 可知應使用未來式，又主詞與動詞的關係為被動關係，應使用被動語態，故選(D) will be。選項(A)的 have been 雖為被動語態，但完成式與句中的時間不符，故不可選。選項(B)為第三人稱現在簡單式，與主詞 all products 不一致，若改為 are 可選填，表示一貫原則或運作，選項(C)若改為 are to be，也同樣可用於本句來表示習慣的原則或規定，但強調未來語氣（to be）。

Quality Control
品質控管 🎧 MP3 023

110 ------- years, the company has been fully devoted to perfecting its quality assurance procedure.
(A) In　(B) For　(C) Since　(D) After

中譯 ▶ (B) 數年間，這家公司全心投入在使其品質保證流程更完善。

速解 ▶ 看到整個句子目光直接鎖定「**----- years, has been**」，空格後為一段時間，且後方為完成式，空格內應填選項(B) For。選項(C) Since 用於完成式，但後面應該接的時間與本句不符，故不選。選項(A) In 與(D) After 後接一段時間，但時態與本句不符，不可選。

進階 ▶ 本題重點為時間前的介系詞或連接詞。當完成式在表達時間時，時常使用 for 與 since，兩者不同在於 for 後面必須接一段時間（如 for 2 days），而 since 後面則必須接過去的一個時間點（如 since 10 days ago 或 since I was young），本題的 years 為一段時間，故不可使用選項(C) Since。選項中的 in 與 after 都可接一段時間（如 in 10 minutes 與 after 10 minutes），然而 in + 時間的句子應該使用未來式，而 after + 時間的句子則通常使用過去式，皆與本句的完成式不符合，皆不可選。

Product Development
研發自動化系統

MP3 023

(111) The division ------- on developing software tools for automation systems since 2009.

(A) focuses　　(B) is focusing
(C) has been focusing　　(D) focused

中譯 (C) 那個部門從 2009 年開始便致力於研發自動化系統的軟體工具。

速解 看到整個句子目光直接鎖定「 **----- since 2009** 」，空格後方為時間副詞 **since 2009**，應選擇表示持續動作的時態，即選項(A) has been focusing。選項(A) focuses 為現在簡單式，選項(B) is focusing 為現在進行式，選項(D) focused 為過去簡單式，皆與句中時間副詞不符，不可選。

進階 本題重點為動詞型態。本句不見主要動詞，表空格須填動詞，而填寫動詞時，需注意時態。句中的時間副詞 since 2009 指「從 2009 年起」，應使用表示「從過去一個時間開始，持續到現在的動作」的時態，如現在完成式，或本題的現在完成進行式（have/has + been + Ving），即 (A) has been focusing。選項(A) 為第三人稱單數現在簡單式，應用來表示「習慣」或「事實」。選項(B)為現在進行式，應用來表示「正在進行的動作」。選項(D)為過去簡單式，應用來表示「過去某個時間發生的動作」。以上皆與時間副詞所要表達的動作不符，不可選。

Product Development
進行市場調查 🎧 MP3 023

112 Don't forget ------- market research before you start designing a product.

(A) conducted　(B) to conduct　(C) conducting　(D) conduct

中譯 (B) 在開始設計產品之前別忘了先進行市場調查。

速解 看到整個句子目光直接鎖定「**forget ----- market**」，空格前為動詞 **forget**，選項中同樣是動詞，應選搭配 forget，且代表事情未完成的形式，即(B) to conduct。選項(A) conducted 為過去分詞，選項(C) conducting 為現在分詞，選項(D) conduct 為動詞原形，皆不可選。

進階 本題考的重點是動詞形態。當有兩個動詞時，第二個動詞必須作變化，故不可選(D)。本題中的 forget 可接不定詞 to + V. 也可接動名詞 Ving，因此也可刪去選項(A)。動詞 forget 後接不定詞與動名詞的意思是不同的。當接不定詞時，表示的是「忘記做某件事」，事情未完成；而接上動名詞時，表示的卻是「忘記做過某件事」，事情已完成（只是忘記了）。本題的 conduct market research 尚未進行，是提醒不要遺忘，故應選不定詞(B) to conduct。

Product Development

UNIT 113
重新設計產品 🎧 MP3 023

⑬ We had the product packaging completely ------- because it didn't match the company's ethos.
(A) redesigned　(B) redesign　(C) redesigning　(D) redesigns

中譯 ▶ (A) 我們完全重新設計產品包裝，因為舊包裝並不符合公司精神。

速解 ▶ 看到整個句子目光直接鎖定「**had the product packaging -----**」，空格前方有使役動詞 **had**，且句中受詞與選項中動詞為被動關係，應選擇過去分詞的(A) redesigned。選項(B) redesign 為原形動詞，表達主動關係，不可選。選項(C) redesigning 與選項(D) redesigns 皆與使役動詞不符，不可選。

進階 ▶ 本題考的重點是使役動詞。使役動詞包含 have, make, let，當後方接受詞時，後方動詞可能使用原形動詞或過去分詞，端看是主動或被動語態（主動如 have the engineer redesign something，被動如 have the product packaging redesigned）。也因此可確定選項(C)與(D)皆不可選。句中執行 redesign 動作的不是受詞 product packaging，表這個受詞與後方動詞 redesign 是被動關係，必須使用過去分詞，即選項(A) redesigned，而非原形動詞的選項(B) redesign。

UNIT
114

Product Development
上市前的試銷 🎧 MP3 023

🄙 We are thinking about ------- test marketing before the launch.
(A) performing　(B) performed　(C) perform　(D) performs

中譯▶ (A) 我們在考慮產品上市前要進行試銷。

速解▶ 看到整個句子目光直接鎖定「**about -----**」，空格前為介系詞 **about**，選項中皆是動詞 perform 的不同形態，應選動名詞，即選項(A) performing。選項(B) performed、選項(C) perform 與選項(D) performs 皆與介系詞不合，不可選。

進階▶ 本題考的重點是介系詞後的詞性。本題選項是動詞，當句中有兩個動詞時，第二個動詞必須做改變，如動名詞、不定詞或過去分詞等，故選項(C)與(D)可先排除。然而空格前方是介系詞，介系詞後方只能接上名詞或代名詞，做為介系詞的受詞（如 Thank you for sending the document. 或 We are interested in working with him.），故不選過去分詞(B)而選動名詞(A)。

Product Development
展示產品功能給客戶 🎧 MP3 023

115 The engineer is asked to create a prototype ------- can demonstrate these features to customers.
(A) who   (B) where   (C) how   (D) which

中譯 (D) 那位工程師被要求做出能展現這些功能給客戶的原型。

速解 看到整個句子目光直接鎖定「**a prototype ----- can demonstrate**」，空格前為名詞 **prototype**，應選替代事物的關係代名詞，即選項(D) which。選項(A) who 用來替代人，而選項(B) where 代替地點，選項(C) how 為代替方法的關係副詞，皆與名詞 prototype 不符，不可選。

進階 本題考的重點是關係代名詞。關係代名詞可視為代名詞，代替先前的名詞（先行詞），也當連接詞引導後方有動詞的從屬子句（關係子句），修飾先行詞。而不同的先行詞需搭配不同的關係代名詞。在先行詞是關係子句的主詞時，以 who 來代替人、which 來代替事物、where 代替地方、when 代替時間。本題先行詞 prototype 為關係子句的主詞，且為事物，故只能選 (D) which 作為關係代名詞。

Renting and Leasing
傢俱設備齊全的狀態出租

UNIT 116

🎧 MP3 023

116 We are renting our property fully furnished ------- it would be more marketable and attract a higher rent.

(A) as well as　(B) so that　(C) instead of　(D) rather than

中譯 (B) 我們要以傢俱設備齊全的狀態出租我們的房子，好讓房子更有市場價值、訂的租金可以更高。

速解 看到整個句子目光直接鎖定「**property fully furnished ----- ...more marketable**」，空格後子句為空格前子句的目的，應使用引導目地的連接詞，即選項(B) so that。選項(A) as well as 帶出附加說明的內容，選項(C) instead of 與選項(D) rather than 連接兩個相比較的事物，並強調較重要的項目，與本句不合，不可選。

進階 本題考的重點是從屬連接詞。從屬連接詞用來連接兩個子句。本句中的 so that 可用來帶出目的或結果，結構會是一個表原因的獨立子句（如本句的 we... fully furnished）加上 so that 後接一個表結果或目的的子句（如本句的 it would... higher rent）。選項(A)為對等連接詞，後方子句的動詞應為 Ving。選項(C)的為介系詞，後方應接上名詞或動名詞。選項(D)的可作連接詞（前後結構須對等，後方動詞應用原形）或介系詞（接名詞或動名詞）。

Renting and Leasing
延長租約
🎧 MP3 023

⑰ There are several routes ------- you can extend your lease and you should always consult your legal advisor.
(A) how　(B) by how　(C) that　(D) by which

中譯 ▶ (D) 有幾種途徑可以延長租約,而你應該諮詢你的法律顧問。

速解 ▶ 看到整個句子目光直接鎖定「**routes ----- you can extend...**」,空格前為名詞 **routes**,後為一個子句 **you**… **extend your lease**,應選表「藉由」的介系詞加關係代名詞,即選項(D) by which。選項(A) how 與選項(C) that 缺少介系詞,不可選。選項(B) by how 介系詞不與 how 使用,同樣不可選。

進階 ▶ 本題考的重點是介系詞加關係代名詞。關係代名詞前必須有介系詞的情況中,有可能是動詞本身就必須搭配介系詞(如 agree with, stop from 等)或是句意必須有介系詞加上關係代名詞一起修飾先行詞,如本句。本句第一部分原為「There are several routes. You can extend your lease by several routes.」,而兩句合併後,須由關係代名詞引領子句修飾 several routes,而介系詞會置於關係代名詞前,而此時關係代名詞只能使用受格的 which/ whom。但 routes 為事物,故只能選(D) by which。

Renting and Leasing
兩次一年的租約 🎧 MP3 023

UNIT 118

⑱ The landlord is demanding that they sign ------- yearly lease after having been there under two one-year leases.
(A) anothers　(B) other　(C) another　(D) others

中譯▶ (C) 房東在他們已經簽過兩次一年的租約後又要求他們再簽一年的租約。

速解▶ 看到整個句子目光直接鎖定「**sign ----- yearly lease**」，空格後為名詞，且為可數單數，空格應填入應對的限定詞，即選項(C) another。選項(A) anothers 為錯誤用法。選項(D) others 為代名詞，與後方名詞不合，不可選。選項(B) other 後方不接可數名詞單數，同樣不可選。

進階▶ 本題考的重點是限定詞。限定詞（如 a, the, one, some 等）置於名詞前，用來限定名詞。選項中的 other 與 another 同樣為限定詞，後方接的名詞有不同。兩者都可接可數名詞，但 other 後方的可數名詞必須為複數（如 other leases），而 another 後方的可數名詞則必須為單數。另外，other 後方才可接不可數名詞（如 other bread）。本題空格後的 lease 屬於可數名詞單數，故前方應該使用 another。而選項(A) 為代名詞 another 的錯誤用法，another 代表一個不特定的單數名詞，選項(D) 為不特定複數的代名詞，兩者後方皆不可再接上名詞。

Renting and Leasing
租下那個辦公室 🎧 MP3 023

119 The tech company is ------- in leasing the office space.
(A) interested　(B) interesting　(C) interest　(D) interests

中譯 (A) 那間科技公司有興趣租下那個辦公室。

速解 看到整個句子目光直接鎖定「**is ----- in**」，空格前為 **be** 動詞 **is** 與主詞 **tech company**，後為介系詞 **in**，應選表感受的形容詞，即選項 (A) interested。選項(B) interesting 為表令人感到...的形容詞，與語意不合，不可選。選項(C) interest 與選項(D) interests 皆為動詞，與本句文法不符，不可選。

進階 本題考的重點是分詞做形容詞使用。空格前為 be 動詞，後方應為名詞或形容詞，若需使用動詞必須有所變化，故選項(C)與(D)可先排除。而過去分詞的選項(A)與現在分詞的選項(B)在此當形容詞用，但過去分詞的形容詞表示的是「感到...的」(如 I'm bored. 表示我感到無聊)，而現在分詞當形容詞表示「令人感到...的」(如 I'm boring. 表示我令人感到無聊、我是個無趣的人)，本題指的是科技公司感到有興趣，故應選(A) interested。

Renting and Leasing
租車公司交車

UNIT
120

🎧 MP3 023

Part 1 新制閱讀 part 6 答題強化

⑳ You should check for damages or scratches when the rental agency hands the car ------- you.
(A) at　(B) to　(C) with　(D) for

中譯 ▶ (B) 在租車公司給你車時，你應該要檢查是否有損傷或刮傷。

速解 ▶ 看到整個句子目光直接鎖定「**hands... -----you**」，空格前方為動詞 **hands**，空格後為受詞 **you**，應選搭配 hands 的介系詞，即選項 (B) to。選項(A) at、選項(C) with 與選項(D) for 皆與本題動詞 handed 不合，不可選。

Part 2 核心文法和單字考點

進階 ▶ 本題考的重點是授與動詞。授與動詞（如 give, buy, hand 等）會有兩個受詞（直接受詞與間接受詞），句中 you 為間接受詞，the car 為直接受詞。這種句型直接受詞可在前或在後（handed the car to you/ handed you the car）。當直接受詞在前時，兩個受詞間必須有介系詞（handed the car to you），依授與動詞的不同，最常見的可能是使用 to 或 for。基本上當有物品直接的給予時會使用 to，本題 hand 有物品直接交付，須使用 to，即選項(B)。

Part 3 精選模擬試題

Selecting a Restaurant
米其林指南上的餐廳 🎧 MP3 024

121 She is devoted ------- every restaurant in the Michelin Guide.
  (A) to try   (B) to trying   (C) try   (D) trying

中譯▶ (B) 她全心投入在嘗試米其林指南上的每一家餐廳。

速解▶ 看到整個句子目光直接鎖定「**is devoted -----**」，空格前為 **is
devoted**，後方的動詞必須有對應的變化，應選 to + Ving，即選項
(B) to trying。選項(A) to try 為不定詞，選項(C) try 為原形動詞，選
項(D) trying 為動名詞，皆與動詞 devote 不合，不可選。

進階▶ 本題考的重點是特殊慣用語。先前章節說過當句中有兩個動詞時，
後續需接動名詞 Ving 或不定詞 to V.，然而有些特殊的動詞、形容詞
或名詞的慣用語為後方加上 to + Ving。本題 devoted （奉獻）作為
形容詞用，為特殊形容詞，用法必須為 be devoted to + Ving，故本
題應選(B)。

Selecting a Restaurant
花大把鈔票用餐 🎧 MP3 024

UNIT 122

122 When ------- a restaurant, remember that you should be able to enjoy good food without breaking the bank.
(A) to select　(B) selected　(C) selecting　(D) having selected

中譯 (C) 在選擇餐廳時，記得你並不需要花大把鈔票也可以享受美食。

速解 看到整個句子目光直接鎖定「**When ----- a restaurant**」，空格前為 **when**，後方為另一子句，且主詞一致、前方為主動語態，應選 Ving，即選項 (C) selecting。選項(A) to select 為不定詞，選項(B) selected 為過去分詞，選項(D) having selected 為完成式分詞，皆與本句不合，不可選。

進階 本題考的重點是分詞構句。本句型為 when + S.+ V., S. + V.，屬於由連接詞 when 帶領的表時間的分詞構句，再加上主要子句。分詞構句為當兩個子句的主詞相同時，從屬子句的主詞可省略，並將動詞改為分詞，主動語態時使用現在分詞 Ving，被動語態時使用過去分詞 Ved。本題主要子句（(you) remember that...）與 when 連接詞子句（When (you) (select) a restaurant）的主詞相同，且 when 後的動作 select 為主動語態，故應選擇 Ving，即選項(C)。

213

Selecting a Restaurant
可愛的餐廳

UNIT 123

🎧 MP3 024

123 While I ------- around the area, I encountered this lovely restaurant.
(A) was walked   (B) walk   (C) was walking   (D) walked

中譯 (C) 我在那附近逛的時候，看見一家很可愛的餐廳。

速解 看到整個句子目光直接鎖定「**while -----**」，空格前為連接詞 **while**，後方主要子句的動詞為簡單過去式，空格應填過去進行式，即選項 (C) was watching。選項(A) was walked 為過去被動、選項 (B) walk 為原形動詞、選項(D) walked 為過去簡單式，皆與本句不符，不選。

進階 本題考的重點是連接詞 while 引導的副詞子句。連接詞 while 經常用來連接兩個子句，用來表示兩個同時進行的動作（如 I was reading while he was cooking.），或是一持續動作途中發生另一動作（如 He came in while I was reading.），在兩種情況下，while 子句的動詞通常為**現在進行式**。本題由連接詞 while 可判斷空格應填入現在進行式動詞。此外，本句 while 連接詞子句在前，主要子句在後（連接詞子句後會有逗號），語意屬於持續動作途中發生另一動作，故主要子句為簡單過去式，而連接詞子句應為現在進行式，故選(B)。

Eating Out
牛排煎久一點

🎧 MP3 024

124 I had to send my steak back and ask them ------- it more because there is still blood in it.

(A) cooking　(B) cooked　(C) cook　(D) to cook

中譯 (D) 我必須退回我的牛排請他們煎久一點，因為裡面還有血色。

速解 看到整個句子目光直接鎖定「**ask them -----**」，空格前 **ask**，接上受詞，後方的動詞必須使用不定詞，故填選項 (D) to cook。選項(A) cooking 為現在分詞、選項(B) cooked 為過去分詞、選項(C) cook 為原形動詞，皆與動詞 ask 不合，不可選。

進階 本題考的重點是特殊動詞用法。本題動詞 ask 屬於特殊動詞，雖與先前提過的使役動詞在意思上很相近，但在用法上卻不同。雖然 ask 與使役動詞都有「要求、讓人做某事」的感覺，但使役動詞後接原形動詞（或過去分詞），而本題的 ask 後面卻需要接不定詞（結構為 ask（人）to + V.）。本題選項皆為動詞，且前方為動詞 ask 與受詞 them，故本題應遵循特殊動詞 ask 的用法並在空格填入不定詞 to cook。

Eating Out
魚子醬與白蘆筍搭配　🎧MP3 024

125 I heard that caviar ------- very good with white asparagus.
(A) tastes　(B) to taste　(C) is tasting　(D) taste

中譯▶ (A) 我聽說魚子醬與白蘆筍配起來很美味。

速解▶ 看到整個句子目光直接鎖定「**caviar ----- very good**」，空格前為 **caviar**，後為 **very good**，為由 that 引導的子句，而選項為動詞 taste，應選現在簡單式的第三人稱單數，即選項(A) tastes。選項(B) to taste 為不定詞，與本句語法不合；選項(C) is tasting 為現在進行式動詞，與動詞 taste 不合；選項(D) taste 為非第三人稱原形動詞，與名詞 caviar 不合，皆不可選。

進階▶ 本題考的重點是狀態動詞。本句有 **that** 帶領子句，故後方動詞應為真正動詞，不使用不定詞，故不選(B)。狀態動詞指用來表達擁有、知覺、感情或想法等的動詞（如 own, smell, hear, love, know 等），因表狀態，不可使用進行式。本句中的 taste 可當動態動詞，表動作「品嚐」，此時可用進行式（如 I'm tasting the soup.），但本題的 taste 表「嚐起來」，屬於狀態動詞，故不選現在進行式的 (C)，且子句的主詞為單數，故應選第三人稱單數的簡單式動詞，即 (A) tastes。

Eating Out
找做桑格力亞酒的材料 🎧 MP3 024

UNIT 126

⑫ He ------- red wine and some fresh fruit to make sangria for half an hour.

(A) to look for
(B) has been looking for
(C) to find
(D) has been finding

中譯 ▶ (B) 他找了紅酒與一些新鮮水果要做桑格力亞酒已經找了半小時了。

速解 ▶ 看到整個句子目光直接鎖定「**He -----…for half an hour**」，空格前為主詞 **he**，後方為受詞，空格應填主要動詞，且後方有表持續動作的時間副詞 for half an hour，應填選項 (B) has been looking for。選項(A) to look for 與選項(C) to find 皆為不定詞，不可選。選項(D) has been finding，動詞不可使用完成進行式，不可選。

進階 ▶ 本題考的重點是瞬間動詞。本題空格前有主詞 he，後方為受詞 red wine and some fresh fruit，缺少主要動詞，空格應填入真正動詞。選項(A)與選項(C)為不定詞，非真正動詞，不可用。瞬間動詞指非延續性的動作，表示動作發生後便結束，例如 find, borrow, kill, marry, open, die, join, buy 等，皆是瞬間的動作，無法表示持續、延續的動作，故雖能使用完成式（可能表經驗或完成，表做過或已經做了），但卻無法接上表持續一段時間的副詞，如 for/since，本題有此類時間副詞，不可使用瞬間動詞 find，應使用 look for，故選可搭本題時間副詞的(B)。

Ordering Lunch
經理付錢
UNIT 127

🎧 MP3 024

⑫ Since the manager is paying, you can order ------- food on the menu.

(A) whenever　　　　(B) whoever

(C) whichever/any　　(D) whomever

中譯 (C) 因為是經理付錢，你可以點菜單上任何一種食物。

....

速解 看到整個句子目光直接鎖定「**order ----- food**」，空格前為動詞 **order**，空格後為名詞 **food**，空格內應填可修飾後方受詞的形容詞或是與受詞相對應的限定詞，即選項 (C) whichever。選項(A) whenever、選項(B) whoever、選項(D)whomever 語意不合，不可選。

....

進階 本題考的重點是複合關係代名詞作為關係形容詞。當關係代名詞 what, which, how, who, when 加上 ever 時，便形成複合關係代名詞 whatever,whichever, however 等，身兼先行詞與關係代名詞的角色，故使用複合關係代名詞時，不需有先行詞（如 The manager will pay for whoever finishes first. = The manager will pay for anyone who finishes first.）。複合關係代名詞中 whichever 與 whatever 可作為形容詞（關係形容詞），後方可接上名詞。本題空格後方為名詞 food，故應選擇(C) whichever，可改為... order any food you want。

Ordering Lunch
收到午餐 🎧 MP3 024

128 Not until we almost finished discussing all matters ------- our lunch.

(A) receive we did　　(B) we did receive

(C) did we receive　　(D) we receive

中譯▶ (C) 直到我們快結束討論所有議題，我們才收到午餐。

速解▶ 看到整個句子目光直接鎖定「**not until... ----- our**」，空格前方為 **not until**，後方主詞與助動詞需倒裝，故選 (C) did we receive。選項(A) receive we did、選項(B) we did receive、選項(D) we receive 都不符合本句倒裝語序的要求，不可選。

進階▶ 本題考的重點是倒裝句。當有否定意思的副詞被放在句首時，需使用倒裝，表強調。本句有否定副詞 not until 在句首，為強調「直到...才...」，後方應使用倒裝句。此種倒裝結構會是 Not only... 助動詞 + 主詞 + 動詞，若是 be 動詞的結構則為 Not only... be 動詞 + 主詞。本句原為「We did not receive our lunch until we almost finished discussing all matters.」，有動詞 receive，應該使用「助動詞+ 主詞 + 動詞」，故選擇 (C) did we receive。

219

Ordering Lunch
餐廳的食物非常棒 🎧 MP3 024

129 The restaurant that offers the best food and each order ------- by its signature chocolate biscuit.

(A) is accompanied　　(B) are accompanied

(C) accompanies　　(D) accompany

中譯▶ (A) 那家餐廳的食物非常棒，且每次訂餐都附餐廳最有名的巧克力餅乾。

速解▶ 看到整個句子目光直接鎖定「**each order ----- by**」，空格前有 **each**，後方有 **by**，空格內的動詞必須符合主詞且有對應的變化，故選 (A) is accompanied。選項(B) are accompanied 為非第三人稱單數被動語態，選項(C) accompanies 為第三人稱單數主動語態，選項 (D)accompany 為非第三人稱單數主動語態，皆與本句不合，不可選。

進階▶ 本題考的重點是主動詞一致。英語的動詞可能會因主詞而有改變，如單數名詞須配上單數動詞，而複數名詞須配複數動詞（如 The order is large. 與 The orders are large.）。而本句第二個子句中的 each 須加上單數名詞，且整體視為單數，故動詞應使用單數動詞。此外，第二個子句的動詞與主詞 each order 為被動關係，後方 by 也可看出此被動關係，動詞需使用被動語態，故本題應選單數被動語態的動詞，即選項(A) is accompanied。

Cooking as a Career
當私人廚師 🎧 MP3 024

130 ------- the person if you are interested in becoming a private chef.

(A) To contact　(B) Contacted　(C) Contacting　(D) Contact

中譯 ▶ (D) 如果你有興趣當私人廚師，聯絡那個人。

速解 ▶ 看到整個句子目光直接鎖定「**----- the person**」，空格後為受詞 **the person**，無主詞，空格內應填原形動詞，即選項 (D) Contact。選項 (A) To contact 為不定詞、選項(B) Contacted 為過去分詞、選項(C) Contacting 為現在分詞，不可選。

進階 ▶ 本題考的重點是祈使句。祈使句用來給予命令或勸告等，對象通常是 you （即主詞為 you），故主詞通常省略，而以原形動詞開頭（如 Finish the project by tomorrow.）。本題是指示，為主詞省略後的祈使句，故句子開頭為動詞，且應使用原形，所以應該填入選項 (D) Contact，完成第一個子句 Contact the person...。

Cooking as a Career
UNIT 131 餐廳的二廚 🎧 MP3 024

⑬ She ------- be the line chef in that famous restaurant, but now she owns three restaurants.

(A) used to　　(B) got used to　　(C) be used to　　(D) was used to

---

中譯 (A) 她原本是那家名餐廳的二廚，但現在擁有三間餐廳。

速解 看到整個句子目光直接鎖定「**She ----- be but now**」，空格後為原形動詞 **be**，且前後子句屬相反關係，空格應填選項 (A) used to。選項(B) got used to、選項(C) be used to 與選項(D) was used to 後方基本上須使用動名詞，皆與本句不合，不可選。

進階 本題考的重點是相似字詞與 to 的用法。本題答案的 used to 表示「過去常做的行為，但現在已不做」（因指過去，必須使用 used），其中的 to 屬於不定詞，不是介系詞，故後方應該使用原形動詞。如本題空格後為原形動詞 be。選項中的 got used to（原形為 get used to）表「從不習慣變習慣」，選項(C) be used to 與選項(D) was used to 皆表「習慣於某事」的狀態，但前者為原形，而後者為過去式。以上詞中 to 屬介系詞，後方應接上動名詞或名詞，本題不可選。

Cooking as a Career
先唸廚藝學校

UNIT 132

🎧 MP3 024

132 To become a chef, you ------- go to a culinary school first if you're willing to work your way up from the bottom.
(A) shouldn't　(B) don't have to　(C) haven't to　(D) mustn't

中譯▶ (B) 要成為廚師，如果你願意從底層做起，你不一定要先唸廚藝學校。

速解▶ 看到整個句子目光直接鎖定「**you ----- go to if you're willing to...**」，空格所在子句表非必要條件，應使用相對的助動詞，即選項 (B) don't have to。選項(A) shouldn't 表建議不應該，選項(D) mustn't 表強烈禁止，選項(C) haven't to 為錯誤型，皆與本句不合，不可選。

進階▶ 本題考的重點是表義務的情態助動詞的否定。情態助動詞置於主要動詞的前面，用來表達義務、責任、意願、能力等。從句意可看出空格所在的子句是表達非必要的條件。否定的情態助動詞 shouldn't 為 should（應該）的否定形，表「不應該」；否定的情態助動詞 don't have to 為 have to（必須）的否定形，注意否定是表「不一定要」；否定的情態助動詞 musn't 為 must（必須）的否定形，表「絕對不可以」，與本題相符的為 don't have to，故本題應選(B)。

223

Events
外燴訂單

🎧 MP3 024

⑬ At this time next week, we will ------- our first catering order for 300 people.

(A) do　(B) doing　(C) be doing　(D) going to do

中譯▶ (C) 下禮拜的這個時間，我們將在為三百人進行我們的第一次外燴訂單。

速解▶ 看到整個句子目光直接鎖定「**At this time next will -----**」，空格前方有 **at this time next week**，後方的動詞必須使用**未來進行式**，空格前有 will，故應填入選項 (C) be doing。選項(A) do 為原形動詞、選項(B) doing 為現在分詞、選項(D) going to do 為不完整的動詞未來式，皆與 will 或前方時間副詞不合，不可選。

進階▶ 本題考的重點是未來進行式。當描述某個動作將在未來某一時刻進行時，會使用未來進行式，如本題的時間副詞 at this time next week 便是指未來的某一時刻，故動詞應使用未來進行式。未來進行式的結構可能是 will be Ving 或是 be going to be Ving，本題空格前已經有 will，無法使用 be going to 形，故只能選擇 (C) be doing。

Events
自己主持派對 🎧 MP3 024

134 She was forced to host the party ------- herself since everyone in the office was busy with other projects.
(A) by　(B) on　(C) to　(D) at

中譯 ▶ (A) 因為辦公室的人都在忙其他案子，她被迫自己主持派對。

速解 ▶ 看到整個句子目光直接鎖定「**host the party ----- herself**」，空格前為動詞與受詞 **host the party**，空格後為 **herself**，空格內應填入適當的介系詞，即選項 (A) by。選項(B) on、選項(C) to、選項(D) at 皆為介系詞，但與 herself 不合，不可選。

進階 ▶ 本題考的重點是反身代名詞。當一個子句的主詞和受詞是同一個人時（如 He hurt himself in the process.），或是需要強調語氣時（如 I can't believe I hosted the party myself.），可使用反身代名詞。而 by + 反身代名詞則是表示「獨自」，本句後方子句可看出只剩主詞 she 一個人，故會使用選項 (A) by 加上反身代名詞表示獨自完成。而其他選項中的介系詞都可視為表地方的介系詞，後方不可接反身代名詞，此外語意也與本句不符合，故不可選。

Events
參加品酒活動 🎧 MP3 024

135 To commit to sustainability, we are asking everyone attending the wine tasting event to bring ------- glass.
(A) you　(B) yours　(C) yourself　(D) your own

中譯 (D) 為致力於永續發展，我們請求參加品酒活動的各位攜帶自己的酒杯。

速解 看到整個句子目光直接鎖定「**bring ----- glass**」，空格前為動詞 **bring**，空格後為名詞 **glass**，空格中可填入形容詞或冠詞，故填選項 (B) to trying。選項(A) she 為主格代名詞、選項(B) yours 為所有格代名詞、選項(C) yourself 為反身代名詞，後方不接名詞，不可選。

進階 本題考的重點是所有格形容詞。所有格形容詞用來表示事物所屬，後方需要加上名詞（如 my book 或 his wine），有時在所有格形容詞與名詞中間會加入 own，用來強調「自己的」。其他選項皆為代名詞，選項(A)會作為一個子句的主詞、選項(B)代替 your + 名詞、選項(C)可作為動詞或介系詞後的受詞，皆用來替代說過或是所知的人事物，後方不接名詞，故本題應選(D)。

General Travel
獨自享受旅行 🎧 MP3 024

UNIT 136

136 Wake up early ------- you want to have the best attractions all to yourself.

(A) although　(B) otherwise　(C) besides　(D) should

中譯▶ (D) 如果你想要獨自享受所有美好的觀光景點，你應該早起。

速解▶ 看到整個句子目光直接鎖定「**wake up early ----- you want**」，空格後的子句為空格前子句的條件，空格內應填入選項(D) should。選項(A) although 為連接詞，選項(B) otherwise 與選項(C) besides 皆為副詞，但與前後子句語意不合，不可選。

進階▶ 本題考的重點是沒有 if 的假設語法倒裝。當表達未來或現在可能發生的假設時，有時為了聽起來較正式，**可省略 if 並倒裝**。如原句是「If you should want to contact the office, please call the number.」（表「萬一...」）可省略為「Should you want to contact the office, please call the number.」。本題第二個子句 you want to... 為條件，整句為省略後的假設句，故空格內應填入 should。選項(A)表「雖然」、選項(B)表「否則」、選項(C)表「此外」，以上連接詞或副詞可連接兩個子句（副詞需使用分號或句號），但語意都不合，不可選。

General Travel
旅行社的建議 🎧 MP3 024

137 The travel agency suggested that he ------- with the hotel to find out what to see in Nairobi.
(A) to check　(B) checks　(C) check　(D) checking

中譯 (C) 旅行社建議他詢問飯店，了解奈洛比可以參觀的景點。

速解 看到整個句子目光直接鎖定「**suggested that he -----**」，空格前的主要動詞為 **suggest**，that 子句中的動詞應為原形，即選項(C) check。選項(A) checked 為不定詞、選項(B) checks 為動詞第三人稱單數、選項(D) checking 為現在分詞，與本句不合，不可選。

進階 本題考的重點是表命令、提議或要求等的動詞的特殊用法。這類動詞包含 suggest, demand, insist, recommend, request, ask 等，後方若接 that 子句，子句中的動詞必須為原形動詞，這是因為前方有個 should 省略（ 本句原為…suggested that he should check with… ），故雖然 that 子句中的主詞為 he，動詞不使用選項(B)的第三人稱單數，而須填入(C)的原形動詞。選項(A)的不定詞與選項(D)的現在分詞都不可直接用在本子句中的主詞後。

General Travel
旅行與當地人互動
UNIT 138

🎧 MP3 024

138 Interacting with locals allows you to gain a deeper understanding of a culture. ------- , it can also give you more memorable experiences.

(A) Beside　(B) Besiding　(C) Besided　(D) Besides

中譯 ▶ (D) 除了能更深入了解一個文化之外，與當地人互動可以給你更難忘的經驗。

速解 ▶ 直接鎖定「**Interacting with locals allows you.... -----, it can also...**」，空格前後為完整句子，且兩個子句為附加的關係，空格內應填入適當的副詞連接詞，即選項(D) Besides。選項(A) Beside 為介系詞，選項(B) Besiding 與選項(C) Besided 皆為錯誤用法，不可選。

進階 ▶ 本題考的重點是副詞連接詞。副詞連接詞為可連接兩個子句的副詞，副詞連接詞前方必須是句號或分號，而後方會是逗號，可用來表達附加、並置、對比、結果、強調等（ 如 besides, however, otherwise, moreover, hence 等 ）。本題中的兩句 gain a deeper understanding 與 give you more memorable experiences 屬於附加關係，所以應該使用副詞連接詞 besides。

Airlines
皮爾森國際機場 🎧 MP3 024

UNIT 139

139 Pearson International Airport has tightened their security procedures ------- the attack that killed 36 people.
(A) since　(B) for　(C) in　(D) at

中譯 (A) 皮爾森國際機場自從一場攻擊造成 36 人死亡後，便加強了安檢程序。

速解 看到整個句子目光直接鎖定「**has tightened ----- the attack**」，空格前方的動詞為現在完成式，空格後為一個表時間點的子句，空格內應填入適當的介系詞，即選項(A) since。選項(B) for 後方需接一段時間，選項(C) in 與選項(D) at 與現在完成式不合，不可選。

進階 本題考的重點是與現在完成式搭配的時間詞。現在完成式的句子當表一段時間時，經常搭配 for 或 since，兩者都表達某事件進行了一段時間。使用 for 時，後方須接上一段時間（如 for 10 years），而 since 後方則配一個過去的時間點（如 since 10 years ago）。本句中的 an attack killed 36 people 表一個過去的時間點（攻擊與傷亡發生的時候），應配上 since 來表示「自從那時候開始」。選項(C)與(D)後方也可接上時間（如 in January, in summer, at 10:00, at midnight），但都與本句的動詞時態（現在完成式）不合，故不可選。

Airlines
墨爾本的機票 🎧 MP3 024

⑭ A ticket to Melbourne now ------- only around USD180 if you're willing to fly red-eye.

(A) costs　(B) spends　(C) pays　(D) takes

中譯 (A) 現在一張去墨爾本的機票只要美金 180 元，如果你願意飛紅眼航班的話。

速解 看到整個句子目光直接鎖定「**A ticket... -----USD180**」，空格前主詞為 **a ticket**，空格後受詞為價錢 **USD180**，空格內應填入適當的動詞，即選項(A) costs。選項(B) spends、選項(C) pays、選項(D) takes 皆與主詞不合，不可選。

進階 本題考的重點是動詞搭配。選項中的動詞的意思都與「花費」相關，但使用的主詞與句子結構會有不同。選項(A)表「價值...」，用於金錢上，主詞必須是事物。選項(B)表「花費」，可用於時間或金錢，主詞必須是人。選項(C)表「付錢」，用於金錢，主詞同樣必須是人。選項(D)表「花費」，用於時間，主詞基本上應為事物或虛主詞 it。以主詞來看，因本句主詞為 ticket，選項(B)與(C)不可選。另，因本句指金錢，選項(D)不可選。故空格應填入主詞可用事物，且表金錢的 (A)。

Airlines
冗長的安檢隊伍 🎧 MP3 025

UNIT 141

⑭ Most fliers find it ------- to wait for hours in lengthy security lines and secretly hope to avoid the wait.
(A) annoyance　(B) annoyed　(C) annoying　(D) annoy

中譯 (C) 大部分的旅客都討厭在冗長的安檢隊伍中等上好幾個小時，並偷偷地希望可以避開。

速解 看到整個句子目光直接鎖定「**find it -----**」，空格前為動詞 **find** 與虛主詞 **it**，空格內應填入適當的形容詞，即選項(C) annoying。選項(A) annoyance 為名詞，選項(B) annoyed 為表感受的形容詞，選項(D) annoy 為動詞，皆與本句不合，不可選。

進階 本題考的重點是不完全及物動詞。不完全及物動詞為後方需要受詞以及補語來完整句子的意思。句中的 find 便是其中一個，作為不完全及物動詞表「發現...是...」，後方可能接上名詞、代名詞、動名詞或虛主詞（作為受詞），再加上形容詞或名詞（作為補語）（如 I found him an interesting actor.）。在本句中的用法是 find 加上虛主詞 it 再接補語，補語可能為名詞或形容詞，不選為動詞的(D)，而名詞應使用 an annoyance（表令人感到不悅的事物），無冠詞，故不選(A)。此外，it 代表的是後方的不動詞 to wait...，故補語無法使用表感受的形容詞，不選(B)，應該使用描述事物的形容詞，即(C)。

Trains
豪華火車 🎧 MP3 025

UNIT 142

⑭These luxury trains are ------- expensive for locals and are meant for international travelers.
(A) to　(B) too　(C) enough　(D) such

中譯▶ (B) 這些豪華火車對當地人來說太貴，原本就是設計給外國旅客的。

速解▶ 看到整個句子目光直接鎖定「**are ----- expensive for locals**」，空格前為 **be** 動詞，而空格後為形容詞，空格內應填入適當的副詞，即選項(B) too。選項(A) to 為介系詞；選項(C) enough 為副詞，須置於形容詞後；選項(D) such 為形容詞，後方應有名詞，以上皆不可選。

進階▶ 本題考的重點是程度副詞。程度副詞可用來修飾形容詞，表達事物的程度。本句中的 too 表「太過...」，含負面意涵（超過原本該有的程度），會置於形容詞之前。本題空格在形容詞前、be 動詞之後，故不可選 (C)的 enough，因為 enough 雖然為副詞，但必須放在形容詞之後（如 It is cheap enough. 或 It is not cheap enough.），本身無正面或負面意涵，須由句子意思判斷。而本句空格後方只有形容詞，故應使用可修飾形容詞的副詞，所以也不選介系詞(A)或形容詞(D)，應該使用置於形容詞前的副詞(B)，且可表示負面的「太...」含義。

Trains
火車上的用餐經驗 🎧 MP3 025

143 Dining on the dinner train is such a special experience ------- I cannot recommend it enough.
(A) that　(B) as　(C) which　(D) but

中譯 ▶ (A) 在火車上用餐的經驗實在太特別，我讚不絕口。

速解 ▶ 看到整個句子目光直接鎖定「**such a special experience ----- I**」，空格前後為兩個子句 **Dining on...** 與 **I cannot...**，且前方有 **such**，空格內應填入適當的連接詞，即選項(A) **that**。選項(B) **as** 為表「當」的連接詞，選項(C) **which** 為關係代名詞，選項(D) **but** 為表對立的連接詞，以上皆與句意或 such 不合，不可選。

進階 ▶ 本題考的重點是從屬連接詞 such... that。句中有兩個子句 Dining on the dinner train... 與 I cannot recommend it enough，需要連接詞相連，故空格內應填入連接詞。另前方有 such，這裡的 such 為形容詞，後接一個名詞片語，而 such 強調此片語裡的形容詞，時常接上連接詞 that 引導一個表結果的子句（即本句中的 I cannot recommend...），組成 such...that，表「如此...以致於」，故本題選(A)。

Trains
火車的兩種座位 🎧 MP3 025

UNIT 144

144 There are two types of seats on the train. One is the cheaper hard seat and ------- is the more expensive soft seat.
(A) other　(B) another　(C) the other　(D) the another

中譯 (C) 這火車有兩種座位，一種是較便宜的硬式座位，另一種是較貴的軟式座位。

速解 看到整個句子目光直接鎖定「**two types...one... and -----**」，空格前後為兩個項目，且第一個項目前方有 **one**，空格內應填入代表第二個項目的代名詞，即選項(C) the other。選項(A) other 可作代名詞，但應配上 the 或複數 -s，選項(B) another 為代替無指定的一個，選項(D) the another 為錯誤用法，以上皆不可選。

進階 本題考的重點是代名詞。選項中的 other 與 another 都可作代名詞使用，another 會用來代替前面說過的名詞，且並無特別指定，因為並無特別指定，故前面不可加 the，選項(D)因此不可選。而 other 為形容詞，若當代名詞時，通常前面加上 the，用來代替特定的「另一個」，或在後方加上複數 -s，代替特定的複數名詞，故(A)也不選。又當事物的數量有兩個時，其中一個會使用 one 代替，而另一個事物則會使用 the other。本題指明有兩種，空格後的事物為第二種，故選(C)，非(B)。

Hotels
飯店費率 🎧 MP3 025

145 When I chose the hotel, I not only looked at rates but also ------- attention to location.

(A) pay (B) paid (C) did pay (D) is paid

中譯 ▶ (B) 我選這家飯店時,不只看了費率,還注意了地點。

速解 ▶ 看到整個句子目光直接鎖定「**not only looked... but also -----**」...,空格前後為連接詞 **not only... but also**,且 **not only** 後為動詞 **looked**,空格內應填相對應的動詞,即選項(B) paid。選項(A) pay 為原形動詞,選項(C) did pay 為助動詞 did 加上 pay,選項(D) is paid 為現在式被動語態,以上皆不可選。

進階 ▶ 本題考的重點是連接詞 not only... but also 的動詞一致。對等連接詞 not only...but also 用來連接兩個單字或子句,且所連接的單字或子句必須要一致(如 not only big but also affordable,兩者都為形容詞)。本句中使用 not only... but also,前後的兩個項目應有一致性,因 not only 後為動詞,but also 後也必須為動詞,且時式也須一致,前方為過去式 looked,後方也應使用過去式,故選擇(B)。

Hotels
訂飯店

UNIT 146

🎧 MP3 025

146 Booking hotels ------- one of the most important but difficult decisions one has to make when organizing trips.

(A) are　(B) is　(C) be　(D) am

中譯▶ (B) 訂飯店是在安排旅遊時最重要但最困難的決定之一。

速解▶ 看到整個句子目光直接鎖定「**Booking hotels ----- one of...**」，空格前為動名詞當主詞，空格內應填入第三人稱單數動詞，即選項(B) is。選項(A) are 為複數 be 動詞，選項(C) be 為原形 be 動詞，選項(D) am 為搭配第一人稱單數的 be 動詞，以上皆不可選。

進階▶ 本題考的重點是動名詞當主詞的主動詞一致。空格前是動名詞 Booking hotels 作為主詞，空格後是補語 one of...，句中缺少主要動詞，可知空格中須填入動詞。又動名詞當主詞時，表這一事件，應視為單數。句中 Booking hotels 雖有複數名詞 hotels，但主詞表示的是「訂飯店」這件事，故應使用第三人稱單數，故選(B)。

147 When you arrive at the hotel, you should familiarize yourself with your hotel's ------- plan.
(A) emergent　(B) emerge　(C) emerging　(D) emergency

中譯 (D) 當你抵達飯店的時候,你應該先熟悉飯店的緊急應變計畫。

速解 看到整個句子目光直接鎖定「**hotel's ----- plan**」,空格前為名詞所有格,空格後為名詞,空格內應填入適當的修飾詞,即選項(D) emergency。選項(A) emergent 與選項(C) emerging 為形容詞,但語意不合,不可選。選項(B) emerge 為動詞,不可選。

進階 本題考的重點是複合名詞。本題空格前為名詞所有格 hotel's,後方為名詞 plan,基本上應置入形容詞,選項(A)與(C)雖為形容詞,可置於名詞前方修飾名詞,但 emerging 表「新興、浮現」,而 emergent 表「緊急」,用來描述一個情況來得突然或緊急(如 emergent event),都與本句語意不合。複合名詞為兩個或多個字形成,可能分開、以連字號相連或合成一個字(如 egg rolls、mother-in-law 或 toothpaste)。本題應填入名詞 emergency 合成**複合名詞 emergency plan**,表如火災等緊急狀況發生時使用的逃生計畫等,緊急時刻會用到的通常都以 emergency 搭配其他詞形成複合名詞(如 emergency exit, emergency room, emergency contact)。

Car Rentals
高額的租車費 🎧 MP3 025

148 It is high rental rates ------- are driving all the customers to other agencies.
(A) where　(B) that　(C) whose　(D) whom

中譯 (B) 正是高額的租車費把客戶都趕到其他租車公司去了。

速解 看到整個句子目光直接鎖定「**it is... rates ----- are driving**」，空格前方有 **it is**，接上想強調的部份 high rental rates，應選(B) that。選項(A) where 指地方，選項(C) whose 與選項(D) whom 都指人，不可選。

進階 本題考的重點為強調句，或稱分裂句。強調句是透過更改語序以強調某一主題，其中一個結構是「it is + 強調部分 + that」，當普通句是「High rental rates are driving all the customers to other agencies.」，強調句便會改成題目的「It is the high rental rates that are driving...」。若強調部分為人，可將 that 改為 who 或 whom，若為地點可改為 where，但本題強調部分為事物 rates，故選(B) that。

Car Rentals
最好的租車價格與服務 🎧 MP3 025

149 Fast Care Hire is said ------- the best deals and services, which is why people always go there when they need to rent a car.
(A) to be offered　(B) offer　(C) to offer　(D) to being offering

中譯▶ (C) Fast Care Hire 據說提供的價格與服務是最好的，也因此大家如果需要租車都去那。

速解▶ 看到整個句子目光直接鎖定「**is said -----**」，空格前為主詞加上 **is said**，且為主動語態，空格應填入 to + V.，即選項(C) to offer。選項(A) to be offered 表被動語態，不可選。選項(B) offer 為原形動詞，會造成句中有兩個主要動詞，不可選。選項(D) to being offering 不符本句型要求，不可選。

進階▶ 本題考的重點是「據說」或「聽說」的句型中的動詞形態。這類句型時常使用虛主詞 it（如 It is said that Fast Car Hire offers the best deals and services.），真主詞後方動詞依照想表達的時態做變化。但除了使用虛主詞外，也可使用真主詞，並將 that 帶領的子句改為不定詞結構，且因 Fast Car Hire 與 offer 為主動關係，應該選擇(C)，並將句子改為 Fast Care Hire is said to offer...。

Car Rentals
租車季節接近

UNIT 150

🎧 MP3 025

⓯ ------- the busy summer car-rental season is approaching, prices are climbing.

(A) Before　(B) While　(C) When　(D) As

中譯 ▶ (D) 隨著夏天的租車季節接近，價錢也在攀升中。

速解 ▶ 看到整個句子目光直接鎖定「**----- ...season is approaching... prices are climbing**」，空格前後為兩個子句，且表同時發展的事件，空格應填正確的連接詞，即選項**(D) as**。選項**(A) Before** 為表「之前」的連接詞，與語意不合，不可選。選項**(B) While** 與選項**(C) When** 表「當」，語意或文法不合，不可選。

進階 ▶ 本題考的重點是語意相似的連接詞的用法。連接詞的題型通常需藉前後子句的關係判斷答案。本句中兩個子句都使用進行式來表示情況的變化，空格中通常只能填入 as，表「隨著」的意思。當 as 表「隨著」時可能用來表示一種狀況隨著另一種狀況變化，或一種狀況是另一種狀況的結果。選項中 when 與 while 則通常表「當」，兩者都可表達一個較長的動作進行過程中，發生另一個較短的動作，但 when 後會接較短的動作（以簡單式表示），而 while 後會接**較長的動作**（以進行式表示）。

Movies
不喜歡科幻片

UNIT **151**

🎧 MP3 025

⓯ The girl doesn't like sci-fi movies. Can you suggest ------- of a different genre?

(A) one　(B) all　(C) it　(D) both

`中譯` (A) 那個女孩並不喜歡科幻片，你可不可以建議另一種類型的電影。

`速解` 看到整個句子目光直接鎖定「**suggest ----- of a different genre**」，空格前為動詞，空格後為可修飾名詞的介系詞片語，空格應填正確的名詞或代名詞，即選項(A) one。選項(B) all 可做代表「全部」的不定代名詞，選項(C) it 為代替先前提及的單數事物的代名詞，即選項(A) one 選項(D) both 可做代表「兩者」的不定代名詞，皆與語意不合，不選。

`進階` 本題考的重點是代名詞。**不定代名詞**是用來代替未明確指定的人事物等，或是先前提及或後述的人事物中的全部或一部份（如 one, all, some, each, both 等），而代名詞如 it, you, they 等則是有明確指定的人事物。本題中並無指定的電影，故不使用代名詞 it。選項中的 one, all 與 both 都可做不定代名詞，one 可用來指代「任何一個或其中一個」、all 則指「某群體的全部」、both 則指「兩個都」。本題語意與 all 或 both 並不合，應選可代表「任何一部」的 one，即選項(A)。

Movies
較少的電影聲效 🎧 MP3 025

152 The director used ------- sound effects in her latest movie because she wanted the viewers to focus on the performance of the characters.

(A) less　(B) fewer　(C) leaset　(D) fewest

中譯 ▶ (B) 導演在她最新的電影裡使用較少的聲效，因為她希望觀眾能專注在角色的演出上。

速解 ▶ 看到整個句子目光直接鎖定「**used ----- sound effects**」，空格前為動詞 **used**，後為可數名詞 **sound effects**，空格應填適當的形容詞比較級，即選項(B) fewer。選項(A) less 為接不可數名詞的形容詞比較級，不可選。選項(C) least 與選項(D) fewest 皆為最高級，不可選。

進階 ▶ 本題考的重點是形容詞搭配的限制。選項中 less 為形容詞 little 的比較級，least 為最高級，搭配的名詞必須是不可數名詞，而 fewer 為形容詞 few 的比較級，fewest 為最高級，搭配的名詞必須是可數名詞。本題空格後的名詞 sound effects 為可數名詞，不可使用 less 或 least。又形容詞最高級前方應有定冠詞 the，空格前不見 the，故不選 fewest，而選 fewer，即選項(B)。

Movies
買到電影票跟零食

🎧 MP3 025

❿ As soon as he ------- the tickets and snacks, he will enter the auditorium to get better seats.
(A) got   (B) get   (C) gets   (D) will get

中譯 (C) 他一買到票跟零食，他就會進場找好位置。

速解 看到整個句子目光直接鎖定「**As soon as ----- will enter**」，主要子句為未來式，而空格前為主詞，後為受詞，空格應填現在簡單式動詞，即選項(C) gets。選項(A) got 為過去式，選項(B) get 為非第三人稱現在式，選項(D) will get 為未來式，皆不可選。

進階 本題考的重點是 as soon as 的用法。連接詞 assoon as 表「一...就...」，可連接兩個幾乎同時發生的動作，結構會是一個主要子句加上由 as soonas 帶領的從屬子句，兩子句可使用同樣時態，強調同時發生，但若主要子句是未來式，從屬子句應使用現在式代替未來式。本句的主要子句 we will enter... 使用未來式，故從屬子句 As soon as he...中的動詞應該使用現在式，故不選(A)或(D)，又從屬子句中的主詞為 he，應使用第三人稱單數形的動詞，即選項(C) gets。

Theater
常上劇場

UNIT
154

🎧 MP3 025

154 I go to the theater very often despite ------- to pay quite a lot for a show.

(A) had　(B) having　(C) have　(D) had had

中譯 ▶ (B) 儘管一場秀不便宜，我還是常常上劇場。

速解 ▶ 看到整個句子目光直接鎖定「**despite ----- to**」，空格前為介系詞 **despite**，空格應填動名詞，即選項(B) having。選項(A) had 為過去式，選項(C) have 現在式，選項(D) had had 為過去完成式，皆與 despite 不合，不可選。

進階 ▶ 本題考的重點是 despite 的用法。本句空格前的 despite 表「儘管」，用來表示對比，屬於介系詞，後方應接上名詞、代名詞（如 Despite this, she...）或由 what 或 who 帶領的子句（如 Despite what he said, she...），前方或後方會有主要子句與 despite 引導的片語形成對比。本題中前方有主要子句 I go to the theater very often，而 despite 後方的片語原為(I) have to pay quite a lot...，因介系詞 despite 後方應使用名詞，故遇動詞應改為動名詞，have 被改為 having，空格應填入選項(B)。

Theater
UNIT 155 雪梨歌劇院 🎧 MP3 025

155 Watching an opera in the Sydney Opera House is ------- I want to do when I arrive in Sydney.
(A) what (B) which (C) that (D) where

中譯 ▶ (A) 在雪梨歌劇院裡看一齣歌劇是我一到雪梨就想做的事。

速解 ▶ 看到整個句子目光直接鎖定「**is ----- I want to do**」，空格前為動詞 **is**，後為不完整子句 **I want to do**，空格應填適當的複合關係代名詞，即選項(A) **what**。選項(B) which、選項(C) that 與選項(D) where 皆為關係代名詞，不可選。

進階 ▶ 本題考的重點是 what 作為複合關係代名詞的用法。前面章節說明過，複合關係代名詞如 whatever, whichever, whenever 等，代表先行詞加上關係代名詞。而 what 也是一個可以代替「事物」的複合關係代名詞，代替先行詞 the thing (s)與關係代名詞 which。本題以動名詞 watching an opera in the Sydney Opera House 當主詞，而後方接上以複合關係代名詞引導的子句。本句原可看成 Watching Opera House is the thing which I want to…，因空格前無並先行詞，無法直接使用關係代名詞，而必須使用可同時代表先行詞與與關係代名詞的選項，故應選擇(A)。

Theater
紐約的百老匯音樂劇 🎧 MP3 025

156 I can't remember which Broadway musical ------- during our last trip to New York.
(A) did we watch
(B) we watched
(C) we did watch
(D) watched

中譯▶ (B) 我想不起來我們上一次到紐約旅行時看的百老匯音樂劇是哪一部。

速解▶ 看到整個句子目光直接鎖定「**I can't remember which -----**」，空格前為一主要子句接上疑問詞 **which**，空格應填適當的間接問句語序，即選項(B) we watched。選項(A) did we watch 為疑問句中的語序，選項(C) we did watch 為有強調語氣的直述句中的語序，選項(D) watched 通常用在直述句，以上皆不可選。

進階▶ 本題考的重點是間接問句。間接問句即是在主要句子裡的問句，而原問句的語序需做變換，即助動詞與主詞調換（問題為「疑問詞＋助動詞＋主詞＋動詞」時改為「疑問詞＋主詞＋助動詞＋動詞」），但若助動詞為 **do/ does/ did** 則需拿掉助動詞，且將時態反映在動詞上。本題由主要句子 I can't remember 加上問句 which Broadway musical did we watch...。間接問句在主要子句裡應改變語序，且因助動詞為 did，拿掉 did 後，過去的時態要表現在動詞上，故在空格應填入 we watched。

Music
紐約的音樂節 🎧 MP3 025

❿ He will go to the Woodstock Festival in New York unless the flight -------.
(A) was canceled　　　(B) will cancel
(C) is canceled　　　　(D) has canceled

中譯 ▶ (C) 除非班機被取消，否則他會去紐約的胡士托音樂節。

速解 ▶ 看到整個句子目光直接鎖定「**unless the flight -----**」，空格前方為連接詞 **unless**，前方主要動詞為未來式，且主詞與動詞為被動關係，空格應填現在簡單式被動語態，即選項(C) is canceled。選項(A) was canceled 為過去式被動語態，選項(B) will cancel 為未來式主動語態，選項(D) has canceled 為現在完成式主動語態，皆不可選。

進階 ▶ 本題考的重點是連接詞 unless 的用法。連接詞 unless 連接兩個子句，用來表示「除非...否則」，連接詞 unless 後的從屬子句裡的動詞可使用現在式、過去式或過去完成式，若講述未來時間，unless 引導的從屬子句需使用現在式代替未來式。本句 unless 連接子句 he will go… New York 與子句 the flight…，前方子句中使用未來式 will go，則 unless 後的動詞應使用現在簡單式，又 flight 與 cancel 為被動關係，故應使用現在式的被動語態，即(C) is canceled。

Music
歌手的合約糾紛 🎧 MP3 025

158 The singer will not be releasing a new album until the contract dispute with the record label -------.

(A) resolves　　　　(B) was resolved

(C) is resolved　　　(D) will resolve

中譯 (C) 那個歌手在跟唱片公司的合約糾紛解決之前不會出新專輯。

速解 看到整個句子目光直接鎖定「**will not be until -----**」，空格前方有連接詞 **until**，且主要子句的動詞為未來式，且動詞與主詞為被動關係，空格應填現在簡單式，即選項(C) is resolved。選項(A) resolves 為現在主動語態，選項(B) was resolved 為過去被動語態，選項(D) will resolve 為未來主動語態，皆不可選。

進階 本題考的重點是 until 的用法。連接詞 until 表「一段時間、直到」，句中的 until 用來連結主要子句 The singer will not... album 與另一個子句 the contract...。當主要子句使用的是未來式時，until 後的動詞應使用現在式代替未來式，故空格中不填選項(B)或(D)。又從屬子句中的名詞 contract dispute 與動詞 resolve 在此應為被動關係，故不選(A)而選(C) is resolved。

Music
聽歌

🎧 MP3 025

159 I always can't help ------- to listen to Sam Smith on a rainy day.

(A) want　(B) wanted　(C) to want　(D) wanting

中譯 (D) 下雨時我總是忍不住想聽 Sam Smith 的歌。

速解 看到整個句子目光直接鎖定「**can't help ----- to...**」，空格前為 **can't help**，空格應填動名詞，即選項(D) wanting。選項(A) want 為動詞原形，選項(B) wanted 為過去式動詞，選項(C) to want 為不定詞，皆不可選。

進階 本題考的重點是 can't help 的用法。本句中的 can't 為 cannot 的縮寫，help 不可解釋為「幫助」，片語 can't help 表達「禁不住、忍不住」，後方若是動詞，需使用動名詞，不使用不定詞或其他動詞形態。本句以主詞 I 開頭，接上 can't help，後方動詞原為 want to listen to，因在 can't help 後方，應使用動名詞，改為 wanting to listen to...，故應選擇(D) wanting。

Museums
博物館關閉 🎧 MP3 025

160 The museum is facing closure ------- the recession and budget cuts and many are preparing to protest.
(A) because of   (B) because   (C) since   (D) so

中譯 ▶ (A) 因為經濟不景氣與預算縮減，博物館將關閉，而許多人正準備抗爭。

速解 ▶ 看到整個句子目光直接鎖定「**facing closure ----- recession and budget cuts**」，空格前後為因果關係，且後為名詞，空格應填適當的詞，即選項 because of。選項(B) because、選項(C) since 與選項 (D) so 皆為連接詞，不可選。

進階 ▶ 本題考的重點是意思相近的詞。本題中有一主要子句 The museum is facing closure，而後方是名詞 recession and budget cuts，在選項中僅能填入 because of 來表達因果關係，因為 because of 為介系詞，後方需使用名詞或動名詞。而其他選項同樣可表達因果關係，但 because 與 since 皆為連接詞，因連接兩個子句，即後方應接上有主詞與動詞的句子，與空格後的名詞不符，不可選。而 so 同樣為連接詞，後方同樣須按上有主詞與動詞的子句，且 so 後方的子句表達的應為結果，而非原因，故本題同樣不可選。

251

Museums
UNIT 161 博物館增加警衛與監視器 🎧 MP3 026

161 The museum is increasing guards and surveillance cameras for fear of ------- again.
(A) burglarized
(B) be burglarized
(C) being burglarized
(D) burglarizing

中譯 ▶ (C) 博物館將會增加警衛與監視器，以免再次遭偷竊。

速解 ▶ 看到整個句子目光直接鎖定「**for fear of -----**」，空格前為 **for fear of**，選項中動詞與省略的主詞為被動關係，空格應填動名詞的被動語態，即選項(C) being burglarized。選項(A) burglarized 為過去動詞主動語態，選項(B) be burglarized 為原形動詞被動語態，選項(D) burglarizing 為現在分詞，皆不可選。

進階 ▶ 本題考的重點是 for fear of 的用法。介系詞片語 for fear of 意指「唯恐...、以免...」，表條件，後方應使用名詞或是動名詞，不可接上動詞或句子等。本句空格前為 for fear of，後方若為動詞，應改為動名詞，故選項(A)與(B)皆不可選。又 for fear of 後方指的是「博物館再次被偷」，動詞 burglarize 應使用被動語態 be burglarized，改為動名詞後為 being burglarized，故不選(D)而選(C)。

Museums
展出品會定期重新安排　🎧 MP3 026

162 As the exhibitions are periodically -------, I recommend visiting the museum whenever you feel like it.
(A) rearrangement　　(B) rearranging
(C) rearranged　　　(D) rearrangeable

中譯▶ (C) 因為展出品會定期重新安排，我建議想去的時候就可以再去參觀。

速解▶ 看到整個句子目光直接鎖定「**exhibitions are periodically -----**」，空格前為副詞，且主詞語動詞為被動關係，空格應填適當的動詞形態，即選項(C) rearranged。選項(A) rearrangement 為名詞，選項(B) rearranging 為現在分詞，選項(D) rearrangeable 為形容詞，皆不可選。

進階▶ 本題考的重點是詞性搭配與語態。本句由連接詞 as 連接兩個子句，故兩部分都會有主詞與動詞。本句空格在從屬子句中，前方有主詞 the exhibition 與副詞 periodically，而副詞修飾動詞或形容詞，故選項(A)的名詞不可選。動詞 rearrange 與主詞 exhibitions 應為被動關係，不應使用主動語態，若選擇(B)會與 be 動詞 are 形成現在進行式的主動語態，應選擇(C)與 be 動詞 are 形成現在簡單式的被動語態。另若填入選項(D)的形容詞，不足以成為主要子句的原因，與語意較不符，不選。

Museums
體倒在路中央 🎧 MP3 026

163 According to the news report, the body was found ------- in the middle of the street with gunshot wounds.
(A) lying   (B) laying   (C) lay   (D) lie

中譯 ▶ (A) 根據新聞報導，屍體發現時倒在路中央，身上有槍傷。

速解 ▶ 看到整個句子目光直接鎖定「**the body was found -----**」，空格前為 **for fear of**，空格應填適當的動詞形態，即選項(A) lying。選項(B) laying 為原形動詞被動語態，選項(C) lay，選項(D) lie 為現在分詞，皆不可選。

進階 ▶ 本題考的重點是分辨易混淆動詞與特殊動詞 find 的用法。動詞 find 為不完全及物動詞，後方必須要加上受詞與補語，句子的意思才會完整。而當後方的補語是動名詞時，通常指受詞正在進行某動作。選項中的動詞 lay 有「放置、下蛋」等意思，變化為 lay-laid-laid，現在分詞為 laying，動詞 lie 有「躺、位於」等意思，變化為 lie-lay-lain，現在分詞為 lying。在本句中應使用表「躺」，且使用 Ving 表主動、發現時正躺著，即選項(A) lying。

Media
媒體的嚴肅報導 🎧 MP3 026

164 Many people feel that the news media are devoting ------- less time to serious news coverage.
(A) more　(B) much　(C) the　(D) very

中譯▶ (B) 許多人覺得新聞媒體報導嚴肅的新聞的時間減少很多。

速解▶ 看到整個句子目光直接鎖定「**devoting ----- less**」，空格前為動詞，後為 形容詞比較級，空格應填適當的副詞，即選項(B) much。選項(A) more 本身為比較級或可與形容詞合成比較級，選項(C) the 用於最高級前，而選項(D)very 修飾最高級，皆不可選。

進階▶ 本題考的重點是修飾比較級的副詞。當需要修飾形容詞時，應使用副詞，即使形容詞為比較級或最高級時，句中空格前為動詞 are devoting，空格後為形容詞 less 加上名詞 time。因為 less 本身為比較級形容詞，故不可加與最高級共用的選項(C) the 或是選項(A) more（與部分雙音節形容詞或三音節以上形容詞組成比較級， 如 mor e c ommon 或 more beautiful）。選項(B)與(D)為副詞，然而 very 不可修飾比較級，故不可選，空格中應填入選項(B) much。

Media
媒體訪談 🎧 MP3 026

165 The president-elect ------- about his vision for the country in his first interview with The Guardian.
(A) mentioned　(B) conveyed　(C) spoke　(D) expressed

中譯 (C) 總統當選人在他與衛報的第一次訪問中談及了他對國家的願景。

··

速解 看到整個句子目光直接鎖定「----- about」，空格前為主詞，後為介系詞 **about**，空格應填不及物動詞，即選項(C) spoke。選項(A) mentioned、選項(B) conveyed 與選項(D) expressed 為及物動詞，皆不可選。

··

進階 本題考的重點是不及物動詞。不及物動詞為後方不需受詞的動詞（如 It doesn't matter. 中的 matter 或 A bird appeared. 中的 appear），有些不及物動詞若後方想加上受詞，可使用介系詞。而及物動詞是後方會直接接上受詞的動詞（如 He likes dogs. 中的 like 或 I just cleaned my room. 中的 clean）。本句空格前為主詞 the president-elect，後為介系詞 about 與受詞 his vision for the country，因為有介系詞，故空格內無法使用及物動詞，選項(A)、(B)與(D)皆為及物動詞，不可選，應填入選項(C)的不及物動詞。

Dentist's Office
醫生準確的診斷 🎧 MP3 026

166 With the help of the latest technology, your doctor can better ------- your condition.

(A) diagnostic　(B) diagnosis　(C) diagnose　(D) diagnosable

中譯 ▶ (C) 有了最新科技的幫助，你的醫生更能準確的診斷你的狀況。

速解 ▶ 看到整個句子目光直接鎖定「**can better -----**」，空格前為助動詞 **can** 與副詞 **better**，空格應填原形動詞，即選項(C) diagnose。選項(A) diagnostic 為形容詞，選項(B)diagnosis 為名詞，選項(D) diagnosable 為形容詞，皆不可選。

進階 ▶ 本題考的重點是詞性分析。better 可作為形容詞，但也可作副詞。在主要子句 your doctor can 中因為有助動詞 can，後方應有動詞，又空格後僅有一名詞片語 your condition，故空格應填入動詞，即選項(C)，而前方 better 則是解釋為副詞，修飾動詞 diagnose。選項(A)與選項(D)為形容詞，由字尾 -ic 與 -able 可推測詞性，而選項(B)為名詞，由字尾 -sis 可推測詞性。英文句子裡必定會有動詞，若填入以上選項中非動詞的字，則句子無主要動詞，故皆不可選。

Dentist's Office
感冒的時候 🎧 MP3 026

167 When you've come down with a cold, ------- is actually no better cure than rest and fluids.
(A) it   (B) when   (C) as   (D) there

中譯 (D) 感冒的時候，最好的治療其實就是休息和補充水分。

速解 看到整個句子目光直接鎖定「----- **is actually no better cure**」，空格後為名詞片語 **better cure**，空格應填適當的主詞，即選項(D) there。選項(A) it 為代替較長的主詞或是講特定主題時使用的虛主詞，與後方名詞片語不符，不選。選項(B) when 與選項(C) as 為連接詞，皆不可選。

進階 本題考的重點是區分虛主詞 there 與 it。英文句子中，除非是祈使句（如 finish your homework now.），否則一定會有主詞。選項(B)與(C)為連接詞，用來連接兩個子句，若填入這兩個選項，則主要子句沒有主詞，不可選。而選項(A)與選項(D)都可作為虛主詞。虛主詞 it 可用來代替較長的真主詞（如 It is hard for me to get up early in the morning.）或是當談論如「天氣或時間」時（如 It's getting cold. 或 It's almost five o'clock.）。而 there 同樣是個虛主詞，用來引出新主題或表達存在，故後方會是名詞或名詞片語（如 There was a seminar and I learned a lot. 或 There are many participants.）。本題空格後方為名詞片語 better cure，故應使用 there，即選項(D)。

Dentist's Office
急診室

UNIT 168

🎧 MP3 026

168 Emergency rooms do not refuse care to people who need it, -------- do they provide the service for free.

(A) nor　(B) so　(C) but　(D) only

中譯 (A) 急診室不會拒絕有治療需要的人，但他們也不會免費提供服務。

速解 看到整個句子目光直接鎖定「**do not ----- do they**」，空格前的句子是否定語氣，後方子句倒裝，且也想表達否定語氣，空格應填適當的連接詞，即選項(A) nor。選項(B) so 與選項(C) but 後方子句不倒裝，選項(D) only 倒裝表強調，皆與本句不合，不可選。

進階 本題考的重點是 nor 的用法。連接詞 nor 可用來連接兩個子句，然而，第一個子句必須是否定句，且由 nor 帶領的子句必須倒裝。本題以一個子句開頭 Emergency rooms do not...，且為否定句，空格後又有另一子句，且為倒裝句 do they provide，故空格應填入 nor，表「也不」，連接一否定句與一倒裝句。連接詞 so 與 but 雖可連接兩個子句，但後面的子句不應倒裝，故不選。而 only 倒裝時，通常放句首，且後方接副詞（如 Only when we are silenced do we realize the importance of our voices.），與本句不符，不選。

Dentist's Office
牙齒定期護理 🎧 MP3 026

❿ Many people in remote areas cannot afford basic needs, ------- visit the dentist for regular dental care.
(A) not to mention　　(B) let alone
(C) to say nothing of　(D) not to speak of

中譯▶ **(B)** 很多在偏遠地區的人無法負擔基本需求，更不用說找牙醫做定期護理。

速解▶ 看到整個句子目光直接鎖定「**cannot afford basic needs, ----- visit**」，空格前為否定句，後方為原形動詞，空格應填適當的字詞，即選項(B) let alone。選項(A) not to mention、選項(C) to say nothing of 與選項(D) not to speak of 雖有類似意思，但後方須接動名詞，皆不可選。

進階▶ 本題考的重點是相似片語的不同用法。片語 let alone 表達「更不用說」，用來講述兩個否定語句，而 let alone 放在第二個否定語句前，強調第二個否定語句的更低可能性。選項中的片語都可表達「更不用說」，然而選項(A)、(C)與(D)因為 mention 以及介系詞 of 的關係，後方必須使用動名詞（或名詞），而 let alone 則基本上會與前方子句的動詞相搭配，使用同樣的形式。本句空格後為原形動詞 visit，故不可填入(A)、(C)或(D)，應填入選項(B)，即 let alone（前方為動詞 afford，故後方也使用原形動詞 visit）。另，以上片語的前方都需逗號。

Dentist's Office
陶瓷製牙齒 🎧 MP3 026

170 Most people prefer using ceramic dental crowns ------- using gold crowns for dental restoration because the former ones look more natural.

(A) from　　(B) to　　(C) of　　(D) more than

中譯 ▶ **(B)** 大部分人的補牙偏愛使用陶瓷，而不是金，因為前者看起來比較自然。

速解 ▶ 看到整個句子目光直接鎖定「**prefer... -----**」，空格前方為 **prefer**，接著兩個比較的事物，空格應填適當的介系詞，即選項(B) to。選項(A) from、選項(C) of 與選項(D) more than 皆與 prefer 不合，不可選。

進階 ▶ 本題考的重點是 prefer 的用法。動詞 prefer 表達「兩個之中更偏好...」，為及物動詞，後方必須有受詞，可接不定詞、動名詞、名詞或 that 子句。當在同一個句子寫出比較的兩樣東西時，基本上會使用 to（如 I prefer coffee to tea.）。本句中主詞 most people 後跟著主要動詞 prefer，後方接著兩樣比較的事物，以動名詞形式出現（using ceramic dental crowns 與 using gold crowns），故中間應該使用介系詞 to，即選項(B)。

Dentist's Office
治療牙周病

UNIT 171

🎧 MP3 026

171 There are two ways to treat gum diseases, receiving dental treatment and practicing good oral hygiene, and the ------- is more important.
(A) last　(B) lately　(C) later　(D) latter

中譯 (D) 治療牙周病有兩種方法：口腔治療與良好的口腔衛生習慣，而後者更加重要。

速解 看到整個句子目光直接鎖定「**two ways, and the ----- is**」，空格前方有兩個選項，空格應填可表示兩者中後者的選項(D) latter。選項(A) last 表「最後」，選項(B) lately 表「最近」，選項(C) later 表「待會」，皆不可選。

進階 本題考的重點是 latter 的用法。形容詞 latter 用來指「兩者中的後者」，也可作為代名詞，會與 the 合用。本句開頭引介兩種方式 there are two ways，並指出此兩種方式 receiving dental treatment 與 practicing good oral hygiene，又空格前為 the，後為 is，應選擇 latter 來表示兩者中的後者。選項中 last 表「排名最後或順序中的最後一個」，也可與 the 連用，來談論三者以上中的最後一項，故本題不選。而副詞 lately 與形容詞/副詞 later 語意上都與本題不合，同樣不選。

Health Insurance
出示健保卡 🎧 MP3 026

172 If you have health insurance, all you need to do is ------- your insurance card when you go to the doctor.
(A) show　(B) showed　(C) shown　(D) showing

中譯▶ (A) 如果你有健保的話，你只需要在看醫生的時候出示你的健保卡即可。

速解▶ 看到整個句子目光直接鎖定「**all you need to do is -----**」，空格前為片語 **all...is**，空格應填不定詞，且 to 省略，即選項(A) show。選項(B) showed 為動詞過去式，選項(C) shown 為過去分詞，選項(D) showing 為現在分詞，皆不可選。

進階▶ 本題考的重點是 all… do 的用法。此類句型中 all do 為主詞，且此種主詞基本上會視為單數整體，故 **be 動詞使用第三人稱單數**，而後方主詞補語中的動詞會使用不定詞，且 to 會省略（如 All she could do was (to) stand there and 本句中的主要子句以 all you need to do 開頭，後方為單數動詞 is，而後方動詞應使用 to 省略後的不定詞，故空格中應填入選項(A) show，而不選其他動詞形態。

Health Insurance
享有健保

UNIT 173 🎧 MP3 026

173 The healthcare system in Taiwan promises that the rich as well as the poor ------- equal access to healthcare.
(A) enjoy　(B) enjoys　(C) enjoyed　(D) is enjoying

中譯 (A) 台灣的健保系統承諾富者與窮者都能平等享有健保。

速解 看到整個句子目光直接鎖定「**the rich as well as the poor -----**」，空格前方有 **as well as**，空格應填搭配遠方主詞的動詞，即選項(A) enjoy。選項(B) enjoys 為動詞第三人稱單數，選項(C) enjoyed 為過去式動詞，選項(D) is enjoying 為進行式動詞，皆不可選。

進階 本題考的重點是 as well as 的用法。連接詞 as well as 表達「以及、是...而且...也是」，用來連接兩個字詞、片語或子句。當 as well as 用來連接兩個主詞時，動詞應該依遠方主詞變化。本句 that 子句中以 as well as 連接兩個主詞 the rich 以及 the poor，而空格後為受詞 equal access to healthcare，故空格應填動詞，且須配合較遠的主詞 the rich。又 the 加上形容詞當名詞時，會視為**複數名詞**，如本句中 the rich 等同 rich people，故使用的動詞應為可搭配複數名詞的動詞，即選項(A)。

Health Insurance
雇主提供的健保 🎧 MP3 026

UNIT 174

174 I'm not going to take the employer-sponsored plan; ------- , I'll look for my own health plan.
(A) because of　(B) rather than　(C) instead of　(D) instead

中譯 (D) 我不會參加雇主提供的健保，而是自己找健保計畫。

速解 看到整個句子目光直接鎖定「**not going to；-----, I'll...**」，空格前後為相反的兩個完整句子，且空格後有逗號，空格應填副詞，選項(D)instead。選項(A) because of 、選項(B) rather than 與選項(C) instead of 為介系詞，皆不可選。

進階 本題考的重點是 instead 的用法。副詞 instead 表「反而、卻」，引導一個替代的選擇，通常置於句首或句尾，在句首時需接著一個逗號。本題為兩個獨立的句子 I'm not going to... 以及 I'll look for，以分號區隔，而空格後方有逗號，空格應填入副詞的 instead。其他選項中的連接詞或介系詞片語後方都應該接名詞或動名詞，不接子句，且後方不使用逗號，故本題不可選。

Hospitals
醫院的死亡機率 🎧 MP3 026

175 The study showed that patients at the worst hospitals were three times ------- to die than patients at the best hospitals.
(A) likely   (B) more likely   (C) most likely   (D) much likely

中譯 ▶ (B) 研究顯示在最差醫院的病人的死亡機率比在最好醫院的病人的死亡機率高出三倍。

速解 ▶ 看到整個句子目光直接鎖定「**three times ----- to die than**」，空格前方有倍數，空格應填比較級形容詞，即選項(B) more likely。選項(A) likely 為形容詞原形，選項(C) most likely 為形容詞最高級，選項(D) much likely 為程度副詞加形容詞，皆不選。

進階 ▶ 本題考的重點是倍數的用法。當要使用倍數來表示差異時，有幾種表示方法，其中之一為「倍數詞 + 形容詞比較級 + than」，表示「是...的幾倍...」，而倍數詞包含 half（一半）、twice（兩倍）與 ...times（三倍以上，如 three times, four times 等）。本句空格前為倍數 three times，後方有與比較級共用的 than，故空格內應使用形容詞比較級，即選項(B)。

Hospitals
竹子蓋成的醫院
UNIT 176

🎧 MP3 026

❶⓱ The state-of-the-art hospital in a remote area in India is in fact ------- bamboo.
(A) made of　(B) made from　(C) made to　(D) made with

中譯 ▶ (A) 那家在印度偏遠地區，擁有最先進技術的醫院其實是以竹子蓋成的。

速解 ▶ 看到整個句子目光直接鎖定「**the state-of-theart hospital is ----- bamboo**」，空格前方主詞為醫院，後方受詞為材料，空格應填可表本質不變的片語，即選項(A) made of。選項(B) made from 表本質有改變，選項(C) made to 表「為...而做」，選項(D) made with 表食材，皆不可選。

進階 ▶ 本題考的重點是不同介係詞與動詞的搭配。不同介係詞表示不同意思，故不同動詞可能會有不同的慣性搭配的介係詞，而有時一個動詞可能使用不同介係詞，且帶有不同意思。動詞 make 則常以被動語態接上不同介系詞，來表達「由...做成」。本句主詞為 hospital，動詞為 make，故應使用被動語態。又受詞為建材 bamboo，本質並不改變，還可看得出此建材的樣子，故應使用 made of。但若製作過程中材料產生了變化，會使用 made from。而 made with 通常在講述食材時使用。介系詞 to 代表「向著某個目標」，made to 表「為...而做」。

267

Hospitals
醫院病史詳查 🎧 MP3 026

⑰ The doctor took a full medical history and performed a detailed ------- to find out the real cause of her abdominal pain.
(A) examined　(B) examine　(C) examination　(D) examining

中譯 (C) 醫生詢問完整的病史並進行詳細的檢查，以找出她腹部疼痛的真正原因。

速解 看到整個句子目光直接鎖定「**performed a detailed -----** 」，空格前方有冠詞與形容詞，空格應填名詞，即選項(C) examination。選項(A) examined 為過去式動詞，選項(B) examine 為原形動詞，選項(D) examining 為動名詞，皆不可選。

進階 本題考的重點是形容詞修飾名詞。本句只需專注在主要部分 The doctor... a detailed -------。主詞為 the doctor，主要動詞有 took（加受詞 a full medical history）以及 performed（加受詞 a detailed）。空格前有不定冠詞 a，後方 detailed 應解讀為形容詞，而後方沒有名詞，故空格應填入名詞 examination 作為受詞選項(B) examine 為動詞，而選項(A) examined 與選項(D) examining 不論解讀為動詞或形容詞，在此都不可使用。另 examining 可做動名詞，而動名詞雖可作名詞使用，卻不以形容詞修飾。

Pharmacy
藥物資訊的說法 🎧 MP3 026

178 Sometimes the information about a medicine given by the doctor is different from ------- given by the pharmacist.
(A) it   (B) they   (C) that   (D) those

中譯 (C) 有時關於某種藥物的資訊，醫生說得和藥師說得不一樣。

速解 看到整個句子目光直接鎖定「**the information... ----- is different from**」，主要動詞 **is** 與形容詞 **different** 前後應為比較的兩樣東西，空格應填適當的指示代名詞，即選項(C)that。選項(A) **it** 為人稱代名詞，選項(B) **they** 為人稱代名詞，選項(D) **those** 為複數指示代名詞，皆不可選。

進階 本題考的重點是指示代名詞。指示代名詞用來指代已知或是特定的名詞，包含 this, that, these, those, such 等，可作主詞，也可作受詞。又當比較同類型事物時，為避免重複，可使用指示代名詞中的 that 與 those 來代替（注意不使用其他代名詞），單數使用 that，複數使用 those，後方接修飾詞。本句中 is different from 可看出是在做比較，前方的事物為 information about a medicine (given by the doctor)，而後方是 information about a medicine (given by the pharmacist)，因 information 重複，且屬於不可數名詞，應使用單數的 that 來代替。

Pharmacy
遵循藥物使用說明 ⌾ MP3 026

179 When it comes to -------, following directions carefully is most important.
(A) medical　(B) medication　(C) medicate　(D) medicated

中譯 (B) 當說到藥物時，小心遵循說明是最重要的。

速解 看到整個句子目光直接鎖定「**When it comes to -----**」，空格前為介系詞，空格應填名詞，即選項(B) medication。選項(A) medical 為形容詞，選項(C) medicate 為原形動詞，選項(D) medicated 為過去分詞，皆不可選。

進階 本題考的重點是 when it comes to 的用法。片語 **when it comes to** 表達「談到...時」，用來指出正在談論的特定主題，其中 **to** 為介系詞，後面應該接名詞或動名詞，後方接主要子句，主要子句可以是肯定句或是疑問句。本句中以 when it comes to 帶出主題，後方接完整子句 following directions carefully is...。空格出現在 when it comes to 後，空格應填入名詞或動名詞，故只能填入 medication。

Pharmacy
假藥事件

UNIT
180

🎧 MP3 026

⑱ In recent years, several cases of counterfeit drugs have been ------- in both developed and developing countries.
(A) reported　(B) reporting　(C) report　(D) reportage

中譯▶ (A) 近年來，好幾起假藥事件在已開發和開發中國家都被報導。

速解▶ 看到整個句子目光直接鎖定「**cases of counterfeit drugs have been -----**」，空格前 **have**，且主詞與動詞的關係為被動，空格應填現在完成被動，即選項(A) reported。選項(B) reporting 為現在分詞，選項(C) report 為原形動詞，選項(D) reportage 為名詞，皆不可選。

進階▶ 本題考的重點是區分主動與被動語態。當主詞是從事某個動作的主事者時，會使用主動語態，而主詞是某個動作的接受者時，則須使用被動語態（即 be 動詞 + p.p.），而時態的變化會表現在 be 動詞上。本句的主詞為 several cases of counterfeit drugs，後方為副詞 in both...countries，句中沒有主要動詞，空格應填入動詞。若將 been 解釋為主要動詞，後方應接形容詞或名詞，但語意不合。動詞為 report，主詞應為動作的接受者，應使用被動語態。又前方有 in recent years，故時態使用現在完成式 have been reported。

規劃三回單字和文法的模擬試題演練，先撰寫試題檢視本身的程度，並於完成試題後觀看解析，背誦各選項的字彙，更完備地應考，最後可利用零碎時間聆聽音檔，快速累積語感，並獲取閱讀高分。

PART 3

READING TEST 1

In this section, you must demonstrate your ability to read and comprehend English. You will be given a variety of texts and asked to answer questions about these texts. This section is divided into three parts and will take 75 minutes to complete.

Do not mark the answers in your test book. Use the answer sheet that is separately.

PART 5

Directions: In each question, you will be asked to review a statement that is missing a word or phrase. Four answer choices will be provided for each statement. Select the best answer and mark the corresponding letter (A), (B), (C), or (D) on the answer sheet.

101. Please be aware that all personal ------- sent from the office computers is subject to review by the management staff.
(A) corresponding
(B) correspondingly
(C) correspondent
(D) correspondence

102. ------- who worked overtime on the weekend to finish the project were given Monday morning off as compensation.
(A) Them
(B) That
(C) Their
(D) Those

103. A monthly newsletter highlighting the achievements of the company will especially be sent out to keep the newcomers better ------- as well as positive on duty.
(A) informative
(B) information
(C) informed
(D) informing

104. Though the company considers the orientation the most efficient method in adjusting rookies to our firm in the very short time, many people find the intensive training schedule rather -------.
(A) exhausting
(B) exhausted
(C) exhaustingly
(D) exhaustion

105. After all applications are received, the city council ------- a meeting to choose new marketing contractors for the new outlet plaza.
(A) held
(B) holds
(C) hold
(D) will hold

106. Concern about the future of many marine animals ------- to a rapid reduction in trading of marine products recently, especially those made from international conserved ones.
(A) leads

(B) has led

(C) leading

(D) lead

107. The sheer variety of products that we offer for sale are ------- unmatched by any of our competitors.

(A) distinctive

(B) distinctively

(C) distinct

(D) distinctness

108. All production is halted, and until the company's profits get improved by 5%, neither side seems ------- to negotiate.

(A) preparation

(B) preparing

(C) prepare

(D) prepared

109. Delegating easier ------- projects to inexperienced workers while leaving challenging ones with veterans is suggesting the office operate more efficiently.

(A) purchased

(B) purchasing

(C) purchase

(D) be purchased

110. All shipment and packaging waste is under the request of -------

of, and collected in the agreed receptacles near the rear entrance of the building.

(A) being disposed

(B) to dispose

(C) disposing

(D) dispose

111. Due to ------- snow in southern England, many flights from Heathrow Airport have been delayed for up to seven hours.

(A) large

(B) heavy

(C) abundant

(D) oversize

112. During the expansion of Hong Kong International Airport, some flights will be ------- to Macau.

(A) sent

(B) transported

(C) reduced

(D) relocated

113. Purchasers would find details of our terms in the price list ------- on the inside front cover of the catalogue.

(A) print

(B) printing

(C) printed

(D) prints

114. Many companies are still reluctant to make major capital investments out of uncertainty over ------- the recovery will continue.
(A) so
(B) which
(C) that
(D) whether

115. This way, your monthly savings deposit takes a small contribution from every paycheck automatically, and you will be surprised ------- quickly this simple trick can make your savings add up.
(A) what
(B) how
(C) why
(D) that

116. A copy of our prospectus containing particulars of our policies ------- householders is enclosed.
(A) for
(B) of
(C) at
(D) by

117. Consequently, we are prepared to offer you a total of £4,800 in full compensation ------- your policy.
(A) by
(B) in

(C) under

(D) between

118. Due to technical problems, our website and mailbox for submission ------- to be inaccessible for an indeterminate delay.

    (A) are convinced

    (B) convinced

    (C) are convincing

    (D) convincing

119. In order to finish the file attachment process, a click on the attach button ------- to be a must.

    (A) is considered

    (B) is considering

    (C) considered

    (D) considering

120. The newly elected administration has launched an aggressive ------- for federal counterterrorism in hopes of solidifying national security.

    (A) transaction

    (B) prejudice

    (C) strategy

    (D) disconnection

121. The research findings about hypnosis healing remain inconclusive and ------- ; therefore, the curing method still has a long way to

go.

(A) potential

(B) anxious

(C) magnificent

(D) controversial

122. Animal rights groups ------- to take more drastic measures unless the cosmetic manufactures stopped inhumane animal tests.

(A) claimed

(B) unraveled

(C) surrendered

(D) liberated

123. The Internet ------- among adolescents brought about serious academic and personality problems and has gradually aroused social attention.

(A) governance

(B) addiction

(C) retreat

(D) provocation

124. Thanks to the decreased costs of 3D printers, the technology of the three-dimensional printing has recently gained ------- among different fields of industry.

(A) richness

(B) popularity

(C) manipulation

(D) capability

125. The financial institution posted an advertisement to offer jobs for business school graduates with ------- consciousness and abilities.

(A) rigid

(B) innovative

(C) optional

(D) retrospective

126. Young generations should be taught from their early childhood to practice the 3R ------- — Reduce, Reuse, and Recycle to protect and sustain the earth.

(A) Groups

(B) Facilities

(C) Principles

(D) Restrictions

127. Mr. Banks is a lawyer ------- in criminal law and is dedicated to defending against criminal charges.

(A) franchised

(B) managed

(C) abolished

(D) specialized

128. The dazzling northern lights, also called "the aurora borealis," display one of nature's greatest spectacles, and are ------- to only

certain regions in Canada, Scotland, Norway, and Sweden.

(A) unique

(B) conceptual

(C) practical

(D) invisible

129. The refined merchandise exhibited in the Trade Fair last month was ------- by Morrison Company and has received great numbers of orders since then.

(A) approached

(B) combined

(C) manufactured

(D) rejected

130. The rich and renowned CEO remained modest and was ------- about charitable affairs by donating millions of dollars each year.

(A) violent

(B) indifferent

(C) popular

(D) enthusiastic

Note

模擬試題（一）

 ## PART 5　中譯與解析 🎧 MP3 027

閱讀原文和中譯	
101. Please be aware that all personal ------- sent from the office computers is subject to review by the management staff. (A) corresponding (B) correspondingly (C) correspondent **(D) correspondence**	請注意所有從辦公室電腦所寄出的個人書信皆需受管理階層的審查。

答案：(D)

 解析

本題考題屬於『名詞』的考法。判斷上下文後優先選『靜態名詞』，亦即不用動作（主、被動）含意的名詞，選項(A) 先排除，所以**選擇(D)**。(B) 選項為副詞，與文法不符，所以不選。(C) 選項是動詞所變化而來的名詞，指的是「記者」，與上下句意不合，所以不選。

102. ------- who worked overtime on the weekend to finish the project were given Monday morning off as compensation. (A) Them (B) That (C) Their **(D) Those**	那些週末超時工作以完成計畫的員工，將給予星期一上午的補休。

答案：(D)

解析

本題考題屬於『代名詞』當主詞的考法。句中主要子句動詞為複數動詞were given，而主要子句主詞為代名詞主格用法，且需用複數形，故**選擇(D)**。(A) 選項為代名詞受詞用法，與文法不符，所以不選。(B) 選項為代名詞主格用法，且為單數形，與文法不符，所以不選。

| 103. A monthly newsletter highlighting the achievements of the company will especially be sent out to keep the newcomers better ------- as well as positive on duty.
(A) informative
(B) information
(C) informed
(D) informing | 強調公司成就的每月通訊將會特別發送給那些新進人員，讓他們持續被妥善告知，並在工作時保持正面態度。 |

答案：(C)

解析

這是『使役動詞(keep)』的考法。keep 的對象為新進人員(newcomers)，inform用來修飾受詞(newcomers)；但是後面並未有受詞，所以用被動的『動態形容詞』，中文解釋為「被告知的」，所以去除(B) **選擇(C)**。選項(A)是『靜態形容詞』，英英解釋為"sb./sth. providing a lot of useful information"，「資訊的主動提供者」，與句意不符，所以不選。選項(D) 是V-ing『動態形容詞』，中文解釋為「（主動）告知的」，不符句意所以不選。

| 104. Though the company considers the orientation the most efficient method in adjusting rookies to our firm in the very short time, many people find the intensive training schedule rather -------.
(A) exhausting
(B) exhausted | 雖然公司認為，新生員工訓練是在很短的時間調整新秀、讓他們適應我們公司最有效的方法，但很多人發現，密集的訓練日程是相當累人的。 |

(C) exhaustingly
(D) exhaustion

答案：(A)

 解析

本題考題屬於『認為(find)』的考法。從上下文得知，find 的主詞為人 (people)，相搭配的動詞選項為exhaust，可以為『情緒動詞』使用。上下文 的句意中，既是指他人的價值判斷，應當用現在分詞(V-ing) 用法，所以**答案 選(A)**，不選(B)。選項(C) 是副詞用法，選項(D) 是名詞用法，與上下文不符， 所以不選。

105. After all applications are received, the city council ------- a meeting to choose new marketing contractors for the new outlet plaza. (A) held (B) holds (C) hold **(D) will hold**	在收到所有的申請文件之後，市議會 將召開會議，為新的購物廣場選擇新 的行銷承包商。

答案：(D)

解析

上下文的句意中，關鍵字句為附屬子句的「現在簡單式」，暗示著「現在時 間」或者「不確定的未來」；而上下文的句意適合用「未來」的動作來表示 將要發生的事件，所以**答案選(D)**。

106. Concern about the future of many marine animals ------- to a rapid reduction in trading of marine products recently, especially those made from international conserved ones. (A) leads **(B) has led** (C) leading (D) lead	最近對於許多海洋動物未來的擔憂， 導致海洋產品交易迅速減少，特別是 那些來自國際保護物種的產品。

答案：(B)

 解析

上下文的句意中，關鍵字句為recently「最近地」，表示從「以前」到「講話時」的動作或經驗持續狀態，應該用「完成式」，所以答案選(B)。

107. The sheer variety of products that we offer for sale are ------- unmatched by any of our competitors. (A) distinctive **(B) distinctively** (C) distinct (D) distinctness	我們的銷售產品多元，對我們的任何競爭對手而言，非常明顯地是無法比擬。

答案：(B)

 解析

空格之後是動詞所變化而來的形容詞用法，而空格之前為be-V; 該空格由本句句意中知道用以強化形容詞(unmatched)，所以該詞性應該用「副詞」。

108. All production is halted, and until the company's profits get improved by 5%, neither side seems ------- to negotiate. (A) preparation (B) preparing (C) prepare **(D) prepared**	所有的生產停止，且在公司利潤提升至5％前，雙方似乎還未能準備好進行協商。

答案：(D)

 解析

空格之前為「連綴動詞」，連綴動詞之後應該用形容詞，而且本句句意中沒有用到修飾句子、動詞或其他結構的用法，所以答案選**(D)**。此句主詞為人或者是擬人化的對象，動詞prepare 應當用過去分詞(V-p.p.)形式，來表達人或者是擬人化的對象接受動作。

Part 1 新制閱讀 part 6 答題強化　Part 2 核心文法和單字考點　Part 3 精選模擬試題

| 109. Delegating easier ------- projects to inexperienced workers while leaving challenging ones with veterans is suggesting the office operate more efficiently.
(A) purchased
(B) purchasing
(C) purchase
(D) be purchased | 委派容易採購項目給沒有經驗的工人，然而留給那些具有挑戰性的項目給老手，是希望（建議）辦公室能更有效地運作。 |

答案：(B)

 解析

本題屬於『動名詞』的考法。由上下文句意判斷，while 所前後連接的部分，兩句的主詞(delegating 與leaving) 與後面的受詞所判斷，空格應當是「動名詞(V-ing)＋N」的結構，意味著是「既定之事實」；所以，後面結構應搭配「動名詞(V-ing)」，以符合上下文句意，所以答案**選(B)**。

| 110. All shipment and packaging waste is under the request of ------- of, and collected in the agreed receptacles near the rear entrance of the building.
(A) being disposed
(B) to dispose
(C) disposing
(D) dispose | 依要求，所有廢棄物的裝運應集中在集收地做處理。該集收地靠近大樓後方入口處，是經同意而選出的地方。 |

答案：(A)

解析

本題屬於『動名詞』的考法。空格因為前有「介系詞」的關係，只能接「動名詞」。由上下文句意判斷，應當用「被動語態」。所以答案**選(A)**。

| 111. Due to ------- snow in southern England, many flights from Heathrow Airport have been delayed for up to seven hours. | 由於英國南部劇烈的降雪，許多從希斯洛機場的航班延誤七小時以上。 |

(A) large
(B) heavy
(C) abundant
(D) oversize

答案：(B)

此題為單字題，依照題意，應該選擇選項(B)heavy 劇烈的最為恰當，一般如雨及雪等的天氣情況會以heavy 形容，例如heavy rain, heavy snow。其他選項單字中文解釋則分別為**(B)大的**、(C)豐富的、及(D)過大的。

112. During the expansion of Hong Kong International Airport, some flights will be ------- to Macau. (A) sent (B) transported (C) reduced **(D) relocated**	在香港國際機場擴建期間，一些航班將會被重新安置到澳門。 (A) 送 (B) 運輸 (C) 減少 (D) 重新安置

答案：(D)

此題為單字題，will be 後面應該加被動式動詞，4個選項皆符合，所以依照題意，應該選擇**選項(D) relocated**重新安置最為恰當。其他選項單字中文解釋則分別為(A)送、(B)運輸、及(C)減少。

113. Purchasers would find details of our terms in the price list ------- on the inside front cover of the catalogue. (A) print (B) printing **(C) printed** (D) prints	買家會在產品目錄封面內頁的價格表上，找到我們所印的產品規範。

答案：(C)

解析

本題屬於『過去分詞』的考法。由上、下文結構判斷，空格雖然為「動詞」選項，但是因為與前句並沒有「連接詞」存在，推測應當是省略「連接詞(which/that)」， 所以選擇「動詞(is printed)」變成「分詞(printed)」的答案；且動詞與名詞的關係應該為「被動」用法，是為「被列印」的對象，所以答案選**(C)**。

114. Many companies are still reluctant to make major capital investments out of uncertainty over ------- the recovery will continue. (A) so (B) which (C) that **(D) whether**	在復甦能否持續的不確定中，許多公司仍不願意作出重大資本投資。

答案：**(D)**

解析

本題屬於『連接詞』中的「名詞子句」考法。由上下文句意判斷，介系詞(over) 後面應用「名詞子句」當受詞，又為「選擇性」句意，所以答案選**(D)**。

115. This way, your monthly savings deposit takes a small contribution from every paycheck automatically, and you will be surprised ------- quickly this simple trick can make your savings add up. (A) what **(B) how** (C) why (D) that	這樣一來，你每月的儲蓄存款會自動從每個月的薪水扣除，而且你會驚奇地發現，這個簡單的技巧可迅速地讓您的儲蓄增加。

答案：**(B)**

解析

本題屬於『連接詞』中的「名詞子句」考法。由上、下文句意判斷，形容詞(surprised)後面應用「名詞子句」結構，空格後面又為副詞(quickly)，所以選擇承接「不完整句意」表示「方式、方法」的**答案(B)**。

116.A copy of our prospectus containing particulars of our policies ------- householders is enclosed. **(A) for** (B) of (C) at (D) by	附件是我們計畫書的副本，上有包含我們房屋所有人的保單詳情。

答案：(A)

解析

本題考題屬於『介系詞』考法中「介系詞＋名詞」的考法。從上下文句意判斷，介系詞的中文翻譯為「為了…」，所以答案**選(A)**。

117.Consequently, we are prepared to offer you a total of £4,800 in full compensation ------- your policy. (A) by (B) in **(C) under** (D) between	因此，我們準備為您提供，在您的保單下，共計4,800英鎊的全額賠償。

答案：(C)

解析

本題考題屬於『介系詞』考法中「介系詞＋名詞」的考法。從上下文句意判斷，介系詞的中文翻譯為「在...之下」，所以答案**選(C)**。

118. Due to technical problems, our website and mailbox for submission ------- to be inaccessible for an indeterminate delay. **(A) are convinced** (B) convinced (C) are convincing (D) convincing	由於技術問題，我們的網站和交付的郵件信箱因為不明原因的延遲，確定是無法進入的。

答案：(A)

 解析

本題屬於『被動式』中「convince」的被動考法。由上下文的句意判斷，應當用「被動式」，中文翻成「被相信...」。所以答案選**(A)**。

119. In order to finish the file attachment process, a click on the attach button ------- to be a must. **(A) is considered** (B) is considering (C) considered (D) considering	為了完成文件附加的過程，對附件按鈕點擊被認為是必須的。

答案：(A)

解析

本題屬於『被動式』中「consider」的被動考法。由上下文的句意判斷，應當用「被動式」，中文翻成「被認為是...」。所以答案選**(A)**。

120. The newly elected administration has launched an aggressive ------- for federal counterterrorism in hopes of solidifying national security. (A) transaction (B) prejudice **(C) strategy** (D) disconnection	新上任的內閣已經推動積極的國家反恐策略，為的是希望鞏固國家安全。 (A) 交易 (B) 偏見 **(C) 策略** (D) 中斷

答案：(C)

解析

這題依句意為侵略性的策略，要選strategy，故答案為**選項C**。

121. The research findings about hypnosis healing remain inconclusive and ------- ; therefore, the curing method still has a long way to go. (A) potential (B) anxious (C) magnificent **(D) controversial**	有關於催眠治療的研究發現依舊是未定且有爭議的；因此，這種治療方式仍有待努力。 (A) 有潛力的 (B) 焦慮的 (C) 壯麗的 **(D) 有爭議的**

答案：(D)

解析

這題依句意為具爭議的，要選controversial，故答案為**選項D**。

122. Animal rights groups ------- to take more drastic measures unless the cosmetic manufactures stopped inhumane animal tests. **(A) claimed** (B) unraveled (C) surrendered (D) liberated	動物權益團體宣稱，除非化妝品製造廠商停止不人道的動物實驗，否則將採取更激烈的手段。 **(A) 宣稱** (B) 闡明 (C) 投降 (D) 解放

答案：(A)

解析

這題指的是宣稱，要選claimed，故**答案為A**。

123. The Internet ------- among ado-lescents brought about serious academic and personality prob-lems and has gradually aroused social attention. (A) governance **(B) addiction** (C) retreat (D) provocation	青少年的網路成癮導致嚴重的課業及人格問題，並且逐漸地引發社會關切。 (A) 管理 **(B) 上癮** (C) 撤退 (D) 挑釁

答案： (B)

這題指的是網路成癮，addiction最符合，故答案為**選項B**。

124. Thanks to the decreased costs of 3D printers, the technology of the three-dimensional print-ing has recently gained ------- among different fields of indus-try. (A) richness **(B) popularity** (C) manipulation (D) capability	幸虧有3D立體印刷機的降價，3D立體印刷科技近日在各個不同產業領域受到歡迎。 (A) 財富 **(B) 受歡迎** (C) 操弄 (D) 能力

答案： (B)

這題指的是受歡迎和流行程度，gain搭配popularity，故答案要選**選項B**。

125. The financial institution posted an advertisement to offer jobs for business school graduates with ------- consciousness and abilities. (A) rigid **(B) innovative**	這家金融機構刊登職缺廣告來徵求具創新意識及能力的商學院畢業生。 (A) 僵化的 **(B) 創新的** (C) 可選擇的 (D) 回顧的

(C) optional
(D) retrospective

答案： (B)

 解析

這題指的是具創新思維的，innovative最符合，故答案為**選項B**。

| 126. Young generations should be taught from their early childhood to practice the 3R ------- — Reduce, Reuse, and Recycle to protect and sustain the earth.
(A) Groups
(B) Facilities
(C) Principles
(D) Restrictions | 年輕世代應從小被教導力行3R原則 — 減量、重複使用，以及回收，以保護並延續地球。
(A) 團體
(B) 設施
(C) 原則
(D) 限制 |

答案： (C)

 解析

這題指的是原則principles，故答案為**選項C**。

| 127. Mr. Banks is a lawyer ------- in criminal law and is dedicated to defending against criminal charges.
(A) franchised
(B) managed
(C) abolished
(D) specialized | 班克斯先生是一名專精於刑事訴訟法的律師，並致力於刑事訴訟的辯護。
(A) 加盟
(B) 設法
(C) 廢除
(D) 專攻 |

答案： (D)

 解析

這題是關係代名詞子句的省略，省略了who is，在此的句意指的是專攻於… 故要選specialized，故答案為**選項D**。

128. The dazzling northern lights, also called "the aurora borealis," display one of nature's greatest spectacles, and are ------- to only certain regions in Canada, Scotland, Norway, and Sweden. **(A) unique** (B) conceptual (C) practical (D) invisible	炫目的極北之光，又稱為「北極光」，展現大自然絕佳的奇觀之一，並且是加拿大、蘇格蘭、挪威，及瑞典特定地區獨具的景觀。 **(A) 獨特的** (B) 概念的 (C) 實際的 (D) 隱形的

答案：(A)

 解析

這題依句意指的是北極光為這個地區獨有的景象，要選獨特的(be unique to)，故答案為**選項A**。

129. The refined merchandise exhibited in the Trade Fair last month was ------- by Morrison Company and has received great numbers of orders since then. (A) approached (B) combined **(C) manufactured** (D) rejected	上個月在貿易展展示的優質商品是由莫里森公司所製造的，並從那時起接獲大量的訂單。 (A) 接近 (B) 結合 **(C) 製造** (D) 排斥

答案：(C)

 解析

這題依句意為由莫里森公司所製造或生產的商品，要選manufactured，故答案為**選項C**。

130. The rich and renowned CEO re-mained modest and was ------- about charitable affairs by do-nating millions of dollars each year. (A) violent (B) indifferent (C) popular **(D) enthusiastic**	這位富有且著名的執行長依舊保持謙遜的態度，並且熱心於每年捐贈數百萬元贊助慈善事業。 (A) 暴力的 (B) 冷淡的 (C) 受歡迎的 **(D) 熱忱的**

答案：(D)

這題依句意為對慈善事業有熱忱的(be enthusiastic about)，要選 enthusiastic，故答案為**選項D**。

In this section, you must demonstrate your ability to read and comprehend English. You will be given a variety of texts and asked to answer questions about these texts. This section is divided into three parts and will take 75 minutes to complete.

Do not mark the answers in your test book. Use the answer sheet that is separately.

PART 5

Directions: In each question, you will be asked to review a statement that is missing a word or phrase. Four answer choices will be provided for each statement. Select the best answer and mark the corresponding letter (A), (B), (C), or (D) on the answer sheet.

101. When Ms. Huang found that the ------- system was out of order, she called the repairman in to look at it right away.

   (A) secure

   (B) security

   (C) secured

   (D) securing

102. No sooner had he arrived at his home than he was called back to the office to deal with a matter of -------.

   (A) urgency

   (B) urge

   (C) urging

   (D) urgent

103. Starting from next week, headquarters will have entrance permits ------- for the use of recruiting employees in the fair.
    (A) issue
    (B) issues
    (C) issuing
    (D) issued

104. Many job opportunities made recent graduates from the community college's business program ------- , for the job fair held by the city government.
    (A) appreciating
    (B) appreciate
    (C) appreciated
    (D) to appreciate

105. The mental reinforcements in ensuring product validity ------- damage throughout the upcoming price-cutting competition.
    (A) minimizes
    (B) will minimize
    (C) minimized
    (D) minimize

106. Although the output situation seems poor at the moment, we ------- a swift improvement once the downturn is over.
    (A) anticipated
    (B) anticipate
    (C) will anticipate

(D) are anticipate

107. Foreign businessmen often express ------- amazement at how far our manufacturer can achieve what they originally think impossible.
(A) unexpecting
(B) unexpect
(C) unexpected
(D) unexpective

108. In spite of consumer objection, Infocus will spend ------- time expanding the potential benefits of building cell phone plants.
(A) consider
(B) considerate
(C) considerable
(D) consideration

109. The problems with the just-in-time supply chain were solved following ------- with the lead suppliers.
(A) demands
(B) arguments
(C) negotiations
(D) concessions

110. The man talking on the phone about the lack of ------- after the accident at the oil refinery is getting increasingly angry.
(A) payment

(B) refunds

(C) remittance

(D) compensation

111. After the accident, all electrical ------- must be checked before any further use.

(A) facilities

(B) hardware

(C) assets

(D) equipment

112. We understand that you are arranging for immediate delivery from stock, and we look forward to ------- from you soon.

(A) hear

(B) hearing

(C) be hearing

(D) to be heard

113. The controversial law regarding team share buying restrictions continues ------- across the country by various local community retailers.

(A) to have protested

(B) to protest

(C) to be protesting

(D) to be protested

114. We highly recommend this book with ------- description of

mysterious creatures in ancient fables, and with insight into the possible origins of them.

(A) detail

(B) detailed

(C) details

(D) detailing

115. Our ------- online stationery shop is committed to providing students and business people with a wide variety of high-quality stationery items as well as PC products and other services.

(A) newly-established

(B) newly-establishing

(C) newly-establish

(D) new-established

116. When ------- to customers' enquiries, be sure you have answered every query in the exhibition.

(A) replies

(B) reply

(C) replying

(D) replied

117. The most attractive yet dangerous aspect of the credit system is that you can buy things -------, at the moment, you do not have enough money.

(A) even if

(B) despite

(C) and

(D) which

118. I am writing in reference to an overdue payment for invoice #5542-87, ------- is now in excess of three months overdue.

(A) what

(B) that

(C) which

(D) who

119. As you propose to ship regularly, we can offer you a rate of 2.48% benefit interest ------- a total cover of £60,000.

(A) for

(B) of

(C) with

(D) from

120. In particular we wish to know whether you can give a special rate ------- return for the promise of regular monthly shipments.

(A) in

(B) for

(C) by

(D) against

121. It is our pleasure to announce that a new campus e-mail program was created recently, and its headquarters ------- in the main building.

(A) was locating

(B) was to locate

(C) located

(D) was located

122. Keeping up with current innovations and new, emerging services in information technology at the same time seems to be a nearly impossible task to ------- with.
(A) get acquainted
(B) acquainted
(C) get acquainting
(D) acquainting

123. It is ------- that producing books in hard copy format may bring several million tons of harmful CO_2 into the atmosphere, so E-books are definitely here to stay.
(A) rebelled
(B) estimated
(C) undertaken
(D) humiliated

124. According to neuroscientists, ------- 20 percent of short-term memory can be improved by regular physical exercise, especially to the elderly.
(A) recently
(B) approximately
(C) perpetually

(D) ironically

125. With ------- pop music superstars creating extraordinary performances, Korean pop music trend has prevailed worldwide.
(A) mandatory
(B) economical
(C) renewable
(D) versatile

126. Music, with its functions of offering soothing feelings and full relaxation, remains a ------- language for all times.
(A) separate
(B) constructive
(C) defiant
(D) universal

127. Some extreme-sports enthusiasts are capable of achieving difficult and challenging extreme tasks with ------- perfection.
(A) synthetic
(B) luxurious
(C) incredible
(D) thorny

128. Due to wide ------- of public opinion, the political figure caught in a dilemma had a hard time getting away from the scandal.
(A) variations
(B) solitude

(C) approaches

(D) isolation

129. The company has recently renewed the computer software, and is working on tests to make sure the new system will be ------- with the existing apparatus.

(A) sympathetic

(B) experimental

(C) compatible

(D) interruptible

130. Martin has lived in comfort and luxury ever since he made successful ------- investments and piled up a considerable fortune.

(A) financial

(B) profound

(C) superstitious

(D) awkward

Note

模擬試題（二）

PART 5　中譯與解析 🎧 MP3 028

閱讀原文和中譯	
101. When Ms. Huang found that the ------- system was out of order, she called the repairman in to look at it right away. (A) secure **(B) security** (C) secured (D) securing	當黃小姐發現負責安全的系統故障時，她立即打電話請維修人員過來檢修。

答案：(B)

解析

本題考題屬於『名詞(片語)＋名詞』的考法。上下文應是指，這系統是屬於『負責「安全」』的系統，與動作（主、被動）、形容詞（內外在特質）無關，所以**選擇(B)**。

102. No sooner had he arrived at his home than he was called back to the office to deal with a matter of -------. **(A) urgency** (B) urge (C) urging (D) urgent	他一到家就被公司用電話召回處理這緊急事件。

答案：(A)

解析

本題考題屬於『介系詞(in) ＋名詞』的考法。因為是句子結尾處，所以判斷上下文後優先選『靜態名詞』，所以**選擇(A)**。選項(B)是動詞，且在一個句子中沒有做適當的變化，與文法不符，所以不選。(C) 選項是動詞所變化而來的形式，判斷上下文後並無需要動作（主動）含意的名詞句意，所以不選。(D)選項是動詞所變化而來的形容詞，與文法用法不符，所以不選。

103. Starting from next week, head-quarters will have entrance per-mits ------- for the use of recruit-ing employees in the fair. (A) issue (B) issues (C) issuing **(D) issued**	從下週起，總部會發出進出許可證，給在商展招募員工的職員所使用。

答案：(D)

解析

本題考題屬於『使役動詞(have)』的考法。從上下文得知，have 的對象為非人的名詞(permits) 時，issue 應該用「被動/ 完成」行為的過去分詞(V-p. p.)，中文解釋為「被發行的」用來修飾受詞(permits)，所以選擇**答案(D)**。選項(B)是名詞複數用法，所以不選。選項(A) 是名詞單數用法或動詞原形用法，與上下文句意不符，所以不選。選項(C) 是V-ing 的主動『動態形容詞』，所以不選。

104. Many job opportunities made recent graduates from the com-munity college's business pro-gram ------- , for the job fair held by the city government. (A) appreciating (B) appreciate **(C) appreciated** (D) to appreciate	近來諸多的工作機會，讓社區學院商業計劃畢業的應屆畢業生相當感謝市政府所舉辦的就業博覽會。

答案：(C)

解析

本題考題屬於『使役動詞(make)』的考法。從上下文得知，make的驅使對象為名詞(graduates)時，appreciate 用來修飾受詞(graduates)，且對象是人，應該用形容詞的過去分詞(V-p.p.)，中文翻成「心懷感激的」，而不是選項(A)代表「主動/ 進行」行為的現在分詞(V-ing)，中文翻成「令人感激的」。所以選擇**答案(C)**。選項(B) 是動詞原形用法，且在一個句子中沒有做適當的變化，與文法不符，所以不選。選項(D)是『不定詞』，與文法不符，所以不選。

105. The mental reinforcements in ensuring product validity ------- damage throughout the upcoming price-cutting competition. (A) minimizes **(B) will minimize** (C) minimized (D) minimize	在心理上強化保證產品的正當性，會在整個即將到來的削價競爭中將損害降到最低。
答案：(B)	

解析

上、下文的句意中，upcoming「即將到來的」，表示「未來」時間，所以答案**選(B)**。

106. Although the output situation seems poor at the moment, we ------- a swift improvement once the downturn is over. (A) anticipated (B) anticipate **(C) will anticipate** (D) are anticipate	雖然輸出的情況目前看來不佳，但衰退一旦結束，我們預計會迅速改善。
答案：(C)	

解析

上、下文的句意中，關鍵字句為once，表示「預計」狀態，屬「未來」時間的用法，所以答案**選(C)**。

| 107. Foreign businessmen often express ------- amazement at how far our manufacturer can achieve what they originally think impossible.
(A) unexpecting
(B) unexpect
(C) unexpected
(D) unexpective | 外國商人對於我們的製造廠商的表現驚訝，因為製造廠商達成了他們原本認為不可能的事情。 |

答案：(C)

 解析

空格之前為一般動詞，空格之後為名詞; 按照本句句意，應當屬形容詞為前位修飾，就進修飾之後的名詞。動詞unpexpected 當形容詞用時，應當用過去分詞(V-p.p.) 形式表達被動語態，所以答案**選(C)**。

| 108. In spite of consumer objection, Infocus will spend ------- time expanding the potential benefits of building cell phone plants.
(A) consider
(B) considerate
(C) considerable
(D) consideration | 儘管消費者的反對，Infocus 還是會花費相當長的時間，擴大建設手機工廠的潛在好處。 |

答案：(C)

解析

空格之前為一般動詞，空格之後為名詞; 所以，按照本句句意，空格應當為修飾不可數名詞的前位修飾語、表示「相當的」的中文意思，所以答案**選(C)**。

109. The problems with the just-in-time supply chain were solved following ------- with the lead suppliers. (A) demands (B) arguments **(C) negotiations** (D) concessions	與即時供應連鎖商的問題被解決，接著與重要的供應商協商。 (A) 請求 (B) 爭論 **(C) 協商** (D) 讓步

答案：(C)

 解析

此題為單字題，選項(A)為請求；選項(B)為爭論；選項(D)為讓步，用法為＋to/from。依照題意，應選擇**選項(C)協商**最為恰當。

110. The man talking on the phone about the lack of ------- after the accident at the oil refinery is getting increasingly angry. (A) payment (B) refunds (C) remittance **(D) compensation**	在廣播上談論有關於在油品精煉廠發生意外之後賠償金不足的男人，愈講愈生氣。 (A) 報償 (B) 退費 (C) 匯款 **(D) 賠償金**

答案：(D)

 解析

此題為單字題，依照題意，應該選擇**選項(D)賠償金**最為恰當。其他選項單字中文解釋則分別為(A)報償、(B)退費、及(C)匯款。

111. After the accident, all electrical ------- must be checked before any further use. (A) facilities (B) hardware (C) assets **(D) equipment**	意外事件之後，所有用電的設備必須在進一步使用之前檢查。 (A) 設施 (B) 硬體 (C) 資產 **(D) 設備**

答案：(D)

解析

此題為單字題，依照題意，應該選擇**選項(D)**設備最為恰當。其他選項單字中文解釋則分別為(A)設施、(B)硬體、及(C)資產。

112. We understand that you are arranging for immediate delivery from stock, and we look forward to ------- from you soon. (A) hear **(B) hearing** (C) be hearing (D) to be heard	我們了解您正在從存貨中安排現貨，以便立即發貨，而我們也期待著能從您那裡儘快得到消息。

答案：(B)

解析

本題屬於『動名詞』的考法。上下文關鍵字是look forward to 的介系詞to，後面結構應當用「動名詞(V-ing)」；且為「主動」用法，所以**答案選(B)**。

113. The controversial law regarding team share buying restrictions continues ------- across the country by various local community retailers. (A) to have protested (B) to protest (C) to be protesting **(D) to be protested**	關於球隊股份購買限制的法律引起極大的爭議，抗議聲浪不斷，遍及全國各零售單。

答案：(D)

解析

本題屬於『不定詞』的考法。上下文關鍵字是continue，後面結構應當用「不定詞(to VR)」。由上下文句意判斷，應當用「被動語態」，所以**答案選(D)**。

114. We highly recommend this book with ------- description of mysterious creatures in ancient fables, and with insight into the possible origins of them. (A) detail **(B) detailed** (C) details (D) detailing	我們強烈推薦這本書，裡面詳細介紹遠古神話中的神秘生物、並以精闢的見解剖析他們的可能來源。

答案：(B)

 解析

本題屬於『過去分詞』的考法。由上下文結構判斷，空格雖然為「動詞」選項，但是因為用來修飾後面「名詞(description)」，所以「動詞(detail)」變成「分詞(detailed)」答案，中文翻譯為「被詳細敘述的...」；且動詞與名詞的關係應該為「被動」用法，所以**答案選(B)**。

115. Our ------- online stationery shop is committed to providing students and business people with a wide variety of high-quality stationery items as well as PC products and other services. **(A) newly-established** (B) newly-establishing (C) newly-establish (D) new-established	我們新成立的網路文具店致力為學生和商務人士服務，提供各種高品質的文具、電腦產品與其他服務。

答案：(A)

解析

本題屬於『複合形容詞』的綜合考法。由上下文句意判斷，動詞(establish)與名詞的關係應當是被動，又搭配副詞加以修飾動詞，所以**答案選(A)**。

116. When ------- to customers' enquiries, be sure you have answered every query in the exhibition.

(A) replies
(B) reply
(C) replying
(D) replied

在回答客戶的詢問時，請確保您已經回答了展場的每個詢問。

答案：(C)

 解析

本題屬於『分詞構句』中的『現在分詞』考法。由上下文結構判斷，空格雖然為「動詞」選項，且有「連接詞(when)」存在，但是因為沒有「主詞」，所以「動詞(reply)」變成「分詞(replying)」答案；且動詞與主詞的關係應該為「主動」用法，所以**答案選(C)**。

117. The most attractive yet dangerous aspect of the credit system is that you can buy things -------, at the moment, you do not have enough money.

(A) even if
(B) despite
(C) and
(D) which

信用體系最吸引人，但也是最危險的地方在於，就算那一刻你沒有足夠的錢，你還是可以買東西。

答案：(A)

 解析

本題屬於『連接詞』中的「副詞子句」考法。由上下文句意判斷，應該選擇「即使、雖然」句意的**答案(A)**。

118. I am writing in reference to an overdue payment for invoice #5542-87, ------- is now in excess of three months overdue. (A) what (B) that **(C) which** (D) who	這封信是要告知您，其中提到的逾期付款發票＃5542-87，目前逾期超過三個月。

答案：(C)

 解析

本題屬於『連接詞』中的「形容詞子句」考法。由上下文句意判斷，空格前面的先行詞為非人(payment)，且空格前有逗點(,)，為「非限定用法」，且不可用that，且空格後面為「動詞」，直接表示空格為關係代名詞的「主詞(which)」用法，所以答案**選(C)**。

119. As you propose to ship regularly, we can offer you a rate of 2.48% benefit interest ------- a total cover of £60,000. **(A) for** (B) of (C) with (D) from	就你提出定期出貨的建議，我們可提供您總計60,000 英鎊的保障與$2.48%的利率優惠。

答案：(A)

 解析

本題考題屬於『介系詞』考法中「介系詞＋名詞」的考法。從上下文句意判斷，介系詞的中文翻譯為「總計...」，所以答案**選(A)**。

120. In particular we wish to know whether you can give a special rate ------- return for the promise of regular monthly shipments. **(A) in**	我們特別想知道，你是否可因每月定期運送貨物的承諾，給一個優惠的價格當作回饋。

(B) for
(C) by
(D) against

答案：(A)

解析

本題考題屬於『介系詞』考法中「介系詞＋名詞」的考法。從上下文句意判斷，介系詞的中文翻譯為「回應／回覆...」，所以答案選**(A)**。

| 121. It is our pleasure to announce that a new campus e-mail program was created recently, and its headquarters ------- in the main building.

(A) was locating
(B) was to locate
(C) located
(D) was located | 我們很榮幸地宣布，新校區的電子郵件程式最近被創立，而它的總部是設在主要大樓。 |

答案：(D)

解析

本題屬於『被動式』中「locate」的被動考法。由上下文的句意判斷，應當用「被動式」，中文翻成「座落於...」。所以答案選**(D)**。

| 122. Keeping up with current innovations and new, emerging services in information technology at the same time seems to be a nearly impossible task to ------- with.

(A) get acquainted
(B) acquainted
(C) get acquainting
(D) acquainting | 要同時熟悉、跟上當前的創新與新興的資科服務，這似乎是一個幾近於不可能達成的任務。 |

答案：(A)

本題屬於『被動式』中「blame」的被動考法。由上下文的句意判斷,後面的動詞變化應該用get + V-p.p. 的變化來表示「被動」的意涵,中文翻成「對…熟悉」。所以答案選**(A)**。

123. It is ------- that producing books in hard copy format may bring several million tons of harmful CO2 into the atmosphere, so E-books are definitely here to stay. (A) rebelled **(B) estimated** (C) undertaken (D) humiliated	據估計,製造硬皮書籍可能將數百萬公噸有害的二氧化碳氣體帶入大氣層,所以電子書當然應該普遍推廣。 (A) 反叛 **(B) 估計** (C) 從事 (D) 羞辱

答案: (B)

這題依句意為據估計,常見的搭配為it is estimated that...,故答案為**選項B**。

124. According to neuroscientists, ------- 20 percent of short-term memory can be improved by regular physical exercise, especially to the elderly. (A) recently **(B) approximately** (C) perpetually (D) ironically	根據神經科學家的說法,將近百分之二十短暫的記憶可以經由規律的體能運動得到改善,尤其是對老年人而言。 (A) 近來 **(B) 將近** (C) 永久地 (D) 諷刺地

答案: (B)

這題依句意為將近,要選approximately,故答案要選**選項B**。

125. With ------- pop music superstars creating extraordinary performances, Korean pop music trend has prevailed worldwide.
(A) mandatory
(B) economical
(C) renewable
(D) versatile

有著多才多藝流行音樂超級巨星創造傑出的表演，韓國流行音樂的潮流遍及全世界。
(A) 命令的
(B) 節約的
(C) 可更新的
(D) 多才多藝的

答案： (D)

 解析

這題依句意為多才多藝的，所以要選versatile，故答案為**選項D**。

126. Music, with its functions of offering soothing feelings and full relaxation, remains a ------- language for all times.
(A) separate
(B) constructive
(C) defiant
(D) universal

音樂，具有提供舒緩情緒及全面放鬆的功用，一直以來是一個世界性的語言。
(A) 分隔的
(B) 積極的
(C) 違抗的
(D) 全世界的

答案： (D)

 解析

這題依句意為世界性的，universal最合適，故答案為**選項D**。

127. Some extreme-sports enthusiasts are capable of achieving difficult and challenging extreme tasks with ------- perfection.
(A) synthetic
(B) luxurious
(C) incredible
(D) thorny

有些極限運動的愛好者有能力以令人難以置信的完美方式達成艱困且具挑戰性的極限任務。
(A) 綜合的
(B) 奢華的
(C) 令人難以置信的
(D) 棘手的

答案：(C)

解析

這題依句意為到了令人難以置信的完美程度，要選形容詞incredible，故答案為**選項C**。

128. Due to wide ------- of public opinion, the political figure caught in a dilemma had a hard time getting away from the scandal. (A) variations (B) solitude (C) approaches (D) isolation	由於輿論的眾說紛紜，這位深陷進退兩難困境的政治人物很難從醜聞中脫身。 **(A) 變化** (B) 孤獨 (C) 方法 (D) 隔離

答案：(A)

解析

這題依句意為眾說紛紜，代表是變化很廣的，**variations**最合適，故答案為**選項A**。

129. The company has recently re-newed the computer software, and is working on tests to make sure the new system will be ------- with the existing apparatus. (A) sympathetic (B) experimental **(C) compatible** (D) interruptible	這家公司最近更新了電腦軟體，並正在測試以確保新的系統與現有的裝置相容。 (A) 同情的 (B) 實驗的 **(C) 相容的** (D) 可中斷的

答案：(C)

解析

這題依句意為與現有的裝置相容，**be compatible with**為常見的慣用語表示「相容」，故答案為**選項C**。

130. Martin has lived in comfort and luxury ever since he made suc-cessful ------- investments and piled up a considerable fortune. **(A) financial** (B) profound (C) superstitious (D) awkward	馬汀自從金融投資成功且積聚可觀的財富後，一直過著舒適奢華的生活。 **(A) 金融的** (B) 深奧的 (C) 迷信的 (D) 笨拙的

答案：(A)

這題依句意為金融投資，要選金融的financial，故答案為**選項A**。

In this section, you must demonstrate your ability to read and comprehend English. You will be given a variety of texts and asked to answer questions about these texts. This section is divided into three parts and will take 75 minutes to complete.

Do not mark the answers in your test book. Use the answer sheet that is separately.

PART 5

Directions: In each question, you will be asked to review a statement that is missing a word or phrase. Four answer choices will be provided for each statement. Select the best answer and mark the corresponding letter (A), (B), (C), or (D) on the answer sheet.

101. I have talked with him about being late for the office twice already, but it hasn't made much of an ------- on him.
    (A) impressing
    (B) impression
    (C) impressive
    (D) impress

102. Nitche Stationery sells a variety of office supplies, and many ------- office appliances for nearly a decade, and has been very satisfied with our quality.
    (A) the other
    (B) another
    (C) others
    (D) other

103. Many workers were left ------- when the company's production facility was shut down due to budget shortfalls.
    (A) unemploy
    (B) unemploying
    (C) unemployment
    (D) unemployed

104. The Avery Career Center offers advice and assistance to get staff ------- in non-technical professions to further ensure their job positions.
    (A) acquirement
    (B) acquiring
    (C) acquired
    (D) to acquire

105. I ------- to inform you that the expired date of your insurance in this product warranty will be further extended as of June 15th for one more year via our promotion campaign.
    (A) write
    (B) will write
    (C) writing
    (D) am writing

106. We ------- several interesting variations on the original business model to you, which we have experienced for a long time.
    (A) presented
    (B) are presenting

(C) have presented

(D) will be present

107. Stunned by the ------- performance of the production yield these years, the magazine critic was at a loss for words when he sat down to write a review of the firm.

(A) impress

(B) impressed

(C) impressively

(D) impressive

108. Setting up plants in the commercial districts brings ------- more profits than in the industrial ones because there is always more consumption in the former ones.

(A) more

(B) even

(C) so

(D) too

109. With so much shipment company information on the Internet, it is difficult to urge users ------- your website, place orders, or even confirm delivery orders precisely.

(A) to be noticing

(B) to notice

(C) noticing

(D) noticed

110. An outsider cannot but ------- to understand the complexity of the development concerning the automated transportation process as it has evolved today.
    (A) struggles
    (B) struggled
    (C) to struggle
    (D) struggle

111. Could you please send me details of the refrigerators ------- in yesterday's 'Evening Post'?
    (A) advertising
    (B) advertised
    (C) advertise
    (D) advertises

112. Visitors in the stadium are quite ------- by our Model Info 2, the newest solar battery.
    (A) impressed
    (B) impressing
    (C) impress
    (D) impresses

113. I appreciate a letter of apology from your department ------- you have verified these errors made by your clients' account management.
    (A) and
    (B) no sooner than

(C) as soon as

(D) before

114. Would you please arrange for $3,000, ------- is to be transferred from our No. 2 account to their account with Denmark Banks, Leadshell Street, London, on the 1st of every month, beginning 1st May this year?

(A) but

(B) and

(C) which

(C) what

115. The personal medical insurance will be effective ------- our receiving the enclosed proposal form which is completed by you.

(A) with

(B) on

(C) within

(D) at

116. Please send me particulars of your terms and conditions ------- the policy and a proposal form if required.

(A) with

(B) on

(C) for

(D) at

117. Doctors believe that the calories you ------- could affect many

aspects of your health.

(A) consume

(B) assume

(C) presume

(D) contract

118. A fully functional version of the program is made ------- the exe files at no cost from the Internet for a 30 day evaluation.

(A) be downloaded

(B) to download

(C) to be downloaded

(D) downloaded

119. Aside from the unbearably high temperatures, global warming is also ------- for the power to go out.

(A) blamed

(B) to be blamed

(C) blame

(D) to blame

120. Irene had better watch out for those of her gossip friends who may once in a while ------- rumors about her.

(A) decorate

(B) spread

(C) pacify

(D) experience

121. At the present time, scientists spare no efforts to find resources of the alternative energy to substitute for the fossil fuels ------- by industry.
(A) occurred
(B) consumed
(C) represented
(D) prospered

122. After most of its safety ------- failed to meet the standards, the mall was seriously penalized, and had to make immediate improvement.
(A) motivation
(B) inspections
(C) purification
(D) concessions

123. Compared with others, people tortured by depression ------- need more care and attention, for they don't easily reveal their emotional problems.
(A) viciously
(B) competently
(C) relatively
(D) punctually

124. To keep healthy, one should be careful not to consume too much the food that ------- additives, such as preservatives, coloring, or artificial flavorings.

(A) contains

(B) digests

(C) huddles

(D) transforms

125. The manager informed the factory that they might ------- or even cancel the original ordes if the goods shipped in continued to be in poor quality.

(A) resolve

(B) approve

(C) withhold

(D) decrease

126. To make both ends meet, Roy had no choice but to take several part-time jobs to ------- additional income.

(A) despise

(B) supervise

(C) generate

(D) overlook

127. The magician's ------- performances attracted full attention of the audience and won him long and loud applause.

(A) marvelous

(B) exclusive

(C) reckless

(D) feasible

128. People who ------- from a migraine headache can relieve the pain effectively by all forms of relaxation, a lot of water-drinking, or keeping away from noises and bright lights.
    (A) guarantee
    (B) suffer
    (C) proceed
    (D) investigate

129. Mr. Cosby had a serious cold and coughed a lot; thus, he could hardly ------- anything because of the painful throat.
    (A) fumble
    (B) console
    (C) swallow
    (D) nominate

130. The movie adapted from a novel was disappointing to the moviegoers because they could hardly find any ------- between the two.
    (A) insistence
    (B) metabolism
    (C) integrity
    (D) consistency

Note

模擬試題（三）

閱讀原文和中譯	
101. I have talked with him about be-ing late for the office twice al-ready, but it hasn't made much of an ------- on him. (A) impressing **(B) impression** (C) impressive (D) impress	我已經跟他提及他2次上班遲到的事情，但這對他好像沒啥印象。

答案：(B)

解析

本題考題屬於『冠詞』的考法。冠詞(a/an)＋單數名詞的應用。且應用『靜態名詞』，與動作（主、被動）無關，且後面有相搭配名詞用法的介系詞(on) 出現，所以**選擇(B)**。(C)選項是動詞所變化而來的形式(-sive)，為形容詞用法，與前後用法不符，所以不選。(D)選項是動詞impress，且在一個句子中沒有做適當的變化，與文法不符，所以不選。

102. Nitche Stationery sells a variety of office supplies, and many ------- office appliances for nearly a decade, and has been very sat-isfied with our quality. (A) the other (B) another (C) others (D) other	尼采文具這公司販售各種辦公室用品，還有許多其他的辦公室器具將近10年的時間，一直以來也十分滿意我們的品質。

答案：(D)

 解析

本題考題屬於『代名詞』的考法。由上下文判斷，應該選「其他的」這個中文，所以為形容詞用法，所以答案**選擇(D)**。選項(A) 可以是代名詞或形容詞用法，因為與文法衝突，所以不選。(B) 選項可以是代名詞或形容詞用法，與文法衝突，所以不選。(C) 選項是others 這個字做代名詞的用法，且是複數形式，也因為與本句題目衝突，直接不考慮。

| 103. Many workers were left ------- when the company's production facility was shut down due to budget shortfalls.
(A) unemploy
(B) unemploying
(C) unemployment
(D) unemployed | 由於預算短缺，該公司的生產設施被迫關閉，留下許多工人失業。 |

答案：(D)

解析

本題考題屬於『使役動詞(leave)』的考法。從上下文得知，leave 的驅使對象為名詞(workers) 時，unemployed 用來修飾受詞(workers)，且對象是人（員工），而且應當是被雇用的對象，應該用形容詞的過去分詞(V-p.p.)，表示動作是因外力所導致的結果；中文翻成「不被雇用的」，與上下文句意符合，所以選擇**答案(D)**。選項(A) 是動詞原形用法，與文法不符，所以不選。選項(B) 與上下文的句意不符，所以不選。選項(C) 是名詞用法，與文法不符，所以不選。

| 104. The Avery Career Center offers advice and assistance to get staff ------- in non-technical professions to further ensure their job positions.
(A) acquirement
(B) acquiring
(C) acquired
(D) to acquire | Avery 就業指導中心提供諮詢和協助，讓員工學會非技術的專業，以進一步確保他們的工作職位。 |

答案：(C)

解析

本題考題屬於『使役動詞(get)』的考法。從上下文得知，get 的驅使對象為名詞(staff) 時，acquire 用來修飾受詞(staff)。因為被驅使的動作(acquire) 後面並沒有對象讓動作去執行，所以用形容詞的過去分詞(V-p.p.) 表示「被動」，中文翻成「學習而來的」，而不是選項(B) 表示「主動/ 進行」行為的現在分詞(V-ing)，也不會是選項(D) 代表不定詞的「主動、企圖、目的性」的用法。選項(A) 是名詞，與上、下文的句意不符，所以不選。

105. I ------- to inform you that the expired date of your insurance in this product warranty will be further extended as of June 15th for one more year via our promotion campaign. (A) write (B) will write (C) writing **(D) am writing**	這封信是為了告訴你，透過我們產品的促銷，您這個產品保固的保險到期日將進一步於6 月15 日起被延長一年。

答案：(D)

解析

本題為TOEIC 書信體中慣用的書信告知/ 通知開頭寫法。用意是，讓讀這封信或訊息的人，在讀時如同告知者正在跟被告知者敘述一件事的原委，所以用「現在時間進行式」。所以答案**選(D)**。

106. We ------- several interesting variations on the original business model to you, which we have experienced for a long time. (A) presented **(B) are presenting** (C) have presented (D) will be present	我們將呈現給你一些、針對原有商業模式的有趣變化，而這已經實驗了一段時間。

答案：(B)

關鍵字句為have experienced，表示「現在時間完成式」，意指「現在當下」的狀態; 而上下文的句意中，「現在時間進行式」指當下行為，所以答案選**(B)**。

107. Stunned by the ------- performance of the production yield these years, the magazine critic was at a loss for words when he sat down to write a review of the firm.

(A) impress
(B) impressed
(C) impressively
(D) impressive

當雜誌評論家坐下來寫這間公司的評論時，對其這些年令人印象深刻的生產良率訝異到說不出話來。

答案：(D)

空格之後為不可數名詞; 修飾不可數名詞的前位修飾語應當用形容詞，所以答案選**(D)**。選項**(B)** 是動詞的V-p.p. 所衍生而來的形容詞用法，暗指所修飾對象的「被動、完成」狀態，與上下文不符，所以不選。

108. Setting up plants in the commercial districts brings ------- more profits than in the industrial ones because there is always more consumption in the former ones.

(A) more
(B) even
(C) so
(D) too

在商業區設廠，比在工業區帶來了更多的利潤，因為在前者的消費量總是較多。

答案：(B)

空格之前為一般動詞，空格之後為形容詞＋名詞的結構；所以，按照本句句意，空格應當為強化形容詞的副詞前位修飾語、表示「更……的」的中文意思，所以答案選**(B)**。

109. With so much shipment company information on the Internet, it is difficult to urge users ------- your website, place orders, or even confirm delivery orders precisely. (A) to be noticing **(B) to notice** (C) noticing (D) noticed	由於網路到處都是貨運公司的資訊，因此很難督促使用者留意你的網站、下訂單，甚至確認訂貨訂單。

答案：(B)

解析

本題屬於『不定詞』的考法。上下文關鍵字是urge，後面結構應當用「不定詞(to VR)」。由上下文句意判斷，應當用「主動語態」，所以答案選**(B)**。

110. An outsider cannot but ------- to understand the complexity of the development concerning the automated transportation process as it has evolved today. (A) struggles (B) struggled (C) to struggle **(D) struggle**	局外人不得不努力去理解自動運輸過程演變至今的複雜發展。

答案：(D)

解析

本題屬於『不定詞』的考法。上下文關鍵字是cannot but，後面結構應當用「不定詞(to VR)」，其中to是省略的。所以答案選**(D)**。

111. Could you please send me details of the refrigerators ------- in yesterday's 'Evening Post'? (A) advertising **(B) advertised** (C) advertise (D) advertises	請你能不能寄給我昨天在「晚間郵報」廣告的冰箱細節？

答案：(B)

本題屬於『過去分詞』的考法。由上下文結構判斷，空格雖然為「動詞」選項，但是因為與前句並沒有「連接詞」存在，推測應當是省略「連接詞（which/that）」，所以選擇「動詞(are advertised)」變成「分詞(advertised)」的答案；且動詞與名詞的關係應該為「被動」用法，是為「被廣告」的對象，所以答案選**(B)**。

112. Visitors in the stadium are quite ------- by our Model Info 2, the newest solar battery. **(A) impressed** (B) impressing (C) impress (D) impresses	展場的參訪者對我們的最新的太陽能電池– 信息2號機型印象深刻。

答案：(A)

本題屬於『情緒動詞』中『過去分詞』的考法。用「過去分詞」修飾人的情緒，是因為人的情緒由外在因素所「被動誘發」，中文翻成「使人感到...」，用以修飾講話者被影響的情緒，所以答案選**(A)**。

113. I appreciate a letter of apology from your department ------- you have verified these errors made by your clients' account management. (A) and	您於確認管理客戶帳戶時所犯得錯誤後，便立即自您部門發出了道歉信函，對此我很感激。

(B) no sooner than
(C) as soon as
(D) before

答案：(C)

解析

本題屬於『連接詞』中的「副詞子句」考法。由上下文句意判斷，應該選擇「一...就...」句意的**答案(C)**。而答案(B)錯在結構錯誤，所以不選。

114. Would you please arrange for $3,000, ------- is to be transferred from our No. 2 account to their account with Denmark Banks, Leadshell Street, London, on the 1st of every month, beginning 1st May this year? (A) but (B) and **(C) which** (C) what	可否請您安排，從今年五月起，每個月的1號從我們的2號帳戶轉移3000美元到他們在倫敦Leadshell 街丹麥銀行的帳戶？

答案：(C)

解析

本題屬於『連接詞』中的「形容詞子句」考法。由上下文句意判斷，空格前面的先行詞為非人($3,000)，為「非限定用法」，空格後面為「動詞」，直接表示空格為關係代名詞的「主詞(which)」用法，所以答案**選(C)**。

115. The personal medical insurance will be effective ------- our receiving the enclosed proposal form which is completed by you. (A) with **(B) on** (C) within (D) at	當我們一收到你所完成的附件申請表，個人醫療保險將生效。

答案：(B)

 解析

本題考題屬於『介系詞』考法中「介系詞＋名詞」的考法。從上下文句意判斷，介系詞的中文翻譯為「一......就......」的句意，所以答案選**(B)**。

| 116. Please send me particulars of your terms and conditions ------- the policy and a proposal form if required.
(A) with
(B) on
(C) for
(D) at | 如果需要的話，請給我你的保單條款、條件與申請表格的詳情。 |

答案：(C)

 解析

本題考題屬於『介系詞』考法中「介系詞＋名詞」的考法。從上下文句意判斷，介系詞的中文翻譯為「為了...」，所以答案選**(C)**。

| 117. Doctors believe that the calories you ------- could affect many aspects of your health.
(A) consume
(B) assume
(C) presume
(D) contract | 醫生們相信你吃進的熱量可能會影響到健康許多面向。
(A) 攝取
(B) 以為
(C) 假定
(D) 訂合約 |

答案：(A)

 解析

此題為單字題，依照題意，應該選擇選項**(A)**攝取最為恰當。其他選項單字中文解釋則分別為**(B)**以為、**(C)**假定、及**(D)**訂合約。

118. A fully functional version of the program is made ------- the exe files at no cost from the Internet for a 30 day evaluation. (A) be downloaded **(B) to download** (C) to be downloaded (D) downloaded	該計劃的全功能版本需從網路免費下載exe 文件，並有30 天的免費評估時間。

答案：(B)

本題屬於『被動式』中「使役動詞」的被動考法。由前面動詞（使役動詞）的被動式判斷，後面的動詞變化應該用to VR 的變化，中文翻成「被下載...」。所以答案**選(B)**。

119. Aside from the unbearably high temperatures, global warming is also ------- for the power to go out. (A) blamed (B) to be blamed (C) blame (D) to blame	除了難耐的高溫之外，全球暖化也導致能源的流失。

答案：(D)

本題屬於『被動式』中「blame」的被動考法。由上下文的句意判斷，後面的動詞變化應該用to VR 的變化來表示「被動」的意涵，中文翻成「為...負責」。所以答案**選(D)**。

120. Irene had better watch out for those of her gossip friends who may once in a while ------- rumors about her. (A) decorate **(B) spread** (C) pacify (D) experience	艾琳最好要小心她那群偶爾會散播有關於她謠言的八卦朋友。 (A) 裝飾 **(B) 散播** (C) 平和 (D) 經歷

答案：(B)

這題指的是散播謠言，要選spread，故答案為**選項B**。

121. At the present time, scientists spare no efforts to find resources of the alternative energy to substitute for the fossil fuels ------- by industry. (A) occurred **(B) consumed** (C) represented (D) prospered	目前來説，科學家們不遺餘力地尋找替代能源的資源來取代工業所消耗的石化燃料。 (A) 發生 **(B) 消耗** (C) 代表 (D) 繁榮

答案：(B)

這題指的是為產業所消耗的石化燃料，消耗要選consumed，故答案為**選項B**。

122. After most of its safety ------- failed to meet the standards, the mall was seriously penalized, and had to make immediate improvement. (A) motivation **(B) inspections** (C) purification (D) concessions	在大部分的安全檢驗無法符合標準之後，這個大賣場被嚴厲地處罰，並且必須做立即的改善。 (A) 動機 **(B) 檢查** (C) 淨化 (D) 讓步

答案: (B)

這題指的是安全檢驗未達標準，要選inspections，故**答案為B**。

123. Compared with others, people tortured by depression ------- need more care and attention, for they don't easily reveal their emotional problems. (A) viciously (B) competently **(C) relatively** (D) punctually	和一般人比較起來，為憂鬱症所苦的人相對地需要更多的關心和注意，因為他們不輕易地透露他們的情緒問題。 (A) 邪惡地 (B) 勝任地 **(C) 相對地** (D) 準時地

答案: (C)

這題指的是「相對地」，指相對地需要更多的關心和注意，故答案為**選項C**。

124. To keep healthy, one should be careful not to consume too much the food that ------- additives, such as preservatives, coloring, or artificial flavorings. **(A) contains** (B) digests (C) huddles (D) transforms	為了維持健康，人們應該小心不要吃太多含有添加物的食物，例如：防腐劑、色素，或者人工調味料。 **(A) 包含** (B) 消化 (C) 蜷縮 (D) 轉變

答案: (A)

這題指的是「含有」，食物中所含的添加物，contain最符合句意，故答案要選**選項A**。

125. The manager informed the factory that they might ------- or even cancel the original orders if the goods shipped in continued to be in poor quality.
(A) resolve
(B) approve
(C) withhold
(D) decrease

經理通知工廠，假使進貨的商品仍舊品質不良的話，他們會減少或甚至取消原有的訂單。
(A) 下定決心
(B) 贊同
(C) 阻擋
(D) 減少

答案：(D)

 解析

這題指的是進貨商品品質不佳會影響到訂單的減少或取消訂單，decrease是四個選項中最符合句意的，故答案為**選項D**。

126. To make both ends meet, Roy had no choice but to take several part-time jobs to ------- additional income.
(A) despise
(B) supervise
(C) generate
(D) overlook

為了收支均衡，羅伊不得不兼職數份兼差的工作來賺取額外的收入。
(A) 鄙視
(B) 監督
(C) 產生
(D) 忽略

答案：(C)

 解析

這題指的是增加或賺取額外的收入，generate最適合，故答案為**選項C**。

127. The magician's ------- performances attracted full attention of the audience and won him long and loud applause.
(A) marvelous
(B) exclusive
(C) reckless
(D) feasible

魔術師奇妙的表演吸引全場觀眾的目光，並且為自己贏得許久響亮的喝采聲。
(A) 奇妙的
(B) 獨家的
(C) 粗率的
(D) 可行的

答案：(A)

這題指的是要選擇能描述魔術師表演的形容詞，四個選項中奇妙的最符合，故答案為**選項A**。

128. People who ------- from a migraine headache can relieve the pain effectively by all forms of relaxation, a lot of water-drinking, or keeping away from noises and bright lights. (A) guarantee **(B) suffer** (C) proceed (D) investigate	罹患偏頭痛的人可以藉由各種放鬆的方式，喝大量的水，或遠離噪音及亮光來有效地紓緩疼痛。 (A) 保證 **(B) 受苦** (C) 行進 (D) 調查

答案：(B)

這題指的是「遭受...」，且空格後為from，suffer from為常見的搭配，故答案為**選項B**。

129. Mr. Cosby had a serious cold and coughed a lot; thus, he could hardly ------- anything because of the painful throat. (A) fumble (B) console **(C) swallow** (D) nominate	寇斯比先生由於嚴重的感冒加上咳嗽咳得厲害，以致於喉嚨疼痛而無法吞嚥任何東西。 (A) 摸索 (B) 安慰 **(C) 吞嚥** (D) 提名

答案：(C)

這題指的是吞嚥任何東西，要選swallow，故答案為**選項C**。

130. The movie adapted from a novel was disappointing to the movie-goers because they could hardly find any ------- between the two. (A) insistence (B) metabolism (C) integrity **(D) consistency**	這部由小説改編的電影讓電影觀賞者感到失望，因為他們幾乎找不出兩者間情節相符之處。 (A) 堅持 (B) 新陳代謝 (C) 廉潔 **(D) 一致性**

答案：(D)

 解析

這題指的是要找出兩者之間的「一致性」，故答案為**選項D**。

Note

Note

國家圖書館出版品預行編目(CIP)資料

新制多益聽力題庫：文法+單字附詳盡解析/
Amanda Chou著. -- 初版. -- 新北市：
倍斯特出版事業有限公司, 2021.03　面；公分.
-- (考用英語系列；30)
ISBN 978-986-06095-0-9 (平裝附光碟片)
1.多益測驗

805.1895　　　　　　　　　　　110000527

考用英語系列 030

新制多益閱讀題庫：文法＋單字附詳盡解析（MP3）

初　　版　　2021年3月
定　　價　　新台幣480元

作　　者　　Amanda Chou
出　　版　　倍斯特出版事業有限公司
發 行 人　　周瑞德
電　　話　　886-2-8245-6905
傳　　真　　886-2-2245-6398
地　　址　　23558 新北市中和區立業路83巷7號4樓
E - m a i l　　best.books.service@gmail.com
官　　網　　www.bestbookstw.com
總 編 輯　　齊心瑪
特約編輯　　陳韋佑
封面構成　　高鍾琪
內頁構成　　菩薩蠻數位文化有限公司
印　　製　　大亞彩色印刷製版股份有限公司

港澳地區總經銷　　泛華發行代理有限公司
地　　址　　香港新界將軍澳工業邨駿昌街7號2樓
電　　話　　852-2798-2323
傳　　真　　852-3181-3973

Simply Learning, Simply Best!

Simply Learning, Simply Best!